An Old Story of My Farming Days
Vol. II

by
Fritz Reuter

An Old Story of My Farming Days
Vol. II
by Fritz Reuter

Copyright © 2024

All Rights reserved.

No part of this publication may be reproduced, stored in a retrieval system, or transmitted in any form or by any means, electronic, mechanical, photocopying or Otherwise, without the written permission of the publisher.
The author/editor asserts the moral right to be identified as the author/editor of this work.

ISBN: 978-93-64281-46-1

Published by

DOUBLE 9 BOOKS

2/13-B, Ansari Road
Daryaganj, New Delhi – 110002
info@double9books.com
www.double9books.com
Tel. 011-40042856

This book is under public domain

ABOUT THE AUTHOR

Fritz Reuter (1810-1874) was a renowned German novelist and a pivotal figure in 19th-century German literature. He is especially noted for his writings in Low German (Plattdeutsch), which vividly portray the rural life and culture of Northern Germany, particularly Mecklenburg. Early Works: After his release, Reuter began his literary career. Major Works: Reuter's major contributions to literature include a series of novels and stories that depict rural Mecklenburg life with a blend of realism and humor. Notable works include: "Ut de Franzosentid" (During the French Period): A collection of stories set during the Napoleonic Wars. "Ut mine Festungstid" (During My Time in Prison): An autobiographical account of his imprisonment. "Ut mine Stromtid" (During My Apprenticeship): A semi-autobiographical novel regarded as one of his masterpieces. "In the Year '13: A Tale of Mecklenburg Life": A historical novel set during the Napoleonic Wars, exploring their impact on rural Mecklenburg. Reuter's use of Low German in his writing was significant in preserving and popularizing the dialect. It added authenticity to his portrayal of rural life and connected deeply with his audience. His works are characterized by their realistic depiction of rural life, combined with humor and a deep understanding of human nature. Reuter's stories often address social issues, reflecting the struggles and resilience of rural communities. Fritz Reuter is celebrated for his contributions to German literature and for promoting Low German. His works continue to be appreciated for their cultural and historical significance. Reuter is honored through numerous schools, streets, and institutions named after him, particularly in Northern Germany. Fritz Reuter remains a significant literary figure, known for his contributions to preserving Low German culture and for his engaging, realistic depictions of rural German life.

CONTENTS

CHAPTER I 7
CHAPTER II 15
CHAPTER III 24
CHAPTER IV 30
CHAPTER V 39
CHAPTER VI 47
CHAPTER VII 63
CHAPTER VIII 78
CHAPTER IX 85
CHAPTER X 94
CHAPTER XI 101
CHAPTER XII 107
CHAPTER XIII 118
CHAPTER XIV 130
CHAPTER XV 138
CHAPTER XVI 145
CHAPTER XVII 155
FOOTNOTES 166

CHAPTER I

On the 23rd of June 1843, the eldest son of David Däsel and the youngest daughter of John Degel were seated on a bench in the pleasure-grounds at Pümpelhagen. They had gone out to enjoy the beauty of the moonlight evening together. Sophia Degel said to her companion: "What made you look so foolish, Kit, when you came back from taking the horses over to meet the squire?"--"It was no wonder if I looked a little foolish. He took me into the sitting-room at the Inn and showed me his wife, and, says he, 'this is your new mistress.' Then she gave me a glass of wine, and made me drink it at once"--"What's she like?" asked the girl.--"Why," said Christian, "it's rather difficult to describe her. She's about your height; her hair is bright and fair like yours, and her colouring is red and white like yours. She has grey eyes like you, and she has just such another sweet little mouth."--Here he gave Sophia a hearty kiss on her pretty red lips.--"Lawk a daisy! Christian!" cried the girl, freeing herself from his embrace, "I suppose then that you gave her just such another kiss as you've given me?"--"Are you crazy?" asked Christian, and then went on soothingly. "No, that would have been impossible. That! sort have something about them that doesn't go with our sort. The lady might have sat here on the bench beside me till doom's day, and I'd never have thought of giving her a kiss."--"I see!" said Sophia Degel, rising and tossing her pretty head; "you think that I'm good enough for that sort of thing! Do you?"--"Sophia," said Christian, putting his arm round her waist again, in spite of her pretended resistance, "that kind of woman is far too small and weakly for us to admire; why if I wanted to put my arm round a creature like that--as I'm doing to you just now, Sophia--I'd be frightened of breaking or crushing her. Nay," he continued, stroking her hair, and beginning to walk home with her, "like mates with like."--When they parted Sophia was quite friends with Christian again. "I shall see the lady in the morning," she said, as she slipped away from his detaining arm, "the girls are all going to make wreaths of flowers to-morrow, and I'm going to help."

Every one at Pümpelhagen was busy weaving garlands, and setting up a triumphal arch across the avenue. Next morning Hawermann saw the last touches put to the arch, to which Mary Möller added a bunch of flowers here, and a bit of green there, as it seemed to be required, and Fred Triddelfitz fluttered about amongst the village-lads and lasses as a sort of volunteer-assistant, in all the grandeur of his green hunting-coat, white leather breeches, long boots with yellow tops, and blood-red neck-tie. While they were employed in this manner, uncle Bräsig joined them in his very best suit of clothes. He wore pale blue summer-trousers, and a brown coat which he must have bought in the year one. It was a very good fit at the back, and was so long in the tails that it nearly reached the middle of his calf, but it showed rather too great an expanse of yellow piqué waistcoat in front. As the coat was the same colour as the bark of a tree, he might be likened to a tree that had been struck by lightning, and which showed a broad stripe of yellow wood in front where the bark had been torn away. He also wore a black hat about three quarters of a yard high. "Good morning, Charles. How are you getting on? Aha! I see that the erection is nearly finished. It looks very nice, Charles--but still, I think that the arch might have been a little bit higher, and you might have had a couple of towers, one on the right hand and the other on the left. I once saw that done at Güstrow in the time of old Frederic Francis, when he came back in triumph! But where's the banner?"--"There's none," said Hawermann, "we hav'n't one."--"Do try to remember where we can get one, Charles. You can't possibly do without a flag of some kind. The lieutenant was in the army, and so he must have a flag flying in his honour. Möller," he called without turning round, "just fetch me two servant's sheets and sew them together lengthwise; Christian Päsel, bring me a smooth straight pole, and you, Triddelfitz, get me the brush you use for marking the sacks, and a bottle of ink."--"Bless me! Zachariah. What on earth are you going to do?" asked Hawermann, shaking his head.--"Charles," said Bräsig, "it's a great mercy that the lieutenant was in the Prussian army, for if he had been in a Mecklenburg regiment we should never have managed to get the right colours. Now it's quite easy to rig up a Prussian flag. Black ink and white sheets! we want nothing more."--Hawermann at first thought of dissuading his friend from making the flag, but on second thoughts he let him go on unchecked, for, thought he, the young squire will see that he meant it kindly.

So Bräsig set to work, and painted a great "vivat!!!" on the sheets. "Hold tight!" he shouted to Mary Möller and Fred Triddelfitz who were helping him, "I want to get 'Lieutenant and Mrs. Lieutenant' properly written on the banner."--He had decided, after much thought, on putting "Lieutenant and Mrs. Lieutenant" after the "vivat", instead of "A. von Rambow and F. von Satrop" as he had at first intended, for von Rambow and von Satrop are merely the names of two noble families, and he had all his life had a great deal to do with people of that kind, while he had never yet known a lieutenant, and therefore thought the title a very distinguished one.

When the flag was finished he trotted across the court with it, and stuck it up on the highest step of the manor-house, and then hastened down stairs again to see how it looked from below. After that, he tried hanging it out at the granary-window, and again from the loft above the stable where the sheep were wintered; but none of these places met with his approval. "It won't do at all, Charles," he said at last; but after a long pause he added: "I have it now!" and pointing at the arch he continued, "That's the very place for it."--"Ah, but," said Hawermann, "don't you see that if you put it there, it'll hide our arch completely. The great poplar over there prevents any wind getting at your banner, and so it's hanging to the pole like an immense icicle that hasn't melted since last winter."--"I'll soon put that right, Charles," cried Bräsig, pulling a quantity of twine out of his pocket, and tying one bit to the upper and another bit to the lower end of his banner. "Gustavus Kegel," he called to the boy who fed the pigs, "are you a good climber?"--"Yes, Sir," answered Gustavus.--"Very well then, my dear pig's Marcary," said Bräsig, laughing heartily at his own joke, and all the grooms, and farm-lads, and lasses laughed because he did, "take the ends of these strings, climb the poplar with them, and then draw tight."--Gustavus did as he was desired, and drew the banner as tight and firm as if he had been setting a main-sail in preparation for Pümpelhagen leaving her moorings and sailing away. Bräsig meanwhile stood by the pole or mast like a captain during a sea-fight, and looked as if he were commanding the whole ship's company: "He may come now as soon as he likes, Charles. I'm quite ready for him."

But Fred Triddelfitz was not ready yet, for he had constituted himself commander-in-chief of the land-forces, and wanted to arrange his army in two lines, one on each side of the road. The first of these lines was formed of the old labourers, the grooms, and the farm-lads. The other of the married women, the maid-servants, and the girls who worked on the farm. After a good deal of trouble he partially succeeded in arranging the men to his mind; but it was otherwise with the women; he could not manage them at all. The married women were each armed with one of their little olive-branches, for, as they said, Josy and Harry ought to see all that was going on at such a time; but unfortunately the said olive-branches required so much dancing and talking to, to keep them quiet, that it spoilt the look of the whole line. The maid-servants refused to acknowledge Fred's authority, and Sophia Degel even went so far as to say that he had better not attempt to order *her* about, for she would obey no one but Mamselle Möller.[1] As for the light infantry of farm-girls, they were never in the same spot for two minutes at a time! There was no managing them, for they seemed to be under the impression that the enemy was in sight, and that it was their bounden duty to take some dapper young foe prisoner on the spot. Fred Triddelfitz struck the crook-stick he had intended to use as his marshal's baton on the ground before them, and said that they were not worth all the trouble he was taking with them. He then went to Hawermann and told him: He would have nothing more to do with it, and as the bailiff did not entreat him to persevere, he asked if he might have the use of his horse to ride out, and see whether the young squire and his wife were coming. Hawermann was rather unwilling to allow him to do so, out of regard for his old horse, but Bräsig whispered: "Let him go, Charles, for our preparations will have a much more imposing effect when we get rid of the grey-hound."

Fred rode off towards Gürlitz; but no sooner was he gone than Bräsig had a new cause of displeasure in the conduct of Strull, the schoolmaster, who now came up followed by all the youthful descendants of the Äsels and Egels who were of an age to go to school, each with his or her hymn-book open. The order which Fred had vainly endeavoured to introduce amongst his forces was effected in a moment with the new-comers, for Master Strull was always accustomed to maintain discipline amongst his scholars. He divided his followers into two parties; one of which was formed of Äsels, for he could count on their singing properly, and the other was composed of Egels, who--as he knew by sad experience--had very peculiar ideas regarding time and tune.

"Bless me, Charles! What does this mean?" asked Bräsig when he saw the schoolmaster arrive on the scene of action.--"Why, Bräsig, Master Strull wants to pay his respects to the squire along with the rest of us, and I don't see any reason why the school-children shouldn't sing what he has taught them as well as they can."--"Much too 'clesiastical for the lieutenant, much too 'clesiastical! Do you happen to have a drum or a trumpet about the place?"--"No," laughed Hawermann, "we hav'n't any instruments of that kind."--"I'm very sorry to hear it," said Bräsig.--"But stop! Christian Däsel come and hold the flag-staff for me, will you? It's all right, Charles," he added as he went away. But if Hawermann had known what he was going to do, he would have made him give up his plan. Bräsig signed to the night-watchman David Däsel to come and speak to him apart, and then asked him if he had brought his instrument with him. David thought for a moment in silence; at last he said: "Here!" and held up the stick which he like all the other workmen had brought by Fred Triddelfitz's orders that they might be waved in honour of the lieutenant. "You stupid old dunder-head!" cried Bräsig impatiently, "I mean your musical-instrument."--"Do you mean my horn? It's at home."--"Can you blow a tune upon it?"--Yes, David said, he could blow *one*.--"No man can do more than he is able!" said Bräsig. "Now go and get your horn and come behind the cattle-shed, and let me hear what it's like."

When they were alone in the meeting place appointed by Bräsig, David put the horn to his lips and blew as loud as if he wanted to announce that the cattle-shed was on fire: "The Prussians have taken Paris," &c., for he was very musical. "*Stop!*" cried Bräsig, "you must blow gently just now, for I want to surprise Hawermann; but when the lieutenant comes you may do it as loud as ever you like. Now, listen. When the schoolmaster has got through all his 'clesiastical nonsense, keep your eye on me, and when you see me wave the flag-staff three times, be sure you blaze away."--"Very well, Sir; but we must see first of all that the old watch-dog is safely on the chain, for he and I are not quite friends just now, and if he sees me with the horn he'll be sure to fly upon me."--"I'll see to that," said Bräsig, and then he went back with Däsel to join the others near the triumphal arch, and when he got there, he resumed his former place as supporter of the flag-staff. They were just in time to see Fred Triddelfitz riding up the hill as fast as the old horse could go, when he was near enough for his voice to be heard, he called out: "They're coming, they're coming! They're at Gürlitz now."

Yes, they were coming. Alick von Rambow and his fair young wife were driving slowly towards their home on that lovely summer-morning. They were in an open carriage, and Alick pointed beyond Gürlitz to the wide green meadows bathed in sunshine and to the shady woods of Pümpelhagen, and said: "Look, dearest Frida, there it is; that is our home."--These words were few and simple, but they did as well as any others to express the pride and happiness he felt in being able to provide such a beautiful home for his young wife, and she understood his meaning perfectly, and rejoiced in feeling how much he loved her.--She was of a calm gentle nature, and might be likened to a quiet brook flowing peacefully by the hill-side and through a cool shady wood far removed from the busy high-way; but now the bright sunshine had found out its secret course, and shone down upon it, lighting up the flowers and grasses on its banks, and showing the brilliant colouring of the pebbles lying under its still waters like treasures before undreamed of. And so the little brook flowed on, making a sweeter and merrier music than before it had been wakened to new life by the magic wand of the sun.

Her appearance was much as Christian Däsel had described it, but he had not seen her cheeks flush with pleasant excitement as they were now doing, while she looked in the direction in which Alick was pointing; nor had he seen her grey eyes swimming with happy tears as she turned them on her husband.

"Ah!" she exclaimed, slipping her hand into Alick's: "How beautiful it is! I never saw such a rich land! Just look at those corn-fields over there!"--"Yes," said Alick, who was much pleased with her delight, "the soil here is a great deal richer than in your province." It was a pity that he did not stop there, but she had alluded to his pet hobby, farming, so he went on: "But there is much room for improvement in our farming operations; sufficient intelligence has never yet been brought to bear on the subject, and so we don't make half as much out of the land as we might. Look there at that wheat-field on the other side of the hill! It is part of the Pümpelhagen estate, and I hope, in a couple of years' time, to have a crop of plants of great mercantile value in that field, and then you'll see that it will bring me in three times as much money as it does now."--Then he launched forth on the commercial value of flax, hops, oil producing plants, carraway and anise-seed, with which, in alternate years, he, as a good farmer, would sow clover and esparcet, "to keep his cattle in good condition, and to make manure." After that he went on to explain what plants were used for dyes, and told his wife that red was extracted from the madder, blue from woad and yellow from weld, and said that he was certain to get a good price for crops of that kind. Just as he had reached this point and was riding his hobby much to his own satisfaction, he was startled by a horse passing the carriage at full gallop. It was Fred Triddelfitz who appeared in all the brilliance of a rainbow, and disappeared with the velocity of a falling star.

"What was that?" cried Frida, and Alick shouted: "Heigh! Heigh!" But Fred took no notice, for he had to bring the news to the people at the triumphal arch, and had only time as he galloped past Gürlitz manor to call out to Pomuchelskopp whom he saw standing at the gate, that they were coming, and would be at the village in five minutes.--"Come, Mally and Sally, it's high time for you to come!" shouted Pomuchelskopp over the garden-hedge, and Mally and Sally threw the bit of worsted work they were doing; down amongst the nettles beside the arbour, put on their Leghorn hats, and took their stand one on each side of their father. Then father Pomuchelskopp said to them: "Don't look round, girls, whatever you do, for we must seem as if we had come out for no other reason than to have a walk this beautiful morning."

But he was doomed to meet with disappointment.--The Pümpelhagen carriage was driving slowly through the village, when Mrs. von Rambow suddenly asked her husband: "Who is that lovely girl who bowed to us just now?" He answered that it was Louisa Hawermann, his bailiff's only daughter, and that the house beside which she was standing was the parsonage. Meanwhile Muchel and his two daughters were going out at their gate as if for a walk, when as ill-luck would have it, our old friend Henny was driven by the demon of housekeeping to go out and feed the chickens. She had on a white cotton cap trimmed with frills round the face, and the inevitable black merino gown which she still considered good enough for morning wear. When she saw Pomuchelskopp and the two girls passing out at the gate, she was very angry with her husband for going without her, and so she rubbed the chickens food off her hands on the old black skirt, and followed them. Her stiff unbending figure clothed in white and black looked exactly like a tombstone going out for a walk.

"Muchel!" she called after her husband.--"Don't look round," said Muchel, "our being here must seem to be accidental."--"Kopp!" she shouted. "Ar'n't you going to wait for me? Do you want me to run myself out of breath?"--"I'm sure I don't care whether you do or not," growled Pomuchelskopp. "Don't look round, girls, I hear the carriage now. It'll be here immediately."--"But, father," remonstrated Sally, "that's mother calling."--"Pshaw! Mother here, mother there!" cried Pomuchelskopp in a rage. "She'll spoil everything. But, my dear children," he continued after a short pause, "don't repeat what I've just said to your mother."--Henny now came up with them, very much out of breath with her run: "Kopp!" she began, but got no further in her speech, for the carriage had now reached them, and Pomuchelskopp stood still, and making a low bow, exclaimed: "A-ah!--I wish you joy, I wish you joy!" and Mally and Sally curtsied at the same time as their father spoke. Alick desired the coachman to stop, and said he was glad to see Mr. Pomuchelskopp and his family looking so well. Whilst this was going on, Muchel was pulling his wife's dress secretly as a sign to her to greet the von Rambows also, but she remained standing as stiff and straight as before, only puffing and blowing a little after her late exertions. Frida leant back in the carriage, and looked as if she had nothing to do with what was going on. Muchel then proceeded to speak of the happy chance which had led to the unexpected pleasure of this meeting, and told how he and his two daughters were taking a walk, and had never .... here he stopped short, for at the same moment he received a sharp pinch from Henny, and heard her whisper savagely: "You're treating your wife with very little respect!"--As soon as Pomuchelskopp came to this abrupt conclusion of his address, Alick signed to the coachman to drive on, saying at the same time that he hoped soon to have the pleasure of seeing his neighbour again.

Pomuchelskopp stood still with a very hang-dog look, and Mally and Sally took their former places at his side, but instead of pursuing their walk as they had intended, they turned their steps homeward, Henny following them, and leading her recalcitrant husband back to his duty after her usual gentle fashion. Never, as long as he lived, did Pomuchelskopp forget the events of that morning, or the admonitions with which his wife overwhelmed him.

"Those seemed to be very disagreeable people," said Frida as they drove away.--"You are quite right in your supposition," answered Alick, "but they are very rich."--"Ah!" cried Frida, "mere riches don't make pleasant companions."--"True, dearest Frida, but the man is an excellent farmer, and for that reason, as well as because he is a near neighbour, we must admit him and his family to our acquaintance."--"Are you in earnest, Alick?"--"Certainly," he replied.--After a little thought, she asked: "What sort of man is the clergyman?"--"I know him very slightly, but my father had a high opinion of him, and my bailiff has a great love and respect for him.--But," he added after a pause, "that is only natural, for the parson has brought up his only child almost from her infancy."--"Oh; the beautiful girl we saw at the parsonage door; but of course the clergyman's wife had more to do with that than he had. Do you know her?"--"Yes--that is to say, I've seen her. She appeared to be a cheery old lady."--"They must be very good people," said Frida decidedly.--"Dear Frida," said Alick settling himself more comfortably in his corner, "how quickly you women jump at a conclusion! You think that because these people adopted a child who was no relation to them, and---and--have brought her up well, that ......" He was going to have enlightened his wife as to the probable double motive which composes every action, however apparently good, by showing her some of the lessons he had learnt in what he called "knowledge of human nature"--for it is a well known fact that puppies which have been blind for nine days of their life, always think they understand more of the ways of the world on the tenth day than all of their surroundings put together.--But before he could go on to prove the wickedness of the world, his young wife started forward on her seat, exclaiming: "Oh, Alick, look. A flag and a triumphal arch. They are preparing a grand reception for us."--And Degel the coachman said, looking over his shoulder at her: "Yes, Madam. I wasn't to tell you, but now you've seen it for yourself. I must drive very slowly now for fear the horses should take fright."

CHAPTER II

At last they drove up to the assembled villagers, and Hawermann approaching the carriage said a few words of welcome that came straight from his heart, and as Alick, in spite of his knowledge of human nature, had nothing ready to say on the spur of the moment, the young lady bent forward and gave the old man her hand with a friendly smile. As she did so, she read in his face as he did in hers, truth, honesty and uprightness. Alick now shook hands in his turn. Then the schoolmaster came forward followed by the line of Äsel, and gave out the key-note of one of the "Hymns of thanksgiving for peculiar mercies." The one chosen was No. 245 in the Mecklenburg hymn-book, and was intended to be used "after a severe thunder-storm." Very wisely, however, Master Strull began at the second verse because he thought it most suited to his squire: "Lord, we praise thy might."--Bräsig now wanted to wave his flag, but Gustavus Kegel held on tight: "Will you let the string go, you young rascal!" he cried.--"We know thy dreadful wrath!" sang the schoolmaster.--"Let the string go; d'ye hear me, boy?" said Bräsig impatiently.--"Yea, in thee do we trust, nor find thee to fail," sang the schoolmaster.--"Wait till I get hold of you, boy, and I'll give you such a thrashing," cried Bräsig.--"Thy kindness how tender, how firm to the end," sang the schoolmaster.--"I say, Sir, the strings have caught in the poplar," cried Gustavus. So Bräsig pulled and tugged at the banner, and in setting it free dragged off some of the small branches and leaves round which the string was entangled. The schoolmaster sang: "Hark, the crash of the storm." Fred Triddelfitz, who had meanwhile taken possession of the dinner-bell that was kept in the passage, rang a violent alarum. Bräsig waved his banner, and all the men and women, young men and maidens, boys and girls shouted at the top of their voices: "Hurrah! Hurrah!" And David Däsel blew on his horn: "The Prussians have taken Paris, &c." so solemnly that it was enough to touch the heart of even a dog. At the last toot of the horn, at the end of the first line, the old watch-dog, which Gustavus Kegel had let loose for fun, rushed at David Däsel's legs, and at the same moment the two brown horses began to dance and snort so much, that it was lucky that Degel the coachman was prepared for something of the kind happening, and at once drove on to the front-door. Alick got out of the carriage, and then helped his young wife out. The house was as grandly decorated within as without, and Mary Möller bustled about amongst the garlands of leaves and flowers in her new red jackonet gown, with a flushed face and red arms. As soon as she had grown a little cooler amongst the flowers, she rushed back to the kitchen to see how the cook was getting on with the dinner, just as if she were an iron heater and must be put in the oven again every time she got cool. As Mrs. von Rambow crossed the threshold, Mary came forward to meet her with her red arms extended as if she were a daughter of Moloch, and placed a wreath of blush-roses on her mistress' head. Then stepping back a few paces, and kneading her arms as if she wanted to make them flash fire, she repeated the following address, which she and Bräsig had been three months in composing:

"Hail to thee our queen and lady dear!
I swear to do all my duty here,
To be of thine ev'ry wish observant,
And to remain thy most obedient,
Ever faithful, humble servant."

She threw open the dining-room door when she had concluded her address, and showed the table ready spread for dinner. Nothing could have been better timed, for it was long past the usual hour. Alick whispered a few words to his wife, who nodded assent, and then turning to the old bailiff with a smile, told him that he must be her guest that day, and asked him to invite the schoolmaster and the young gentleman, who was learning farming, to dine with them also; adding that she hoped the good old gentleman, who had waved the banner, would likewise give her the pleasure of his company. After that she left the room and went to thank Mary Möller for her address, and for the excellent way in which she had managed the household during their absence, and said that now that she had come home, she would herself help Mary to continue as she had begun. Mary Möller blushed so red with pleasure, that she might be said to resemble a baker's oven filled with glowing red-hot coals.

The guests soon afterwards assembled. Hawermann brought Bräsig into the dining-room with him, and introduced him to the squire and his wife as a very dear old friend of his, adding, that he had known the late squire well, and that he had always taken a warm interest in the joys and sorrows at Pümpelhagen. Then Bräsig went up to Alick, and seizing his hand whether he would or not, shook it heartily and assured him with many an emphatic nod, of his eternal friendship, saying in conclusion: "I'm delighted to see you looking so well, Sir. And as I was just saying to Charles, I hope and trust that you will follow in the footsteps of your worthy father."--He now went up to Mrs. von Rambow, and taking her hand, said: "Honoured Mrs. Lieutenant von Rambow," here he was on the point of kissing her hand, but suddenly changing his mind, went on: "No, I will not. I was always expected to kiss the Countess' hand as a sort of courtly duty; I should never be able to bring myself to do it again if I were to treat you in the same way, you look so good and kind. But remember if ever you want anyone to do you a service--my name is Zachariah Bräsig--send for me--I live a short five miles from here at Haunerwiem--and I promise that the day shall not be too hot, nor the night too dark for me to help you."

This sort of talk is either understood or misunderstood according to the character of the hearer. Bräsig, like an honest man spoke out of the fulness of his heart without fear of misconception, but Alick did not take his speech to him as it was meant. He thought it very impertinent of a man like old Bräsig to hold up any one--even his own father who had always been so good to him--as an example for him to follow, so he remained silent and displeased.--Frida, on the contrary, had the gift of reading character, and saw the real kindness of heart below the eccentricity of diction, and so laying her hand again in that of the old gentleman she made him sit beside her at table.

Fred Triddelfitz arrived soon after Hawermann. He was dressed like a young squire in a blue coat and brass buttons, that looked exactly like a child of Pomuchelskopp's best blue coat. The schoolmaster came next. He was a tall muscular man, who appeared to be better fitted by nature for hewing wood, than for thrashing children. With his round black head and seedy black clothes he resembled nothing so much as a huge nail that fate had stuck crookedly in a wall, and which had now grown rusty in its unnatural position. His face also was somewhat rusty. The only thing about him that might be said to look cheerful was his shirt front, and that was because his mother, seeing that it had grown yellow with lying in the drawer had freshened it up by rubbing some laundry blue on it, under which process it had gained a lovely sea-green colour.

These two last guests were received with more cordiality by Alick than the two first; he made them sit one on each side of him at dinner, and was much pleased when he heard that Fred's father was the apothecary at Rahnstädt, and that he understood chemical analysis. When uncle Bräsig heard the word analysis, he said in a low voice to Hawermann: "Annalissis! Annalissis! What in all the world is that? Is it an insect?" Then, without waiting for an answer, he turned to Alick, and said: "For that sort of thing, my dear Sir, you should get the apothecary's son to bring you a pot of 'urgent Napoleon' (unguentum Neapolitanum)."--Naturally enough Alick did not understand what he meant, and even if he had understood he had not time to explain, for by this time they were all seated and dinner had begun. The schoolmaster looked rather uncomfortable, for he was seated on the extreme edge of his chair.--Alick now introduced his favourite subject of conversation, farming as it ought to be at Pümpelhagen. He told his guests that he intended to manure the land with bone-dust, nitre and guano, and to make a large hop-garden in the field below the flower-garden. Poor old Hawermann listened to all these plans in silence, saying to himself that he had never imagined that the new squire had such strange views of agriculture, and that he wondered how Bräsig could laugh as he was doing. But it was only natural that Bräsig should laugh, he regarded the whole thing as a joke, and a very good joke too; it never occurred to him that Alick could possibly be in earnest, and when he said in conclusion: "But of course the ground must be thoroughly prepared first," Bräsig answered with a hearty laugh: "Yes--and when we've had a good crop of hops, we'll plant raisins and almonds there to feed the pigs. And then, Madam," turning to Mrs. von Rambow, "you'll see what capital pork a pig fattened on raising and almonds will produce."

Of course Alick did not like that; he looked straight at his plate, and drew his eye-brows together, but he was riding his hobby too gallantly to give in for so slight a check, and went on to explain his views about agricultural machines. He described the plough and clod-breaker in one, which he was trying to invent, addressing his remarks chiefly to Triddelfitz, who replied in such learned terms that Mary Möller listened with open mouth, and beat upon her breast, murmuring: "God be merciful to me a sinner! And I really, fool that I was, thought myself a fit wife for a man like that! Nay, one might as soon, expect a goose and an eagle to set up house together."--As soon as dinner was finished, Mrs. von Rambow rose to leave the dining-room, saying to Hawermann as she did so, that she and Alick had agreed to walk over the farm on the next morning, and that she hoped Hawermann would go with them. He was only too delighted to do as she asked. When she had left the room the wine was passed round, and Daniel Sadenwater--whom Alick had retained in his service at his wife's request--was desired to bring cigars.

Bräsig helped himself to a "ceegar" as he called it, and told Mr. von Rambow that he smoked such things now and then, but not one of those that Bröker, the sexton, had in his shop; no, they were too strong, and besides that, they didn't look nice, and some people even went so far as to say that Bröker rubbed them up in the same way as the old women at the apple-stalls do their apples, to make them look fresh, which to say the least was very nasty. Alick made no reply to this remark, for--somehow or other--he did not like Bräsig. The old man was too satirical when other people's notions of farming did not agree with his own. Fred Triddelfitz was a very different sort of person; he had nodded and shaken his head, had looked astonished, had Oh'd and A'd at the proper times, and had altogether seemed so much impressed by the wisdom of what he had heard, that Alick began to look upon himself as a good useful tallow-candle, stuck in a tall candle-stick, and set where it could give light to Pümpelhagen and the neighbouring villages--and perhaps even to the whole world. But in spite of his foibles, Alick was really a good-hearted man, he only wanted to enlighten the world at large, and to make the little world over which he reigned happy and comfortable in his own way. He called Hawermann to join him in the window, and asked him how Fred was getting on. Hawermann replied that he was pretty well satisfied with him, and that he hoped he would be a reasonably good farmer in course of time. That was sufficient to confirm Alick in his good opinion of the young man, and he next enquired what salary he received, and whether a horse was kept for his use. No, Hawermann said, he hadn't a horse, and he neither paid nor received any money.

Alick then went to Fred, and said to him: "I'm very much pleased, Triddelfitz, to hear from Mr. Hawermann that he is perfectly satisfied with the progress you are making, I, therefore, intend to offer you a small salary of ten pounds a year, and the keep of a horse."--Fred hardly knew whether he was standing on his heels or his head: Hawermann so much pleased with him! Could it be possible? Ten pounds a year of pocket-money! That was very delightful, but a horse! His breath was so taken away with surprise and pleasure, that he could only stammer out a few words of thanks. Alick did not give him time to recover his presence of mind, but retired once more to the window with Hawermann. Fred could think of nothing but his good fortune. His head was as full of all the horses in the neighbourhood, black and brown, chestnut and bay as if the Mecklenburg government had suddenly determined that the Rahnstädt horse-market should be held in it. Bräsig sat opposite, watching him with a smile of amusement. At last Fred exclaimed: "Oh, Mr. Bräsig, I *must* have her before the Grand-Duke comes to Rahnstädt next month, for it has been arranged that his Royal Highness is to be received and conducted into the town by a company of young farmers."--"Who must you have?" asked Bräsig.---"Augustus Prebberow's sorrel-mare, Whalebone."--"I know her," said Bräsig indifferently.--"She's a beauty!"--"An old r ...." radical, he was going to have called her, but stopped himself because he thought it too vulgar an expression to be used in the aristocratic mansion in which he then was. "She's an old democrat, and won't be of any use to you when the Grand-Duke makes his entrance into Rahnstädt, for she'll never hear the people cheering him."--That was a pity, because there would be a great deal of shouting and hurrahing at such a time, but then Fred knew how fond Bräsig was of opposing everything he did too well to let his ridicule turn him from his fixed intentions.

Meanwhile Alick had been giving his old bailiff a short lecture on the immense advance that had been lately made in the science of agriculture, and when he had finished what he had to say, he pressed a book into Hawermann's hand, saying: "I hope you will like this book, which I have much pleasure in giving you, and which, I firmly believe, will henceforth be the only recognised authority in agricultural matters."--Hawermann thanked him for his gift, and then as it was beginning to grow dusk, he and his companions took leave of Mr. von Rambow. Bräsig and Master Strull accepted the bailiff's invitation to accompany him home. And Fred went to the stables.

Why he went there no one knew, not even he himself. He went there by instinct to look at the horses; he wanted to bring his inward feelings into more conformity with his outward circumstances, and so he visited the old farm-horses that he had already seen a thousand times, and examined their legs carefully. He thought of all the horses he knew that had anything the matter with them. One had spavin--*he* would take care not to buy a horse that had spavin. Another horse's legs were not quite so straight as they might be, and a third had string-halt--he had learnt to distinguish that, within the last two years. A fourth had the staggers--any man would be a fool to buy that horse. A fifth had been fired for another illness, and so on, and so on. But there was another thought uppermost in his mind as he stood in the door-way of the stables. And that thought was of the wonderful beauty and refinement of Mrs. von Rambow. The young rascal imagined that he had fallen over head and ears in love with her, and now in spite of Alick's kindness to him about the horse, he did not hesitate to cause him unhappiness--in thought. "Yes," he said, as he stood in the door-way in the gathering darkness, "what is Louisa Hawermann in comparison with that angelic lady? Ah, Louisa, I'm sorry for you! I don't know how on earth I came to fall in love with you. And then Mina and Lina. They're poor little bits of things. And Mary Möller--pah! That would never have done. She looked like a great red plum to-day, and Mrs. von Rambow like a delicately tinted peach. When the sorrel-mare is mine, I can perhaps go on a message for the lady--to the post or somewhere. And then, when she comes home at night from a ball at Rahnstädt, I may perhaps open the carriage-door for her, if Daniel Sadenwater happens to be out of the way. If she has forgotten her handkerchief or--or her goloshes at Rahnstädt, I'll mount my sorrel-mare, and--tch, tch--I'll get back with her things in half an hour; ten miles in half an hour!---'Here are your goloshes, Madam,' I'll say. 'Thanks, Triddelfitz,' she'll answer, 'your attention .....' The devil take that beastly pole!" he exclaimed; for as he was going home in the dark immersed in dreams about his new love-affair, he tripped over a pole that had been left in the yard through his own carelessness, and now he lay at full length on ground that felt wonderfully cool and soft. What he had fallen on he could not tell, though his nose made him suspect what it was, and he thought it might be better to go to his own room, and find out before joining Hawermann in the parlour.

The three old gentlemen on arriving at the bailiff's house, seated themselves comfortably in the parlour, and then Bräsig asked: "Is that book a no-vell, Charles, to amuse you on winter evenings?"--"I hardly know what it is, Zachariah, but I'll light the lamp and look."--When the lamp was lighted, Hawermann was going to look at the title of the book, but Bräsig took it out of his hand, saying: "Nay, Charles, we have a learned man here, Strull must read it to us."--The schoolmaster drew a long breath, and began to read as if it were Sunday and he were reading the gospel for the day; and whenever he paused for breath, it was when he came to a word he did not know. "'Printing and Paper from Frederic Vieweg & Son in Brunswick Chemistry in relation to A-gri-culture and Phy-si-ology.'"--"Stop!" cried Bräsig. "That's not the word, it's fisionomy."--"No," said Stroll, "it's pronounced 'phy-si-ology' here."--"Well, it doesn't much matter," said Bräsig. "Foreign words are rather peculiar, one man pronounces them in this way, and another in that.--Please go on!"--"'By Justus Liebig Drrr of Medicine and Philosophy Professor of Chemistry in the Ludwig University at Giessen Knight of the Ludwig-order of the Grand-duchy of Hesse and of the third class of the order of S-t-Anne of the Russian Empire Foreign member of the Royal Society of Science at Stockholm of the'--there's something in Latin that I can't read--'in London Honorary member of the Dublin Academy--cor-res-pon-d .....'"--"Stop!" cried Bräsig. "Preserve us all, Charles! What a lot of things that fellow is."--"But that isn't nearly all," said the schoolmaster, "there's as much again to come yet."--"Then we'll skip all that. Go on!"--"'Fifth revised and enlarged edition Published by Vieweg & Son Brunswick 1843.' Now comes a preface."--"We'll skip that too," said Bräsig, "begin where the book begins."--"There's a heading 'Subject' and it has got a stroke under it"--"All right!" said Bräsig. "Fire away!"--"'The task of organic chemistry is to investigate the chemical conditions of life and the completed development of all organisms.' End of the sentence."--"*What* did you say?" asked Bräsig.--"'Of all organisms,'" repeated the schoolmaster.--"Well!"

exclaimed Bräsig. "I've heard many an outlandish word, but Organism, Organ ..... Stay! Charles, do you remember the bit of Gellert we had to learn by heart for parson Behrens: 'Mr. Orgon went to the door.' Perhaps this Orgon has something to do with that one."--"Do let the schoolmaster read on, Bräsig, otherwise we'll never understand."--"Why, Charles, talking of a thing is great use in teaching us what it means. You'll see that this book is just like those I tried to read about the water-cure, and begins with all kinds of incompr'ensible things. Now go on!"--"'The duration of all living things is dependent upon their reception of certain materials which we call food and which are necessary for the development and reproduction of every organism.' End of the sentence."--"The man's right enough there," said Bräsig. "All living creatures require food, and"--here he took the book from Strull---"'it is necessary for every organism.' I know what he means by organism now, it's the stomach."--"Yes," assented the schoolmaster, "but you forget that he uses the word 'reproduction' also."--"Ah!" said Bräsig, with a wave of his hand. "'Production.' That's a thing that has only been known in the last few years. When I was a child no one ever heard of production, and now they call every bushel of wheat and every ox a production. I'll tell you what it is, Master Strull, they only use these words as a flower of speech and to show how learned they are."--When they had read a little more of the book the schoolmaster rose to go home, and then the two old friends were left alone together, for Bräsig was to spend the night at Pümpelhagen.--At last Hawermann said with a deep sigh: "I'm very much afraid, Zachariah, that bad times are beginning for me."--"Why, what do you mean? Your young squire is a merry light-hearted sort of man, and is fond of a joke too. Didn't you notice that in the way he was talking about farming at dinner to-day?"--"What *you* thought a joke, Bräsig, *he* meant in earnest"--"*In earnest!*"--"Most certainly. He has studied farming; in new-fashioned books which don't at all approve of our old-fashioned ways, and I can't undertake the management of these new ways of farming at my age, for I don't understand them well enough."--"You're right there, Charles. People who have been accustomed to climb high towers from the time they were little children, don't get dizzy when they are called upon to do it in their old age, and people who have been brought up to learn science in their childhood find it quite easy to dance on a scientific tight rope when they are old. Do you understand me?"--"Perfectly. And, Bräsig,"--pointing to the book--"we were never taught to dance on that rope when we were young, and now my old bones are too stiff to attempt it. I've nothing to say against the new ways, I don't understand them, and if Mr. von Rambow will tell me how he wants things to be done, I'll carry out his views as well as I can; but I'm afraid that that kind of farming will require a great deal of money if it is to be done properly, and our purse is not a very heavy one. I thought at first that he would get something with his wife, but he didn't.[2] He had to get all new things in Rahnstädt himself, and they're not paid for yet"--"Don't distress yourself about that, Charles. He has made a good choice all the same. I was much taken with the young lady."--"So was I, Bräsig."--"You see what a woman can do in keeping things straight in what your sister has done. I'm going to call on her to-morrow, for those two young parsons seem to have been getting into a scrape of some kind. Good-night, Charles."--"Good-night, Bräsig."

CHAPTER III

Next morning Fred Triddelfitz swam about the farm-yard at Pümpelhagen like a pickerel in a fish-pond, for he had put on his green hunting-coat and grey breeches, in order that--as he said to himself--Mrs. von Rambow might have something pleasant to look at. His eyes which used to glance ever and anon at Hawermann's window when he was at work in the yard, were now turned often and curiously in the direction of the manor-house, and when the squire opened his window and called him, he shot across the yard as if he were indeed a pickerel and Alick were the bait he wanted to catch.

"Triddelfitz," said Mr. von Rambow, "I have determined to make a short address to my people this morning, will you tell them to come up to the house at nine o'clock."--"Aye, aye, Sir," said Fred, who thought that answer more respectful than any other he could have used.--"Where is the bailiff? I want to speak to him; but there's no hurry."--"He has just gone out at the back gate with Mr. Bräsig."--"Very well. When he comes back will do perfectly."--Fred made as grand a bow as he could, and turned to go, but after walking away a few steps, he went back and asked: "Pray, Sir, do you want to see the women as well as the men?"--"No, only the men. But wait a moment--yes, you can tell the married women to come too."--"Aye, aye, Sir," said Fred, who then set off round the village, and desired all the married women, and the men who worked on the farm to go up to the manor-house in their Sunday-clothes.--It was now eight o'clock, and if the ploughmen who were at work in the more distant fields were to get up to Pümpelhagen in time, they must be called at once, so he set off to fetch them.

Hawermann had accompanied his old friend a little bit of the way towards Rexow, and then crossing the fields, he went to see how the ploughmen were getting on with their work. Whilst he was there, Fred came over the hill and made towards him in as straight a line as he could, considering his way of walking and the roughness of the ploughed land. "Mr. Hawermann," he said, "the men must unyoke their horses at once, for the squire wants all the workmen to be up at the manor-house at nine. He is going to make them a speech."--"What is he going to do?" asked

Hawermann surprised.--"Make a speech," was the answer. "All the other men and the married women have received orders to be ready. He had forgotten the women, but I reminded him of them."--"You'd better," ....--"have left it alone," Hawermann was going to have said, but he stopped himself in time and added quietly: "Go and give the men your message."--"But you're wanted too."--"Very well," answered the old man turning to go home with a heavy heart.--That bit of land ought to have been finished that morning, and now nothing to speak of could be done till the afternoon.--And there was another thing. His master had made this arrangement on the very first day without telling him of his intention. He had consulted Triddelfitz, not him, and yet there was no such desperate need of hurry.--Still that did not grieve him so much as the thought of the speech. What on earth was he going to say? Was he going to lecture them about their duty? If he was it was unnecessary to do so. The people went to their work as naturally as to their dinner ..... they did not think about their duty, they just did it. It would be a great pity to speak to them either in praise or blame upon the subject. Too much talk did more harm than good. Labourers were like children, if they were praised for doing their duty, they began to think that they had done more than their duty.--Or was he going to give them some proof of his generosity? He was quite good-natured enough for that.--But what could he give them?--They had all they needed. He could give them nothing tangible, for he knew too little of their position to do so, he would, therefore, be obliged to content himself with vague figures of speech and meaningless promises, which everyone would of course interpret according to his own hopes and wishes, and which it would be impossible ever to realize.

These were Hawermann's thoughts as he went to join his master in his study. Mrs. von Rambow was in the room ready dressed for her walk over the farm. She went forward to meet him as he came in and said: "We must wait for a little, Mr. Hawermann, Alick wants to speak to the people before we go."--"That won't take long," said Alick who was turning over some papers.--There was a knock at the door.--"Come in."--And Fred entered with a letter in his hand: "From Gürlitz," he said.--Alick broke the seal and read the letter. It was from attorney Slus'uhr to say that when David and he happened to be passing Gürlitz that morning they had gone in to see Mr. Pomuchelskopp, from whom they had accidentally heard of Mr. von Rainbow's return home, and as they wished to speak to him on particular business, they would do themselves the pleasure, &c. &c. There was also a postscript to say that the business was very pressing. Alick was in a very painful position, for he could not refuse to receive the two men however much he might wish to do so. He went out to the door, and told the messenger that he would be glad to see the gentlemen, but when he returned to the study he looked so grave and anxious that his wife asked him what was the matter. "Oh, nothing," he answered. "I'm thinking about my speech. I'm afraid that it will last longer than I thought at first, and so perhaps it would be better if you and Mr. Hawermann were to set out at once without waiting for me."--"Oh, Alick, without you! I had been looking forward ...."--"But you see, my dear child, I can't help it. I know the whole place perfectly, and--and I will follow you as soon as I possibly can."--It seemed to Hawermann that the squire was nervously anxious to get rid of them both, so he came forward and asked Mrs. von Rambow if she would go with him now. She consented and followed him somewhat gravely.

Soon after they were gone Alick addressed the assembled villagers, but his whole pleasure in making his speech from the throne was destroyed by the remembrance of the disagreeable letter in his pocket. The speech was much what Hawermann had imagined it would be. It was made up of good advice and promises couched in such long words and high-flown language, that the villagers were quite puzzled as to what it all meant; the only thing they understood was that the squire had promised them all sorts of good things, and had said that any one who had a favour to ask was to go at once to him, and his request would meet with fatherly consideration.--"Ah!" said Päsel to Näsel. "That's a good look out for us. He'll do that, will he? I'll go to him to-morrow, and ask if I may bring up a calf this year."--"You got one last year."--"That doesn't matter, I can sell it to the weaver at Gürlitz."--"Well," said Kegel to Degel, "I'll go to him to-morrow, and ask him to give me another bit of potato-ground next spring, and tell him that my piece isn't big enough to supply my family."--"That was because you didn't hoe your potatoes at the right time; the bailiff gave you a bit of his mind about it you remember."--"What does that matter? The devil a bit he knows about that, and he's our master now, and not the bailiff."--So the people went away restless and discontented with their present condition, and Alick himself was anxious and unhappy because of the visit that was hanging over him that morning. The only person at Pümpelhagen who was perfectly contented was Fred Triddelfitz, so the young squire had not cast the pearls of his speech entirely before swine.

Slus'uhr and David arrived, and what can I say about their visit? They sang the same song as before, and Alick had to renew his bills again. From long practice he had grown quite expert at this. Borrowing money is a dreadful thing, nothing comes up to it except perhaps being beheaded or hung, neither of which is precisely a pleasant experience; still I have known people who never rested till they had borrowed from all the Jews and Christians they could persuade to lend them money. Alick was not as bad as that, but yet he thought it as well to make use of the present opportunity, and get a new loan from David of sufficient money to pay for the refurnishing of the house. His excuse was that it was better "to have to do with one usurer than with several," and it never seemed to occur to him that that one was as bad as a dozen.

Meanwhile Hawermann and Mrs. von Rambow were walking over the farm. The beauty of the summer-morning soon chased away the slight shadow of displeasure from the lady's fair face, and she began to look about her, and try with right good will to learn something about farming in Mecklenburg. Hawermann soon discovered to his great delight that she was by no means so ignorant of agricultural matters as she thought herself. She had been brought up in the country, and had always taken an intelligent interest in what was going on around her. She liked to know why this or that was done, a mere superficial knowledge did not content her. So it was that she already knew enough about farming to understand the reasons for the differences she noticed between the crops at Pümpelhagen and those at her old home. The soil on her father's estate was light and sandy, while here it was a rich clay, well suited for the cultivation of wheat. The old bailiff gave her many simple little hints which helped her very much. They were both delighted with their walk, and a friendly confidence in each other was the result of their common enjoyment of the same subjects.

When they reached the Gürlitz march, Hawermann showed her the glebe-lands, and told her that the late squire had taken a lease of them.--"And the barley over there," asked Mrs. von Rambow. "That's part of the Gürlitz estate, and it belongs to Mr. Pomuchelskopp."--"Ah, that was the gentleman who met us yesterday with his family," cried Frida. "What sort of man is he?"--"I never see anything of him," said Hawermann, rather confused.--"Don't you know him?" asked Mrs. von Rambow.--"Yes--no--that is, I used to know him; but we hav'n't seen anything of each other since he came here," replied the old man, and then he introduced another subject of conversation, but Frida laid her hand upon his arm, and asked: "Mr. Hawermann, you know that I am a stranger in this neighbourhood, and Alick seems to know very little about these people. Tell me, are they proper acquaintances for us?"--"No," said Hawermann shortly.--They walked on silently, at last Mrs. von Rambow stood still, and asked: "Can you, and will you tell me the reason why you broke off your old acquaintance with that man?"--Hawermann looked at her long and earnestly. "Yes," he said at length, but more as if he were speaking to himself than to her. "And if you believe me as the late squire did, it will perhaps be better for you to know it."--He then told her his story plainly and quietly, hiding nothing and exaggerating nothing. Mrs. von Rambow listened attentively and without interrupting him. When he had finished she merely said: "I didn't like what

I saw of these people yesterday, and now I dislike them."--They had been walking through the glebe-lands for some time, and had reached the hedge at the end of the parsonage-garden; suddenly they heard a sweet young voice at the other side of the hedge exclaim: "Good-morning, father, good-morning," and at the same moment the lovely girl that Mrs. von Rambow had seen at the parsonage-door on the preceding day sprang through the garden-gate towards her father. But on seeing who was with him she blushed deeply and stopped short, so that if Hawermann wanted to have his good-morning-kiss, he would have to go and help himself to it.

The old man introduced his daughter to Mrs. von Rambow with much loving pride, and the squire's young wife, after a few kindly words of greeting, asked her to come up to Pümpelhagen to see her father and herself. When Hawermann had charged his daughter with messages to Mr. and Mrs. Behrens, they took leave of Louisa, and continued their walk.--"The clergyman and his wife are very good people, are they not?" asked Frida.--"Madam," said Hawermann, "I can't give you an impartial answer to that question. They have saved all that remained to me after my misfortunes. They have brought up my only child with loving care, and have taught her all the good she knows. I can never think of them without the greatest reverence and the deepest gratitude. But if you want to know more about them, ask any one you like in the parish. Rich and poor, high and low will all speak of them with affection."--"Mr. Pomuchelskopp too?" asked the lady.--"If he were to speak honestly and without prejudice, he would bear the same testimony," answered the old man; "but unfortunately he had a disagreement with the parson when he first came here about the glebe. It was not Mr. Behrens' fault. I was the real cause of it, for it was I who persuaded the late squire to take a lease of the land. And, Madam," he continued after a pause, "Pümpelhagen can never pay so well without the glebe; having the lease of it is an advantage that cannot be given up without great loss."--Frida made the bailiff explain to her in what this advantage consisted, and as soon as she understood the whole case, she determined that she would do her best to keep the glebe for Pümpelhagen.

When they got home, they saw attorney Slus'uhr and David driving away from the door, and Alick bowing and smiling as much as if Slus'uhr had been his colonel, and David had been a young count.--"Who is that?" Frida asked of Hawermann.--He told her.--When she came up to her husband, she said: "What have you to do with these people, Alick, and why were you so extraordinarily polite to them?"--"Polite?" repeated Alick rather confused. "Why not? I am polite to every body," glancing at Hawermann as he spoke.--"Of course you are," said his young wife, slipping her hand within his arm, "but these were common Jew traders, and ...."--"My dear child," interrupted Alick, who did not wish her to finish her sentence, "the man is a wool-stapler, and I've no doubt I shall often have to do business with him."--"And the other?" she asked,--"Oh, he is--he only happened to come with his friend. I've nothing to do with him."--"Good-bye, Mr. Hawermann," said Frida, shaking hands with the old man, "and thank you so very much for having gone with me this morning." She then went into the house, and Alick followed her; but he looked round again when he had reached the door-way, and saw that the old bailiff's eyes were fixed on him sorrowfully. He could not meet that sad gaze, and turning away he followed his wife into the house.

In that look of honest sorrow lay the future of the three people who had just parted. Alick had told a lie, he had betrayed the confidence of his young wife for the first time, and Hawermann knew it; and Alick knew that Hawermann knew it. A stone was now lying in the way, over which any one passing by that road might easily stumble, for the way had grown dark through untruth and deceit, and none could warn the traveller of the hidden danger. Frida as yet walked on in innocent fearlessness, but sooner or later her foot would strike against that stone. Alick, moreover, deceived himself, he thought he could guide Frida safely past the stone that lay in her path without her ever being aware of its existence, and he knew that the road was clear on the other side of it. Hawermann saw the danger distinctly that menaced the family at Pümpelhagen, and he would willingly have done what he could to help them out of it, but when he would have stretched out his hand to assist and warn, Alick thrust it away with outward calmness, but inward displeasure. It is said that a wicked man grows to hate any one who shows him forbearing kindness, that may be the case, but such hatred is nothing to the gnawing impatient dislike which a *weak* man feels towards him, who alone in all the world knows some mean action of which he has been guilty. This kind of dislike does not come all at once, like the hatred born of open strife; no, it creeps slowly and gradually into the heart in like manner as the wood-louse bores its tunnels into the wainscoting, till at last it gains as complete possession of the heart as the insect does of the wood.

CHAPTER IV

Bräsig went to Rexow that morning to see Mrs. Nüssler as he had intended. The crown-prince was in the doorway when he arrived, and came forward to meet him with such a hearty wag of the tail that anyone would have thought him a most christian-minded dog, and would have imagined that he had quite forgiven Bräsig the fright he had given him the last time he was at Rexow. There was a look of such quiet satisfaction in his yellow brown eyes that one would have thought that everything was going on well in the house; that Mrs. Nüssler was busy in the kitchen, and that Joseph was comfortably seated in his own particular arm-chair. But it was not so. When Bräsig went into the parlour he certainly found Joseph in his old place, but Mrs. Nüssler was standing in front of him, and was giving him a lecture about caring for nothing, and never interfering when things were going wrong, although it was his duty to do so. As soon as she saw Bräsig, she went up to him and said angrily: "And *you* keep out of the way, Bräsig. Everyone may be standing on their heads here for anything *you* care, and it's all your fault that we ever took those two lads into the house."--"Gently!" said Bräsig. "Gently! Don't excite yourself, Mrs. Nüssler! Well what's all this about the divinity students?"--"A very great deal! But I should never have said a word about it, for they're Joseph's relations, and 'it's an ill bird that files its own nest!' There has been no peace or comfort in the house since the two young men have been here, and if it goes on like this much longer, I'm afraid that I shall have a quarrel with Joseph himself."--"Mother," said young Joseph, "what can I do?"--"Hold your tongue, young Joseph," cried Bräsig, "it's all your fault. Why didn't you teach them better manners?"--"Come, come, Bräsig," said Mrs. Nüssler, "just leave Joseph to me if you please, and remember it's your fault this time. You promised to keep an eye on the young men, and see that they didn't get into mischief, and instead of that, you let one of them do what he likes and never trouble your head to see what he's after, while you encourage the other to spend all his time in fishing and such like nonsense, instead of minding his books, so that he's always out in the fields, and comes home in the evening with a lot of perch about the length of my finger, and when I think the day's work is over, I'm expected to go back to the kitchen and cook that trash!"--"What!" cried Bräsig. "Does he only bring you in such tiny little fish? That's queer now, for

I've shown him all the best pools for catching large perch. Then you must .....!--Just wait!"--"I'll tell you," interrupted Mrs. Nüssler, "you must forbid him to fish, for he didn't come here to do that. His father sent him here to learn something, and he's coming to see him this very afternoon."--"Well, Mrs. Nüssler," said Bräsig, "I can't help admiring the presistency with which he has followed my advice about fishing. Hasn't he done anything else though?"--"A great deal, both of them have done a great deal. I've never spoken about it because they're Joseph's relations, and at first everything went on *pretty* well. It was an idle, merry life at first; my two little girls were very much brightened up by the change and all went on smoothly. Mina here, and Rudolph there, Lina here, and Godfrey there. They talked sense with Godfrey and nonsense with Rudolph. The two lads worked away properly at their books in the morning; Godfrey indeed sometimes read so long that it gave him a headache, and Rudolph did quite a fair amount of study. But that did not last long. They soon began to quarrel and wrangle about theological questions, and Godfrey, who knows more than the other, said that Rudolph did not speak from a Christian standpoint."--"Did he say 'standpoint'?" put in Bräsig.--"Yes, that was his very word," answered Mrs. Nüssler.--"Oho!" said Bräsig. "I think I hear him. While other people end with standpoint, Methodists always begin with it. And then I suppose he wanted to convert him?"--"Yes," said Mrs. Nüssler. "That's just what he wanted to do. But you see the other lad is much cleverer than Godfrey, and made so many jokes about all that he said, that at last Godfrey quite lost his temper, and so the discomfort in the house grew worse and worse. I don't know how it was, but my two girls mixed themselves up in the quarrel. Lina who is the gravest and most sensible took Godfrey's side of the argument, and Mina laughed and giggled over Rudolph's jokes."--"Yes," interrupted Joseph, "it's all according to circumstances!"--"You ought to be ashamed of yourself, young Joseph," said Bräsig, "for allowing such a Hophnei to remain in the house."--"Nay, Bräsig," said Mrs. Nüssler, "let Joseph alone, he did his best to make matters comfortable again. When Godfrey talked about the devil till we all felt quite eerie, Joseph believed in his existence; and when Rudolph laughed at, and ridiculed all belief in him, Joseph laughed as heartily as anyone. When the dispute ran highest, my little Mina took all Godfrey's books to Rudolph's room, and all Rudolph's to Godfrey's, and when the young men looked rather cross, she said quickly, that they'd better both study the subject thoroughly, and then perhaps they might agree better about it than at present."--"Mina's a clever little woman," cried Bräsig.--"Well," continued Mrs. Nüssler. "They didn't like it at all at first; but whatever Godfrey's faults may be, he's a good-natured lad, so he began to study Rudolph's books. And the other at last set to work at Godfrey's, for you see it was wintry weather and it gave him something to do. You should have seen them a short time afterwards! They had changed as much as their books. Godfrey made poor jokes about the devil, and Rudolph sighed and groaned, and spoke of the devil as if he knew him intimately, and as if he were accustomed to sit down to dinner with us every day and to eat his potatoes like any other honest man. Then my little girls turned right round. Mina took Godfrey's part; and Lina took Rudolph's, for Rudolph said that Godfrey didn't speak from a Christian standpoint."--"Ugh!" said Bräsig, "he oughtn't to have said that. But wait a bit! Is he really that sort of fellow, and can't he ever catch a good-sized perch?"--"And then," cried Mrs. Nüssler indignantly, "they were all at sixes and sevens again, because of that horrible perch fishing, for as soon as spring returned and the perch began to bite, Rudolph cared no more about the Christian standpoint. He took his fishing-rod, and went out after you all day long. The other went back to his old opinion about the existence of the devil, you see he was preparing for his examination and couldn't get through it properly without that. My two girls didn't know which of their cousins to trust to."--"They're a couple of rascals," cried Bräsig, "but it's all the Methodist's fault, what business had he to bother the other about the devil and the Christian standpoint?"--"No, no, Bräsig, I've nothing to say against him for that. He has learnt something, has passed his examination, and may be ordained any day. But Rudolph does nothing at all, he only makes mischief in the house."--"Why, what has he been after now? Has he been fishing for whitings?" asked Bräsig raising his eyebrows.--"Whitings!" said Mrs. Nüssler scornfully. "He has been fishing for a sermon. You must know that, Mrs. Baldrian wanted to hear her son preach, so she asked the clergyman at Rahnstädt to let him preach in his church, and he said he might do so. She then went and told her sister what she had done, and Mrs. Kurz was very much put out that her son wasn't as far on as his cousin, so she went to the old parson too and asked him to allow Rudolph to preach for him some day soon. Well the clergyman was so far left to himself as to arrange that Rudolph should preach on the same day as Godfrey. The two young men had a great argument as to which was to have the forenoon and which the afternoon, but at last it was settled that Rudolph should preach in the morning. Well, Godfrey set to work as hard as he could, and spent the whole day from morning till evening in the arbour. As he has a bad memory he learnt his sermon by repeating it aloud. Rudolph did nothing but amuse himself as usual, till the two last days, when he seated himself on the grass bank behind the arbour, and seemed to be thinking over his sermon. On the Sunday morning, Joseph drove the two young clergymen and us to Rahnstädt. We went into the parsonage pew, and I can assure you I was in a great fright about Rudolph, but the rogue stood there as calmly as if he were quite sure of himself, and when the time came for him to preach, he went up into the pulpit and began his sermon. He got on so well that everyone listened attentively, and I was so pleased with the boy that I turned to whisper to Godfrey, who sat next to me, how relieved and overjoyed I was, when I saw that he was moving about restlessly in his seat, and looking as if he would like to jump up and pull Rudolph out of the pulpit: 'Aunt,' he said, 'that is *my* sermon.' And so it was, Bräsig. The little wretch had got it by heart from hearing his cousin learning it aloud in the arbour."--"Ha, ha, ha!" laughed Bräsig. "What a joke! What a capital joke!"--"Do you call it a *joke*?" said Mrs. Nüssler angrily. "Do you call playing a trick like that in God's house a joke?"--"Ha, ha, ha!" roared Bräsig. "I know that it's wicked to laugh, and I know that only the devil could have prompted the lad to play such a trick, but I can't help it, I must laugh at it all the same."--"Oh, of course," said Mrs. Nüssler crossly, "of course *you* do nothing but laugh while we are like to break our hearts with grief and anger."--"Never mind me," said Bräsig soothingly, "tell me, what did the Methodist do? Ha, ha, ha! I'd have given a good deal for a sight of his face!"--"You would, would you? Of course he couldn't preach the same sermon in the afternoon, so the parson had to give his people one of his old sermons over again; but he was very angry, and said that if he chose to make the circumstance public, Rudolph might go and hang himself on the first willow he came across."--"But the Methodist?"--"The poor fellow was miserable, but he didn't say a word. However his mother said enough for two, and she spoke so harshly to her sister Mrs. Kurz about what had happened, that they're no longer on speaking terms. There was a frightful quarrel. I was both ashamed and angry at the way they went on, for both Baldrian and Kurz joined in the squabble, and even Joseph began to mix himself up in it, but fortunately our carriage drove up, and I got him away as quickly as I could."--"What did the duellist say?"--"Oh, the wretch was wise enough to run away here as soon as he had concluded his stolen sermon."--"And you gave him a regular good scolding, I suppose," said Bräsig.--"Not I indeed," said Mrs. Nüssler decidedly. "I wasn't going to put my finger in that pie. His father is coming to-day and he is 'the nearest' to him, as Mrs. Behrens would say; and I've told Joseph that he's not to mix himself up in the affair or to talk about it at all. He's quite changed latterly. He has got into the habit of putting up his back and meddling with things with which he has nothing to do. Now just keep quiet, Joseph."--"Yes, Joseph, hold your tongue," said Bräsig.--"And my two girls," continued Mrs. Nüssler, "are quite different from what they used to be. Since that unlucky sermon their eyes have always been red with crying, and they've gone about the house as quietly as mice. They hardly ever say a word to each other now, though they used never to be separate, and when one of them was happy or unhappy the other had to know all about it immediately.

My household is all at odds."--"Mother," said young Joseph rising from his chair with a look of determination, "that's just what I say, and I *will* speak; you'll see that the boys have put it into their heads."--"What have they put into their heads, Joseph?" asked Mrs. Nüsller crossly.--"Love affairs," said Joseph, sinking back into his corner. "My dear mother always used to say that when a divinity student and a governess were in same house ...... And you'll see the truth of it with Godfrey and Mina."--"Law, Joseph! How you do talk to be sure! May God preserve you in your right mind! That's all nonsense, but if it were the case, the divinity student should leave the house at once and Rudolph too. Come away, Bräsig, I've got something to say to you."

As soon as they had left the house, Mrs. Nüssler signed to Bräsig to follow her into the garden, and when they were seated in the arbour, she said: "I can't stand Joseph's eternal chatter any longer, Bräsig. It was Rudolph who taught him to speak so much continually encouraging him to talk last winter, and has got into the habit now and won't give it up. But, tell me honestly--remember you promised to watch--have you seen anything of the kind going on?"--"Bless me! No. Not the faintest approach to anything of the sort."--"I can't think it either," said Mrs. Nüssler thoughtfully. "At first Lina and Godfrey, and Mina and Rudolph used to go about together. Afterwards Mina took to Godfrey, and Lina to Rudolph, but ever since the examination Lina and Godfrey have been on their old terms with each other once more, while Mina and Rudolph have never made friends again; indeed I may say that she has never so much as looked at him since the day he preached in Rahnstädt."--"Ah, Mrs. Nüssler," said Bräsig, "love shows itself in most unexpected ways. Sometimes the giving of a bunch of flowers is a sign of it, or even a mere 'good-morning' accompanied by a shake of the hand. Sometimes it is shown by two people stooping at the same moment to pick up a ball of cotton that one of them has dropped, when all that the looker-on sees is that they knocked their heads together in trying which could pick it up first. But gradually the signs become more apparent. The girl blushes now and then, and the man watches whatever she does; or the girl takes the man into the larder, and gives him sausages, or cold tongue, or pig's cheek, and the man begins to wear a blue or a red neck-tie; but the surest sign of all is when they go out on a summer-evening for a walk in the moonlight, and you hear them sigh without any cause. Now, has anything of that kind been going on with the little roundheads?"--"No, I can't say that I've noticed them doing that, Bräsig. They used to go to the cold meat-larder sometimes it's true, but I soon put an end to that; I wasn't going to stand that sort of thing; and as for blushing, I didn't notice them doing that either, though of course I've seen that their eyes are often red with crying."--"Well," said Bräsig, "there must have been a reason for that--I'll tell you what, Mrs. Nüssler: you just leave the whole management of the affair in my hands, for I know how to arrange such matters. I soon put an end to that sort of nonsense in Fred Triddelfitz. I'm an old hunter, and I'll ferret the matter out for you, but you must tell me where they generally meet."--"Here, Bräsig, here in this arbour. My girls sit here in the afternoon with their work, and then the other two join them. I never thought any harm of it."--"All right!" said Bräsig, going out of the arbour, and looking about him. He examined a large cherry-tree carefully which was growing close by, and seeing that it was thickly covered with leaves he looked quite satisfied. "That'll do," he said, "what can be done, shall be done."--"Goodness, gracious me!" said Mrs. Nüssler, "I wonder what will happen this afternoon! It's very disagreeable. Kurz is coming at coffee-time, and he is desperately angry with his son for playing such a trick on his cousin. You'll see that there will be a terrible scene."--"That's always the way with these little people," said Bräsig, "when the head and the lower part of the constitution are too near each other, the nature is always fiery."--"Ah!" sighed Mrs. Nüssler as she entered the parlour, "it'll be a miserable afternoon."

She little knew that misery had long ago taken up its abode in her house.

Whilst these arrangements were being made downstairs the twins were busy sewing in their garret-room. Lina was seated at one window, and Mina at the other; they never looked up from their work, and never spoke to each other as in the old days at Mrs. Behren's sewing-class. They worked away as busily as if the world had been torn in two, and they had to sew up the rent with their needles and thread, while their serious faces and deep sighs showed that they were fully aware of the gravity of their employment. It was strange that their mother had not told Bräsig how sadly pale they had grown. The change must have been very gradual for her not to have noticed it. But so it was. The two apple-cheeked maidens looked as if they had been growing on the north-side of the tree of life, where no sun-beams could ever come to brighten their existence, and tinge their cheeks with healthful colour. They could no longer be likened to two apples growing on one stalk. At last Lina's work fell on her lap, she could go on sewing no more, her eyes were so full of tears, and then large drops began to roll slowly down her pale cheeks; Mina took out her handkerchief and wiped her eyes, for her tears were falling upon her work, and so the two little sisters sat weeping each in her own window, as if all her happiness were gone past recall.

Suddenly Mina jumped up, and ran out of the room as if she must go out into the fresh air, but she stopped short on the landing, for she remembered that her mother might see her and ask her what was the matter, so she remained outside the door crying silently. And then Lina started up to go and comfort Mina; but she suddenly remembered that she did not know what to say to her, so she remained standing within the room beside the door, crying also. It often happens that a thin wall of separation rises between two loving hearts, and while each would give anything to get back to the other, neither will be the first to turn the handle--for in every such partition wall there is a door with a handle on each side of it--and so they remain apart in spite of their longing to be reconciled.

But fortunately the twins were not so selfishly proud as to allow this state of matters to go on for ever. Mina opened the door, and said: "Why are you crying, Lina?" and Lina immediately stretched out both hands to her sister, and said: "Oh, Mina, why are you crying?" Then they fell upon each other's necks and cried again, and the colour returned to their cheeks as if a sunbeam had kissed them, and they clung to each other as if they were once more growing on the same stalk.--"Mina, I will let you have him. You must be happy," said Lina.--"No, Lina," said Mina, "he likes you most, and you are much better than I am."--"No, Mina. I've quite made up my mind. Uncle Kurz is coming this afternoon, and I'll ask father and mother to let me go home with him, for I couldn't remain here and see it all just yet."--"Do so, Lina, for then you'll be with his parents, and when you both come back, I'll ask Godfrey to get his father to look out for a situation for me as governess in some town far, far from home, for I couldn't stay here either."--"Mina!" cried Lina, holding her sister from her at arm's length, and looking at her in amazement, "with *his* parents? With *whose* parents?"--"Why--Rudolph's."--"You meant Rudolph?"--"Yes, why who did you mean?"--"I?--Oh, I meant Godfrey."--"No, did you really?" exclaimed Mina, throwing her arms round Lina's neck, "but is it possible? How is it possible? We don't mean the same after all then!"--"Ah!" said Lina who was the most sensible of the two, "what a great deal of unnecessary pain we have given each other!"--"Oh, how happy I am," cried Mina, who was the least sensible, as she danced about the room. "All will be well now."--"Yes, Mina," said Lina the sensible, joining in the dance. "Everything will go on happily now."--Then silly little Mina threw herself into her sister's arms again--she was so happy.

If people would only turn the handle of the door that divides them from their friends while there is yet time, all would go well with them, even though it might not bring such intense joy as it did to the two girls in the little garret-room.

The sisters cried one moment and laughed the next; then they danced round the room, and after that they sat on each other's knees, and told how it all happened, and sorrowed over their own stupidity, which had prevented them seeing the true state of the case. They wondered how it was that they had not had an explanation sooner, and then they confessed to each other exactly how matters stood between them and their cousins, and ended by being more than half angry with the two young men, whom they accused of being the real cause of the misunderstanding. Lina said that she had been in great doubt before, but that ever since last Sunday she had been quite certain that Mina cared for Godfrey because of her constant tears; and Mina said that she had been miserable because of the wicked trick Rudolph had played in church about the sermon, and that she had been puzzled to account for Lina's tears. Lina then explained that she had been so very sorry for poor Godfrey's disappointment. All was made up now between the sisters, and when the dinner-bell rang they ran down-stairs together arm in arm, looking as sweet and fresh as two roses. Bräsig, who had seated himself with his back to the light that he might see them better, was very much astonished when he caught sight of their happy faces. "What," he said to himself, "these two girls changed and shy, and suffering from some secret grief? In love? Not a bit of it! They're as merry as crickets."

The sound of the dinner-bell brought Godfrey Baldrian, or the methodist, as Bräsig called him. Lina blushed and turned away from him, not in anger, but because she remembered the confession she had just made in the garret. And Bräsig said to himself "That's very odd now! Lina seems to have taken the infection, but how can she care for a scare-crow of a methodist?"--Bräsig expressed himself too strongly but still it must be acknowledged that Godfrey was no beauty. Nature had not given him many personal advantages, and he did not use those that he had in the wisest possible way. For example his hair. He had a thick head of yellow hair that would have provoked no criticism, and indeed would have looked quite nice if it had only been cut properly, but unfortunately he had taken the pictures of the Beloved disciple John as his model, and had parted his hair down the middle, and brushed it into ringlets at the ends, though the upper part of his head showed that the real nature of his hair was to be straight. I have nothing to say against little boys of ten or even twelve going about with curls, and the mothers of these same little boys would have still less objection to it than I should, for they delight in stroking the curls lovingly out of their children's faces, and in combing them out smooth when visitors come to the house. Some mother have even gone so far, when their children's hair did not curl naturally as to screw it up in paper or use tongs, but that was a mistake on their part. If it were the fashion, I should have nothing to say against even old people wearing curls, for it looks very nice in some ancient pictures, but there are two remarks I should like to make while on this subject, and these are: a man with thin legs ought never to wear tight trousers, and he whose hair does not curl naturally should cut it short. Our poor Godfrey's hair, which hung down his back, was burnt to a sort of dun colour by the sun, and as he liked it to look smooth and tidy, he put a good deal of pomade on it, which greased his coat-collar considerably. Beneath this wealth of hair was a small pale face with an expression of suffering on it, which always made Bräsig ask sympathisingly what shoemaker he employed, and whether he was troubled with corns. The rest of his figure was in keeping with his face. He was tall, narrow-chested, and angular, and that part of the human body which shows whether a man enjoys the good things of life, was altogether wanting in him. Indeed he was so hollowed out where the useful and necessary digesting apparatus is wont to show its existence by a gentle roundness of form, that he might be said to be shaped like the inside of Mrs. Nüssler's baking-trough. For this reason Bräsig regarded him as a sort of wonder in natural history, for he eat as much as a ploughman without producing any visible effect. Let no one imagine that the methodist did not do his full duty in the way of eating and drinking; I have known divinity students, and know some now, with whom I should have no chance in that respect. But the fact is that young men whose minds are employed in theological studies are generally somewhat thin, as will be seen in any of the numerous divinity students to be met with in Mecklenburg; when they have been settled in a good living for a few years, they begin to fill out like ordinary mortals. Bräsig remembered this, and did not despair of seeing Godfrey a portly parson one of these days, though how it was to come about was rather a puzzle to him. Such was Godfrey Baldrian in appearance; but his portrait would not be complete if I did not add that he had the faintest possible tinge of Phariseeism in his expression. It was only a tinge, but with Phariseeism as with rennet, a very small quantity is enough to curdle a large pan of milk.

They sat down to dinner, and Joseph asked: "Where is Rudolph?"--"Goodness gracious me, Joseph, what are you talking about!" said Mrs. Nüssler crossly. "I'm sure you might know by this time that Rudolph is always late. I daresay he's out fishing; but whatever he's about I can assure him that if he doesn't come in in time for dinner, he may just go without."-- The meal was a very silent one, for Bräsig was too much occupied watching what was going on to be able to talk, and Mrs. Nüssler had enough to do wondering over the cause of the remarkable change in her daughters' appearance. The twins sat side by side, and looked as happy as if they had just awakened from a disagreeable dream, and were rejoicing that it was only a dream, and that the warm sun-beams were once more shining upon them.

CHAPTER V

When dinner was over, Mina whose turn it was to help her mother to clear away the dishes, tidy the room, and prepare the coffee, asked her sister: "Where are you going, Lina?"--"I'll get my sewing and go to the arbour," answered Lina.--"Very well," said Mina, "I'll join you there as soon as I'm ready."--"And I'll go too," said Godfrey, "for I've got a book I want to finish."--"That's right," said Bräsig, "It'll be a deuced good entertainment for Lina."--Godfrey felt inclined to take the old man to task for using such a word as "deuced," but on second thoughts refrained from doing so, for he knew that it was hopeless to try to bring Bräsig round to his opinion, so he followed the girls from the room.--"Bless me!" cried Mrs. Nüssler. "What can have happened to my girls? They were as quiet as mice and never said a word to each other till this afternoon, and now they are once more one heart and one soul."--"Hush, Mrs. Nüssler," said Bräsig, "I'll find out all about it for you to-day. Joseph, come with me; but mind you're not to talk."--Joseph followed him to the garden, and when they got there Bräsig took his arm: "Now hold your tongue, Joseph," he said, "don't look round, you must appear to be taking a walk after dinner." Joseph did as he was told with much success. When they reached the cherry-tree beside the arbour, Bräsig stood still and said; "Now then, Joseph, give me a back--but put your head close to the stem of the tree." Joseph was about to speak, but Bräsig pressed down his head, saying: "Hold your tongue, Joseph--put your head nearer the tree." He then stepped on his back, and when standing there firmly, said; "Now straighten yourself--It does exactly!" Then seizing the lower branch with both hands, Bräsig pulled himself up into the tree.--Joseph had never spoken all this time but now he ventured to remark: "But, Bräsig, they're not nearly ripe yet."--"What a duffer you are, Joseph," said Bräsig, thrusting his red face through the green leaves which surrounded him. "Do you really think that I expect to eat Rhenish cherries at midsummer. But go away now as quickly as you can and don't stand there looking like a dog when a cat has taken refuge in a tree."--"Ah well, what shall I do?" said Joseph, going away and leaving Bräsig to his fate.

Bräsig had not been long in his hiding-place, when he heard a light step on the gravel walk, and, peering down, saw Lina going into the arbour with such a large bundle of work in her arms that if she had finished it in one day it would have been difficult to keep her in sewing. She laid her work on the table and, resting her head on her hand, sat gazing thoughtfully at the blue sky beyond Bräsig's cherry-tree.--"Ah, how happy I am," she said to herself in the fulness of her grateful heart. "How happy I am. Mina is so kind to me; and so is Godfrey, or why did he press my foot under the table at dinner. What made Bräsig stare at us so sharply, I wonder? I think I must have blushed. What a good man Godfrey is. How seriously and learnedly he can talk. How decided he is, and I think he has the marks of his spiritual calling written in his face. He isn't the least bit handsome it is true; Rudolph is much better looking, but then Godfrey has an air with him that seems to say: 'don't disturb me by telling me of any of your foolish worldly little vanities, for I have high thoughts and aspirations, I am going to be a clergyman.' I'll cut his hair short though as soon as I have the power."--It is a great blessing that every girl does not set her heart on having a handsome husband, for otherwise we ugly men would all have to remain bachelors; and pleasant looking objects we should be in that case, as I know of nothing uglier than an ugly old bachelor.--Lina's last thought, that of cutting Godfrey's hair, had shown so much certainty of what was going to happen, that she blushed deeply, and as at the same moment she heard a slow dignified step approaching, she snatched up her work and began to sew busily.

Godfrey seated himself at a little distance from his cousin, opened his book and began to read, but every now and then he peeped over the edge of it, either because he had read it before, or because he was thinking of something else.--That is always the way with Methodistical divinity students even when they firmly believe what they teach. Before the examination they think of nothing but their spiritual calling, but after the examination is well over human nature regains its sway, and they look out for a fitting wife, before they begin to think of a parsonage.--Godfrey was like all the rest of his kind, and as no other girls except Mina and Lina had come in his way, and as Lina attended to his admonitions far more docilely than her sister, he determined to make her his help-meet. He was ignorant as to how such matters ought to be conducted, and felt a little shy and awkward. He had got no further in his wooing than pressing his lady-love's foot under the table, and whenever he had done so he was always much more confused than Lina, whose foot had received the pressure.

However he had determined that the whole matter should be settled that day, so he began: "I brought this book out entirely for your sake, Lina. Will you listen to a bit of it just now?"--"Yes," said Lina.---"What a slow affair it's going to be," thought Bräsig, who could hardly be said to be lying on a bed of roses, his position in the cherry-tree was so cramped and uncomfortable.--Godfrey proceeded to read a sermon on Christian marriage, describing how it should be entered into, and what was the proper way of looking upon it. When he had finished he drew a little nearer his cousin and asked: "What do you think of it, Lina?"--"It's very nice," said Lina.--"Do you mean marriage?" asked Godfrey.--"O-oh, Godfrey," said Lina, her head drooping lower over her work.--"No, Lina," Godfrey went on drawing a little closer to her, "it isn't at all nice. I am thankful to see that you don't regard the gravest step possible in human life with unbecoming levity. Marriage is a very hard thing, that is to say, in the Christian sense of the word."--He then described the duties, cares and troubles of married life as if he wished to prepare Lina for taking up her abode in some penal settlement, and Bräsig, as he listened, congratulated himself on having escaped such a terrible fate. "Yes," Godfrey continued, "marriage is part of the curse that was laid on our first parents when they were thrust out of paradise." So saying he opened his Bible and read the third chapter of Genesis aloud. Poor Lina did not know what to do, or where to look, and Bräsig muttered: "The infamous Jesuit, to read all that to the child." He nearly jumped down from the tree in his rage, and as for Lina, she would have run away if it had not been the Bible her cousin was reading to her, so she hid her face in her hands and wept bitterly. Godfrey was now quite carried away by zeal for his holy calling; he put his arm round her waist, and said: "I could not spare you this at a time when I purpose making a solemn appeal to you. Caroline Nüssler, will you, knowing the gravity of the step you take, enter the holy estate of matrimony with me, and become my Christian help-meet?"--Lina was so frightened and distressed at his whole conduct that she could neither speak nor think; she could only cry.

At the same moment a merry song was heard at a little distance:

> "One bright afternoon I stood to look
> Into the depths of a silver brook,
> And there I saw little fishes swim,
> One of them was grey, I look'd at him.
> He was swimming, swimming and swimming
> And with delight seemed overbrimming;
> I never saw such a thing in my life
> As the little grey fish seeking a wife."

Lina struggled hard to regain her composure, and then, in spite of the Bible and the Christian requirements demanded of her, she started up and rushed out of the arbour. On her way to the house she passed Mina who was coming out to join her with her sewing. Godfrey followed Lina with long slow steps, and looked as much put out as the clergyman who was interrupted in a very long sermon by the beadle placing the church key on the reading desk and saying that he might lock up the church himself when he had done, for he, the beadle, must go home to dinner. Indeed he was in much the same position as that clergyman. Like him he had wished to preach a very fine sermon, and now he was left alone in his empty church.

Mina was an inexperienced little thing, for she was the youngest of the family, but still she was quick-witted enough to guess something of what had taken place. She asked herself whether she would cry if the same thing were to happen to her, and what it would be advisable for her to do under the circumstances. She seated herself quietly in the arbour, and began to unroll her work, sighing a little as she did so at the thought of the uncertainty of her own fate, and the impossibility of doing anything but wait patiently.--"Bless me!" said Bräsig to himself as he lay hidden in the tree. "This little round-head has come now, and I've lost all feeling in my body. It's a horribly slow affair!"--But the situation was soon to become more interesting, for shortly after Mina had taken her seat a handsome young man came round the corner of the arbour with an fishing rod over his shoulder and a fish basket on his back.--"I'm so glad to find you here, Mina," he exclaimed, "of course you've all finished dinner."--"You need hardly ask, Rudolph. It has just struck two."--"Ah well," he said, "I suppose that my aunt is very angry with me again."--"You may be certain of that, and she was displeased with you already, you know, even without your being late for dinner. I'm afraid, however, that your own stomach will punish you more severely than my mother's anger could do, you've neglected it so much to-day."--"All the better for you to-night. I really couldn't come sooner, the fish were biting so splendidly. I went to the black pool to-day, though Bräsig always advised me not to go there, and now I know why. It's his larder. When he can't catch anything elsewhere he's sure of a bite in the black pool. It's cram full of tench. Just look, did you ever see such beauties?" and he opened the lid of his basket as he spoke, and showed his spoil, adding: "I've done old Bräsig this time at any rate!"--"The young rascal!" groaned Bräsig as he poked his nose through the cherry-leaves, making it appear like a huge pickled capsicum such as Mrs. Nüssler was in the habit of preserving in cherry-leaves for winter use. "The young rascal to go and catch my tench! Bless me! what monsters the rogue has caught!"--"Give them to me, Rudolph," said Mina. "I will take them into the house, and will bring you something to eat out here."--"Oh no, never mind."--"But you mustn't starve," she said.--"Very well then--anything will do. A bit of bread and butter will be quite enough, Mina."--The girl went away, and Rudolph seated himself in the arbour.--"The devil take it!" muttered Bräsig, stretching his legs softly, and twisting and turning, in the vain endeavour to find a part of his body which was not aching from his cramped position. "The wretch is sitting there now! I never saw such goings on!"

Rudolph sat buried in thought, a very unusual circumstance with him. He was easy-going by nature, and never troubled himself beforehand about vexations that might come to him. He was not in the habit of brooding over his worries, but on the contrary always tried to forget them. He was tall and strongly made, and his mischievous brown eyes had sometimes a look of imperious audacity which was in perfect keeping with the scar on his sunburnt cheek that bore witness that he had not devoted his whole time and energy to the study of dogmatic Theology. "Yes," he said to himself as he sat there waiting for his cousin, "I must get myself out of this difficulty! I could bear it as long as it was far off, for there was always plenty of time to come to a decision, but two things must be settled to-day beyond recall. My father is coming this afternoon. I only hope that my mother won't take it into her head to come too, or I should never have courage to do it. I'm as well suited to be a clergyman as a donkey is to play the guitar, or as Godfrey is to be colonel of a cavalry-regiment. If Bräsig were only here, he'd stand by me I know--And then Mina--I wish it were all settled with her."--At this moment Mina appeared carrying a plate of bread and butter--Rudolph sprang up, exclaiming: "What a dear good little girl you are, Mina!" and he threw his arm round her waist as he spoke.--Mina freed herself from him, saying: "Don't do that. Ah, how could you have been so wicked? My mother is very angry with you."--"You mean about the sermon," he answered, "well yes, it was a stupid trick."--"No," said Mina quickly, "it was a wicked trick. You made game of holy things."--"Not a bit of it," he replied. "These trial sermons are not holy things, even when they are preached by our pious cousin Godfrey."--"But, Rudolph, it was in *church*!"--"Ah, Mina, I confess that it was a silly joke. I didn't think sufficiently of what I was doing. I only thought of the sheepish look of amazement Godfrey's face would wear, and that tickled me so much that I was mad enough to play the trick. Now don't let us talk any more about it, Mina," he said coaxingly, as he slipped his arm round her waist again.--"No, I won't allow that," said Mina. "And," she went on, "the parson said that if he were to make the story known, you'd never get a living all your life."--"Then I hope that he'll tell everyone what I did and it'll end all the bother."--"What do you mean?" asked Mina, pushing him from her and staring at him in perplexity. "Are you in earnest?"--"Never more so in my life. I've entered the pulpit for the first and last time."--"Rudolph!" cried Mina in astonishment.--"What's the use of trying to make me a clergyman," said Rudolph quickly. "Look at Godfrey and then look at me. Do you think I should make a good parson. And then, there's another thing, even if I were so well up in theology that I could puzzle the learned professors themselves, they would never pass me in the examination. All that they care about is having men who can adopt all their cant phrases. If I were the apostle Paul himself they'd refuse to pass me, if they caught sight of this little scar upon my cheek."--"What are you going to do then?" asked Mina anxiously, and laying her hand upon his arm, she added: "Oh, *don't* be a soldier!"--"I should think not! No, I want to be a farmer."--"The confounded young rascal!" muttered Bräsig.--"Yes, my own dear little Mina," continued Rudolph, drawing her to his side on the bench, "I intend to be a farmer; a real good hard-working farmer, and you, dear Mina, must help me to become one."--"What!" said Bräsig to himself, "is she to teach him to plough and harrow?"--"I, Rudolph?" asked Mina.--"Yes, my sweet child," he answered, stroking her smooth hair and soft cheeks; then taking her chin in his hand, he raised her face towards him, and looking into her blue eyes, went on: "If I could only be certain that you'd consent to be my little wife as soon as I'd a home to offer you, it would make everything easy to me, and I should be sure of learning to be a good farmer. Will you, Mina, will you?"--Mina began to cry softly, and Rudolph kissed away the tears as they rolled down her cheeks, and then she laid her little round-head on his shoulder. Rudolph gave her time to recover her composure, and after a few minutes she told him in a low whisper that she would do as he asked, so he kissed her again and again.--Bräsig seeing this exclaimed half aloud: "The devil take him! Stop that!"--Rudolph found time to tell her in the midst of his kissing that he intended to speak to his father that afternoon, and said amongst other things that it was a pity, Bräsig was not there, as he was sure he would have helped him to make his explanation to his father, who, he knew, thought a great deal of Bräsig's advice.--"The young rascal to catch my fish!" muttered Bräsig.--Then Mina said: "Bräsig was here this morning and dined with us. I daresay he is enjoying an after dinner sleep now."--"Just listen to little round-head," said Bräsig to himself. "An after dinner sleep indeed! But everything is settled now, and I needn't cramp my bones up here any longer."--And while Rudolph was saying that he would like to see the old man before he went into the house, Bräsig slipped out of his hiding-place in the cherry-tree, and clinging with both hands to the lowest branch, let his legs dangle in the air, and shouted: "Here he is!"--Bump! He came down on the ground, and stood before the lovers with an expression on his red face which seemed to say that he considered himself a competent judge on even the most delicate points of feeling.

 The two young people were not a little startled. Mina hid her face in her hands as Lina had done, but she did not cry; and she would have run away like Lina if she and uncle Bräsig had not always been on the most confidential terms with each other. She threw herself into uncle Bräsig's arms, and in her desire to hide her blushing face, she tried to burrow her little round-head into his waistcoat-pocket, exclaiming: "Uncle Bräsig, uncle Bräsig, you're a very naughty old man!"--"Oh!" said Bräsig, "you think so, do you?"--"Yes," answered Rudolph, who had mounted his high horse, "you ought to be ashamed of listening to what you were not intended to hear."--"Moshoo Rudolph," said the old bailiff stiffly, "I may as well tell you once for all, that shame is a thing that must never be mentioned in connection with me, and if you think that your grand airs will have any effect upon me, you're very much mistaken."--Rudolph saw clearly that such was the case, and as he did not want to quarrel with the old man for Mina's sake, he relented a little, and said more gently that he would think nothing more of what had occurred, if Bräsig could assure him that he had got into the tree by accident, but still he considered that Bräsig ought to have coughed, or done something to make his presence known, instead of sitting still and listening to the whole story from A to Z.--"Oh," said Bräsig, "I ought to have *coughed*, you say, but I *groaned* loud enough, I can tell you, and you couldn't have helped hearing me if you hadn't been so much taken up with what you yourself were about. But *you* ought to be ashamed of yourself for having fallen in love with Mina without Mrs. Nüssler's leave."--Rudolph replied that that was his own affair, that no one had a right to meddle, and that Bräsig understood nothing about such things.--"What!" said Bräsig. "Have you ever been engaged to three girls at once? *I* have, Sir, and quite openly too, and yet you say that I know nothing about such things! But sneaks are all alike. First of all you catch my fish secretly in the black pool, and then you catch little Mina in the arbour before my very eyes. No, no, let him be, Mina. He shall not hurt you."--"Ah, uncle Bräsig!" entreated Mina, "do help us, we love each other so dearly."--"Yes, let him be, Mina, you're my little god-child; you'll soon get over it."--"No, Mr. Bräsig," cried Rudolph, laying his hand on the old man's shoulder, "no, dear good uncle Bräsig, we'll never get over it; it'll last as long as we live. I want to be a farmer, and if I have the hope before me of gaining Mina for my wife some day, and if," he added slyly, "you will help me with your advice, I can't help becoming a good one."--"What a young rascal!" said Bräsig to himself, then aloud: "Ah, yes, I know you! You'd be a latin farmer like Pistorius, and Prætorius, and Trebonius. You'd sit on the edge of a ditch and read the book written by the fellow with the long string of titles of honour, I mean the book about oxygen, nitrogen and organisms, whilst the farm-boys spread the manure over your rye-field in lumps as big as your hat. Oh, I know you! I've only known one man who took to farming after going through all the classes at the High-school, who turned out well. I mean young Mr. von Rambow, Hawermann's pupil."--"Oh, uncle Bräsig," said Mina, raising her head slowly and stroking the old man's cheek, "Rudolph can do as well as Frank."--"No, Mina, he *can't*. And shall I tell you why? Because he's only a grey-hound, while the other is a man"--"Uncle Bräsig," said Rudolph, "I suppose you are referring to that silly trick that I played about the sermon, but you don't know how

Godfrey plagued me in his zeal for converting me. I really couldn't resist playing him a trick."--"Ha, ha, ha!" laughed Bräsig. "No, I didn't mean that, I was very much amused at that. So he wanted to convert you, and perhaps induce you to give up fishing? He tried his hand at converting again this afternoon, but Lina ran away from him; however that doesn't matter, it's all right."--"With Lina and Godfrey?" asked Mina anxiously. "And did you hear all that passed on that occasion too?"--"Of course I did. It was for her sake entirely that I hid myself in that confounded cherry-tree. But now come here, Moshoo Rudolph. Do you promise never to enter a pulpit again, or to preach another sermon?"--"Never again."--"Do you promise to get up at three o'clock in the morning in summer, and give out the feeds for the horses?"--"Punctually."--"Do you promise to learn how to plough, harrow, mow and bind properly? I mean to bind with a wisp, there's no art in doing it with a rope."--"Yes," said Rudolph,--"Do you promise when coming home from market never to sit in an inn over a punch-bowl while your carts go on before, so that you are obliged to reel after them?"--"I promise never to do so," said Rudolph.--"Do you promise--Mina, do you see that pretty flower over there, the blue one I mean, will you bring it to me, I want to smell it--do you promise," he repeated as soon as Mina was out of hearing, "never to flirt with any of those confounded farm-girls?"--"Oh, Mr. Bräsig, do you take me for a scoundrel?" asked Rudolph, turning away angrily.--"No, no," answered Bräsig, "but I want you to understand clearly from the very beginning that I will strangle you if ever you cause my little god-child to shed a tear." And as he spoke he looked so determined, that one might have thought he was going to begin the operation at once. "Thank you, Mina," he said, taking the flower from her, and after smelling it putting it in his button-hole. "And now come here, Mina, and I will give you my blessing. Nay, you needn't go down on your knees, for I'm not one of your parents, I'm only your god-father. And, Moshoo Rudolph, I promise to take your part this afternoon when your father comes, and to help you to free yourself from being bound to a profession you don't like. Come away both of you, we must go in now. But, Rudolph, remember you mustn't sit on the grass and read, but must see to the proper manuring of your fields yourself. Look this is the way the farm-lads ought to hold their pitch-forks, not like that. Bang! and tumble off all that is on it; no, they must shake the fork gently three or four times, breaking and spreading the manure as they do so. When a bit of ground is properly spread it ought to look as smooth and clean as a velvet table-cover."--He then went into the house accompanied by the two young people.

CHAPTER VI

Towards the middle of the afternoon Kurz, the general-merchant, and Baldrian, the rector of the academy, set out for Rexow. Kurz very soon repented having asked the rector to accompany him, for it is an extremely uncomfortable thing for a short man to have a long-legged friend as companion in a walk. As they went along the road, the rector said jestingly that their way of walking made a capital verse of the kind the Romans loved, and which they called a dactyle, for they went long, short short; long, short short. This witticism made Kurz angry, for he regarded it as a reflection on his legs, and on his power of walking, so he tried hard to lengthen his steps.--"Now we are making a spondee," said the rector.--"Do me the favour, brother-in-law," said Kurz angrily, and gasping for breath, "not to thrust your learning down my throat; I'm too hot to bear it"--Then he passed his handkerchief over his heated face, took off his coat and hung it over his walking-stick. Kurz's principal trade was that of druggist, but he also dealt in drapery and other goods, and as in this latter branch of trade there were always remnants left of various materials, he found his short stature very convenient in using up any odd pieces of cloth that might be left on his hands. About a year and a half before this when clearing his shop of old and useless goods, he found a remnant of stuff that had once been in fashion for ladies' cloaks, the pattern of which was a giraffe browsing on a tall palm-tree. He considered the piece of cloth too good to throw away, and as he could not induce any one to buy it, he had it made into a summer-coat for himself. And now he walked along the Rexow road carrying it like a banner, as if he were the youngest ensign in the army of a small German prince, whose coat of arms was a giraffe and a palm-tree. Rector Baldrian stalked on by his side in a yellow nankin-coat, and looked as if he were the leader of the right wing of the same prince's bodyguard, always supposing that the said prince had chosen to dress his body-guard in yellow nankin for a little change.

"Bless me!" said Mrs. Nüssler, who was in the parlour, "Kurz is bringing the rector with him."--"So he is," answered Bräsig, "but he won't be much in our way this afternoon, for I intend to interrupt him whenever I see fit."--They were both afraid, and not unreasonably so, of Baldrian's love of making long speeches.

The two visitors now came into the room, and the rector began to talk about his pleasure in seeing his old friends again, and told them how he had embraced the opportunity of Kurz's going to Rexow to accompany him as he could not have a better excuse. Bräsig answered shortly that his long legs were the best excuse he could have for the walk, and then turned away from him. As Mrs. Nüssler was busy talking to Kurz the rector had to content himself with addressing the rest of his remarks to Joseph, who listened to the stream of words with the most praiseworthy attention, and when it ceased, merely said: "How-d'ye-do, brother-in-law; won't you sit down."--Kurz was in a bad humour. Firstly, because he wanted to give his son a scolding; secondly, because Baldrian had nearly walked him off his legs; and thirdly, because he had got a slight chill from taking off his coat, and was suffering from hiccough. His bad temper, however, was nothing unusual, for he had almost always something to displease him. He was a radical, not with regard to the affairs of the state, for such people were then unknown in Mecklenburg, but as far as the municipal government of the town in which he lived was concerned. He had long made it the task of his life to get the charge of the town-jail out of the hands of the long-nosed baker who was so shamefully favoured by the mayor. He gasped and hiccoughed, and his heated face crowned with stubbly grey hair might, without too great a stretch of imagination, be likened to a freshly cut spiced ham that had been thickly strewed with pepper and salt on the top. The resemblance was incomplete in one particular, for there was no knife to be seen, but Bräsig took care to put that right. He went to the knife-basket, took a sharp dinner-knife out of it, and going up to the spiced ham, said: "Come, Kurz, sit down there for a moment."--"What do you want?" asked Kurz.--"To show my sympathy for your hiccough. Now, Keep your eyes fixed on the sharp edge of the knife. I shall bring the edge of the knife nearer and nearer to you, so; but you must be frightened or it will do no good. Nearer--and--nearer, as if I wanted to stab you on the nose. Nearer and--nearer till I almost touch your eyes."--"Hang it!" cried Kurz, springing to his feet "Do you mean to put out my eyes?"--"Capital!" said Bräsig. "Capital! I've given you a fright, and that ought to have cured you."--It really had the effect of sending away his hiccough, but did not lessen his ill-humour.--"Where's my son?" he asked. "I've got a crow to pick with him. Ah, brother-in-law," he went on, turning to Joseph, "I've had enough to anger me. There's my son here; then at the court-house about the management of the jail; at home with my wife because of that silly affair of the sermon; in the shop with a stupid apprentice, who when asked for a penny-weight of black silk-thread gave the customer half an ounce instead! And again on the road here with the rector's long legs."--"Mother," said young Joseph, pushing a coffee-cup nearer his wife, "give Kurz some coffee."--"Oh, brother-in-law," said

Mrs. Nüssler, "there's plenty of time for all that. Let us talk over the matter quietly first, and don't speak to the boy about what he did until your anger has cooled a little, or you will only be pouring oil on the flames."--"I'll ...." began Kurz passionately, but he got no further, for at the same moment the door opened, and Godfrey came in.

Godfrey looked unusually solemn as he went up to his father and wished him good-day. His pompous manner, and the severe gravity of his deportment were enough to make one imagine, that his patron saint had taken care to clothe him in unapproachable dignity, that he might the more easily keep himself unspotted from the world.--"How-d'ye-do, papa. I hope you are well," he said giving his father a kiss in the hollow of his cheek, which the latter returned by making a kiss in the air thereby reminding one of a carp when he puts his head out of the water. "How is mama just now?" the son continued, for Godfrey had been taught to say "papa and mama" from his earliest years, because though the rector thought it quite right and proper for tradesmen's children to call their parents "father and mother," he did not consider it seemly that the children of well educated people should do so. Kurz was always indignant at "such affectation," for his son of course said "father and mother"--"How-d'ye-do, uncle," continued Godfrey addressing Kurz, "and how are you, Mr. bailiff Bräsig," then turning to his father he went on: "I am particularly glad that you have come to-day, for I want to speak to you about a matter of the deepest interest to myself."--"Aha!" said Bräsig to himself. "He's making a good beginning."

The rector went out into the yard with his son, and Bräsig placed himself in the window that he might watch them. Mrs. Nüssler came up to him and said: "Well, Bräsig, have you found out anything this afternoon with regard to my children?"--"Don't be anxious, Mrs. Nüssler, the mystery is unravelled."--"What do you mean?" cried Mrs. Nüssler. "What have you discovered?"--"You'll soon hear what it is, for look put there, that has got something to do with it. Why do you think that the rector shakes hands with and embraces the Methodist so warmly? Is it because of his Christian faith? No, I will tell you why. It is because you are such a good manager."--Bräsig had as great a knowledge of human nature and of the human heart as if he had been a soothsayer, but like all soothsayers he spoke darkly, and so Mrs. Nüssler was unable to understand what he meant. "But," she exclaimed, "why does he embrace Godfrey because I am a good manager?"--Bräsig had another fault in common with all soothsayers and that was that he never answered a direct question unless it suited him to do so. "Look!" he said. "Why does he give his son his blessing? Is it not because he knows that money can buy everything that a man can desire, and that there is plenty of it here?"--"But what has that got to do with my children?"--"You'll soon see. Look! The Methodist is going away now, just watch his father. Preserve us all! He's preparing a speech, and it's sure to be a long one, for everything about him is long, especially his cer'monious politeness."--When the rector came in he proved what a good judge of human nature Bräsig was, for no sooner had he entered the room than he began: "Ladies and gentlemen, a wise man of old gave utterance to this incontestable proposition, that that household is to be regarded as the happiest in which peace and comfort are to be found. That is the case here. I have not come to disturb your peace--my worthy brother-in-law Kurz may do as he likes--I have come here by chance, but chance is often only another name for destiny, and it sometimes leads us without our knowledge to the most important events of our lives. Such has been the case to-day. This chance may lead to good or it may lead to ill, but as I do not wish to say too much just now, I will allude to this part of the subject no more for the present. Dear brother-in-law Joseph, I address myself to you as the real head of this happy family"--Joseph stared at him in as blank amazement as if the rector had said that he was the autocrat of all the Russias, and that he ought by rights to sit on a throne in the royal palace at Moscow--"Yes," repeated the rector, "I address myself to you as the *real* head of the family, and you will, I am sure, pardon me if I also turn to my dear sister-in-law, who has ever conducted the affairs of her own immediate circle with so much wisdom and love that the blessed effects of her rule have extended themselves to other families, related to her's by the ties of consanguinity--I allude more particularly to the kind reception my son Godfrey met with here and which has been of the greatest possible advantage to him.--You, my dear brother-in-law Kurz, also belong to the family, at least on the female side, through--but we will say no more about that in this happy hour--suffice it to say that I know you will rejoice with me in my joy. But now," approaching Bräsig, "'πος τ' αρ' ιω τον προστυξομαι αυτον? [Transl.: pos t' ar' io, ton prostuxomai auton?]' which signifies: How shall I address you, Mr. bailiff Bräsig? for though you cannot be called a member of the family in the strict sense of the word, yet you have always been so helpful in deed, and so wise in counsel ...."--"If that's the case," interrupted Bräsig, "I'll give you some good advice now. If you don't keep a better hold of the reins you'll never get to the end."--"End!" ejaculated the rector, whose inborn sanctimoniousness was only covered by a thin crust of scholastic pedantry. "End!" he repeated, raising his eyes to heaven. "Will it lead to a good or a bad end? Who can tell what the end will be?"--"I can," answered Bräsig, "for I heard the beginning in that confounded cherry-tree this afternoon. The end is that the Methodist will marry our Lina."

What an uproar there was!--"Goodness gracious me!" cried Mrs. Nüssler. "Godfrey!--our child!"--"Yes," said the rector, who now that he had been stopped in his harangue stood before them with much the same dazed expression as Klein the engineer at Stavenhagen had worn, when on trying some engines to see whether they would answer, a pipe burst unexpectedly and his glory was suddenly eclipsed.--Kurz started up, exclaiming: "The rascal! Godfrey evidently thinks no small beer of himself!"--And Joseph also rose, but more slowly, and asked: "Was it Mina you said, Bräsig?"--"No, young Joseph, only Lina," answered Bräsig quietly.--"So you knew all about it, Bräsig, and yet you never told me," said Mrs. Nüssler reproachfully.-- "Oh, I know more than that," he replied, "but why should I have told you? It could make no difference whether you knew it a quarter of an hour sooner or later, and besides that, I thought it would have been a pleasant surprise for you."--"Here he is," said the rector, bringing Godfrey in from the front hall where he had been awaiting the result of the interview, "and he relies on your kindness for a favourable decision."

Godfrey's manner was so totally different from what it had been a short time before that he looked like another man. He had got rid of his pomposity and look of self-sufficiency, for he was too thoroughly in earnest at that moment to put on any little airs, and was contented to show himself as he really was, namely, a man full of doubt and hope, of fear and love; in short, a human being and not a machine. And assuredly true love is in itself so beautiful, being one of the deepest and tenderest feelings of humanity, that he could not have made it more beautiful by retaining his grave clerical manner. Godfrey had not felt this to be the case at first, but now his love had gained such power over him that he told Mrs. Nüssler and Joseph his tale so simply and naturally, that Bräsig said to himself: "What a change there is in that young fellow! If Lina has improved him so much in this short time, there are great hopes for the future. He may become a very pleasant, agreeable man in course of time."

Mrs. Nüssler listened silently to what Godfrey had to say for himself. Although she really liked her nephew, she did not feel at all sure that she could give him her daughter, and was very much puzzled and distressed. "Good gracious, Godfrey," she at last exclaimed, "I know that you are a good lad, and that you've been working hard for your examination, but ....." Here she was interrupted by her husband for the first time in her life. As soon as Joseph understood that it was not Mina he became calm, and sat down again; he collected his thoughts while Godfrey was speaking, and when he saw all eyes fixed on him he determined to speak, and so interrupting his wife, he said: "Ah, Godfrey, it all depends upon circumstances. I will do my duty as father of the family. If my wife gives her consent, so do I, and if Lina gives her consent, I will do so too."--"Bless me, Joseph!" cried Mrs.

Nüssler. "What on earth are you saying? *Do* be quiet. I must speak to my daughter first. I must hear what she says before anything is settled."--And she hastened from the room.

They had not to wait long till she came back with Lina, and followed by Mina and Rudolph, who probably intended making their confession when they saw that matters were going smoothly with the other two. Lina blushed as red as a rose when, letting go her mother's hand, she returned Godfrey's kiss, and then threw herself into her mother's arms. After that she seated herself on her father's knee, and tried to give him a kiss, but could not for coughing, and no wonder, for Joseph in his excitement was smoking as if for a wager, so she only said: "Father," and he answered: "Lina." When she got up Bräsig was standing at her side, and he patted her shoulder, and said: "Never mind, Lina, I'll give you a present too."--Godfrey now came up to her, and taking her by the hand led her up to his father, who stooped down so low to give her a paternal embrace, that the others all thought he wanted to pick a hair-pin off the floor. The rector then prepared to make another speech, but Bräsig put a stop to it by drumming "The old Dessauer" so loud on the window-pane that no one could hear a single word, and as he drummed he stared out of the window as fixedly as if the way the sunlight fell on the fruit-trees in Joseph's garden were particularly worthy of his attention. He was thinking of the apple-tree which might have been his, long, long ago, but which Joseph had planted in his own garden, while he had had to look on. But in spite of that he had always taken as great care of the tree as if it had been his, had tended it, and watched over it. And the tree had borne fruit, two round rosy apples, which as time went on grew ripe and beautiful in his eyes, and then two boys saw them, climbed over the wall, and one of them plucked an apple and put it in his pocket, while the other prepared to follow his example. Well, well, boys are boys, and apples and boys always go together. He knew that, and had often told himself that it would come to pass sooner or later, but it made him sad to think that the care of the little apple-cheeked maidens was passing out of his hands, and he could not yet bring himself to consent to give his little round-heads up to other people, so he drummed more vehemently than before on the window.

Kurz here blew his nose so loudly that one might be pardoned for thinking he wanted to blow a trumpet in accompaniment to Bräsig's drum. He did not do it however because his feelings were touched by what was going on, but because he was very angry. He felt as much out of place in this quiet scene of domestic happiness, as a fifth wheel in a carriage, but as he knew that good manners required him to congratulate his relations, he advanced to do so with a forced smile which made him look as if he were eating a plum pickled in vinegar. He passed his son Rudolph without even glancing at him, and made his civil speeches to the right hand and to the left with the worst possible grace. When he reached the rector he could restrain himself no longer, for the thought of his son's misdeeds overwhelmed him, and he turned to Rudolph, saying: "Ar'n't you ashamed of yourself?" Then to the others: "Pardon me, but this business must be settled first--Ar'n't you ashamed of yourself? Hav'n't you cost me more money than Godfrey ever cost his father? Have you learnt anything? Tell me what you have learnt."--"Dear brother-in-law," said the rector, laying his hand on Kurz's head as kindly as if he had been a little boy, and had done his latin exercise well, "he can't tell you all that he has learnt at a moment's notice."--"What!" cried Kurz, jerking his head from under the rector's hand. "Did *you* bring me here, or was it I who brought you? I think that I brought you, and so have a right to have my business done."--"Ar'n't you ashamed of yourself?" he cried, turning again to Rudolph. "Look, there's Godfrey. He has passed his examination, and is engaged to a pretty girl--and a nice girl too," here he made a bow which he intended for Lina, but in his excitement he directed it to Mrs. Nüssler. "He may get a church to-morrow," bowing to Bräsig instead of Godfrey, "whilst you--whilst you--have gone about fighting, and have done nothing. You have also contracted debts, but I won't pay them," and then although no one had contradicted him, he repeated: "I won't pay them! No, I won't pay them!" After which he joined Bräsig at the window, and began to help him to drum.

Poor Rudolph stood on thorns during this address. It is true that he was naturally of an easy going disposition, and that he generally took his father's admonitions as they were intended, for let no one imagine Kurz meant all he said when he was angry with his son. No. It was that he loved his boy so dearly, he could not bear to acknowledge that the rector's son had done so much better than he had. But although Rudolph was quite aware that that was the case, he felt hurt and angry with his father for having taken him to task before so many witnesses, and if his eyes had not fallen on Mina, he would have said some of the bitter words which rushed to his lips. Mina was very pale, and was trembling violently in her intense sympathy for him, who since that afternoon, was bone of her bone, and flesh of her flesh, and Rudolph seeing it swallowed down the hasty words he was about to have uttered, feeling for the first time that he must no longer be swayed by impulse, but read in Mina's eyes her opinion of his every action. And I think that is one of the greatest blessings true love brings to the young.

"Father," he said after he had regained his self-command, and then unheeding the grave faces round him, he went up to his father and laid his hand on his shoulder, "Come, father! I've done with silly tricks and practical jokes from this time forward."--Kurz went on drumming on the glass, and Bräsig ceased to do it. "Father," Rudolph went on, "you're quite right to be displeased with me, I know that I deserve it, but ...."--"*Do* stop that confounded drumming," said Bräsig, pushing Kurz's hand down.--"Father," continued Rudolph, seizing his father's hand, "let all be forgiven and forgotten!"---"No," said Kurz, thrusting both his hands into his pockets.--"What!" cried Bräsig, "you won't do that? I know quite well that nobody has any business to interfere between a father and son, but all the same I intend to interfere, for it's your own fault that the dispute is such a public one. Do you mean to tell me that you won't forgive and forget your own son's folly? Don't you remember sending me that nasty sweet Prussian kümmel long ago? And didn't I forgive you, and go on dealing with you, and paying my debts honourably?"--"I have always served you honestly," answered Kurz.--"Oh, indeed!" said Bräsig sarcastically, "when you sold me that pair of trousers for instance? Young Joseph, you remember them, and can bear me witness how they changed colour."--"Pshaw! That stupid story of yours about the trousers," cried Kurz. "You've talked about them often enough, and ...."--"Well, you know, them," interrupted Bräsig. "Now confess. Wasn't it pure wickedness on your part to let me take them, when you knew they would turn red, and yet, have I not forgiven and forgotten? That's to say I hav'n't forgotten, for I've a distinct recollection of the whole affair. And you needn't forget the young man, you need only forgive him."--"Dear brother-in-law," began the rector, who thought it incumbent on him to preach peace as he had formerly been a clergyman, but Kurz stopped him short, and said: "Say no more for pity sake! You're engaged to a pretty girl, and will soon get a living--I mean that your son Godfrey will--while we--we--have learnt nothing, and so will never have a chance of either!" And so saying he began to walk rapidly up and down the room.--"Father," cried Rudolph, "listen to me."--"Yes," said Mrs. Nüssler whose heart was sore for the lad; then going up to Kurz she took him by the arm, and went on, "you must and shall listen to what he has to say, for although that was a very wrong and silly trick he played about the sermon--and no one could have been more angry with him than I was--still he is a dear good boy, and many a father would be proud of having such a son."--"Very well," replied Kurz, "I will hear what he has to say." Placing himself opposite his son, and sticking his thumbs in the arm-holes of his waist-coat, he went on: "What have you to say? Go on. What have you to say for yourself?"--Rudolph looked entreatingly but firmly at his father as he answered: "Dear father, I know that you will be sorry, but I can't help it, I cannot be a clergyman, and I intend to be a farmer."

It is said that bears are taught to dance by being put on a heated iron floor, where they are obliged to keep jumping about continually to prevent their feel being burnt. On hearing his son's words, Kurz began to dance round Rudolph as spasmodically as if the devil had heated Mrs. Nüssler's parlour floor, as the bear keepers are in the habit of doing. "Well, this is delightful!" he said at every jump he gave. "The nicest thing I ever heard. My son, after having cost me so much money, after having had such an excellent education wants to be a farmer! a clod-breaker! a country-bumpkin! a lout!"--"Young Joseph," cried Bräsig, "shall we allow that to pass? Get up, young Joseph! Sir!" he continued going up to Kurz. "Do *you*, a mere herring-dealer, a seller of molasses, dare to look down upon us farmers? Sir, do you know what we are? We are the backbone of the nation. If we did not exist, and did not give you employment, you tradesmen would have to go about the country with packs on your backs. And yet you think that your son has had too good an education to be a farmer! You sometimes say that he has learnt too much, and then again you say that he has not learnt enough, just as it suits you. Sir, do you really think--come here and stand beside me, Joseph--do you think that it is necessary for a man to be a fool or an ass before he can be a good farmer?"--"Dear brother-in-law," began the rector once more.--"Do you wish to kill me with your long speeches?" snapped Kurz. "You've shorn your lamb; I came here to shear my black sheep, and everyone falls upon me and wants to shear me instead."--"Now, Kurz," said Mrs. Nüssler, "do try to be sensible. What can't be cured must be endured. If Rudolph doesn't want to be a clergyman, he is the 'nearest' as Mrs. Behrens would say, and ought to be the best judge. It seems to me that if he is only a good man, it doesn't matter whether he preaches or ploughs."--"Father," said Rudolph, seeing that the old man appeared to be impressed by what he had heard, "do give your consent, you don't know how much the happiness of my life depends upon it."--"Who'll teach you?" asked Kurz still crossly. "No one I'll be bound!"--"That's my affair," said Bräsig, "I know a man, who'll do it. Hilgendorf in Tetzleben, who understands the most learned the'ries in agriculture, and who has made some great scholars into good practical farmers. He once had a poet amongst his pupils, who used to write verses under the hedge, and who, instead of saying that the sun had risen, used to say that Aurora was looking down upon the fields and meadows. Then, when he wanted to describe how the black storm clouds were rising, he said that cloud citadels were being piled up in the western heavens, and instead of saying that it was dropping, he used to say that a few drops of rain were falling softly from the sky. But in spite of all this Hilgendorf succeeded in making the poet a useful member of society. Rudolph must go to him."--"Yes," answered Kurz, "he shall go to him, but I will tell Hilgendorf ...."--"Tell him whatever you like father," said Rudolph, seizing his father's hand, "but there's one thing I want to ask you ...."--"Stop! Stop!" cried Kurz. "I know you're going to speak of your debts, but don't tell me about them to-day. I've had enough to bear with hearing that you're going to be a mere country bumpkin. I won't pay them I tell you," pushing his son away from him as he spoke.--"And you shan't have to do it, father," said Rudolph drawing himself up to his full height, and looking at the old gentleman, with an expression of such manly determination that all eyes were fixed on him. "You shan't have to do it. I have contracted new obligations today and have sworn to myself that I will fulfil them at any cost. This is the person to whom I am indebted," he continued, going up to Mina, who had hidden her face on her sister's shoulder at the beginning of the quarrel, and who felt as if the Last Judgment had begun. He put his arm round her waist, and went on: "And if I'm ever good for anything, you must thank her for it--it will all be her doing," his eyes filled with tears as he spoke, "and she has promised to be my wife."--"The young rascal!" said Bräsig passing the back of his hand across his eyes, then taking his former place in the window he began to drum "the old Dessauer" once more, and he was the only one who was able to make music on the occasion.--The others all stood as though they had been turned to stone.--"Goodness gracious me!" Mrs. Nüssler at last exclaimed. "What does all this mean?"--"What?" cried Joseph. "Did he say, Mina?"--"Mercy on us, Joseph!" interrupted Mrs. Nüssler. "I wish you'd be quiet. Mina, tell me what it means."--But Mina looked so white and still as she stood there, her head resting on Rudolph's shoulder, that it seemed as if she would never raise it, and never speak again.--Kurz had grasped the whole meaning of the situation in a moment, and before speaking did up a couple of sums in addition in his head. He was so much pleased with the result of his calculation of Joseph's savings that he began to dance again, but no longer like a polar bear; no, this time he resembled a red Indian dancing his war-dance in sign of victory while Bräsig supplied the music. Rector Baldrian's face was the only one that remained calm and composed during all this excitement, and his expression was as inscrutable as my own when I look into a Hebrew Bible.--"What is it? What does it mean? What is all this?" cried Mrs. Nüssler throwing herself into a chair. "My two children! Both my little girls on one and the same day! And didn't you promise me," she said, turning suddenly upon Bräsig, "that you would be on the watch?"--"Did I not watch, Mrs. Nüssler," remonstrated Bräsig, "till all my bones ached? But misfortunes never come single, and who can prevent them? What do you say, Joseph?"--"I say nothing, but my dear mother always used to say that a candidate for the ministry, and a governess....."--"Joseph," cried Mrs. Nüssler, "you're talking me to death! You've learnt to chatter since that wretched Rudolph came to the house."--"What a fool you were not to tell me before," said Kurz to his son as he danced round him and Mina, "I would have forgiven you long ago for the sake of the dear little daughter-in-law you're giving me." As he said this he took Mina's face between his hands and kissed her.--"Mercy me!" exclaimed Mrs. Nüssler. "Kurz is calling her his daughter-in-law, and kissing her, and yet his son has nothing to do, and Mina is such an inexperienced little thing!"--"Oh?" asked Bräsig. "You mean because she's the youngest? Come away with me, I want to speak to you in private for a moment," and he drew her away to a corner of the room where they both stood still and stared into the match-box which was hanging on the wall. "Mrs. Nüssler," he said, "what's right for one is equally right for the other. You've given Lina your blessing, why won't you give it to Mina also? It's quite true that she's the most inexperienced of the two because she's the youngest, but Mrs. Nüssler you must rec'lect that the difference in age between twins is so small that it's hardly worth counting. You have agreed to give your daughter to the Methodist, although the devil alone knows how he will treat her--none of us can tell, for neither you nor I nor Joseph have ever studied for the priesthood--while the duellist--didn't you notice how determined he looked, as if he would defend Mina against the whole world--is a capital young fellow. And more than that, he's going to be a farmer, so we can look after him, and you, Hawermann and I, and even Joseph if he chooses, can keep him up to the mark. There's another thing I want to say, Mrs. Nüssler, and that is, I always thought that Joseph would grow to understand things better as he grew older, but he doesn't. No, he doesn't, and so you may look upon the lad as the best son-in-law you could have had, and quite a blessing to you, for you see that we are getting old, and if I were to die--not that I'm going to do so just yet--it would be a great comfort to me to know that you had some one belonging to you, who could take care of you."--When he had finished speaking Bräsig continued to stare into the match-box, and Mrs. Nüssler threw her arm round his neck and gave him the first kiss he had ever had from her, then she said gently and quietly: "Bräsig if you really think it right, I'm sure that it can't be against the will of God."--Many an arbour has been the scene of a more passionate kiss than that one, but if the old match-box in the corner could have spoken I do not think that it would have changed places with it.

Mrs. Nüssler turned, and going to Rudolph, said: "Rudolph I will say no more against it; I consent." She took Mina in her arms and then drew Lina to her, so that the twins were clasped together in her embrace as they used to be when they were children; she called them by the old pet names she had given them long ago, and yet everything was quite different to-day from what it had been then. In that old time she had given them all they had, and now she had to receive from them; but hope is not to be overcome, like the bee it makes its way into every flower and helps itself to the honey it contains.

Meanwhile Bräsig was pacing the room with long strides; he held his nose very high in the air, blowing it loudly every now and then, arched his eyebrows, and pointed his feet straight out to the right and left with as much dignity as if he were the father of the two girls, and their forgiveness lay in his hands. As he walked up and down the picture of a beautiful young woman came to his remembrance, he saw her as once of old, her head crowned with a garland of ferns and yellow corn-flowers, and he thought how well they suited the quiet loving eyes. She seemed to take him by the hand, to lead him gently to the mother and children, and laying his hands upon their heads to whisper: "Never mind, they belong to you too."

Rudolph went up to Godfrey, held out his hand and said: "You're not angry with me now, are you Godfrey?"--And Godfrey pressing his cousin's hand warmly, replied: "How can you think so, dear brother. Forgiveness is a Christian duty."--The rector coughed preparatory to making another speech, and Kurz caught him by the coat tails and entreated him not to meddle with the affair.--It was then that Joseph's absence was discovered.--"Where was he?"--"Goodness gracious me!" cried Mrs. Nüssler suddenly. "What's become of my Joseph?"--"Bless me! Where's Joseph?" asked all the others, but Bräsig was the first who thought of going in search of him. He hastened out of the front door into the yard, shouting: "Joseph!" and then he ran to the back door and called: "Joseph!" On his way back, he peeped into the kitchen where he caught sight of a red face watching the coals under the great copper kettle, and he saw that it was Joseph.

While Joseph was in the parlour, he was suddenly overwhelmed by the feeling that it behoved him to do something under such peculiar circumstances, and his heart felt so hot and heavy that 80° F. in the shade was too cold for him, and so he had taken refuge in the kitchen, in order to bring his outward and inward temperature more nearly to the same degree. There was another reason for his having gone there, and that was that he could not imagine a family festival without a bowl of punch, so he was busy making it when his friend found him. Bräsig helped him by taking the tasting part of the business off his hands, and when they returned to the parlour they looked exactly like two fiery dragons guarding a treasure, for they came in carrying Mrs. Nüssler's largest soup-tureen between them. When Joseph put the tureen on the table, he merely said: "There!" so Bräsig turning to the twins, said: "Go and thank your father. He has thought of everything."

While the old gentlemen gathered round the punch bowl, and the young people were amusing themselves in their own way, Mrs. Nüssler slipped out of the room. She needed a little quiet time to speak to a much older friend than even Bräsig, before she could rejoin the others. The twins were full of happy anticipations of the future, and blushed rosy red whenever uncle Bräsig called attention to them in any joking speech, and that pleased him so much that he was often guilty of doing so. "Yes," he said to Godfrey, "there are all kinds in the world, that mischievous thing Methodism amongst others. You wanted to convert *me*; take care, I intend to convert *you*. I'll convert you through Lina."--And when Godfrey was about to answer him, he rose, and shaking hands with him heartily said: "Never mind you shall have it all your own way when once you have a living. I mean you well at heart, we've smoked the pipe of peace together."--Then he said to Rudolph: "Wait a bit! You caught my tench, you rascal, but Hilgendorf will take your fishing-rod from you," so saying he went up to the lad and whispered in his ear: "I don't mean you harm! You must think of Mina whenever you have to weigh out a bushel of corn; and next spring when you've to stand amongst a dozen harrows, while a high east-wind is blowing no end of lime dust down your nose, and closing it up as if a swallow had built her nest in it; and when the sun, seen through the lime dust flying about you looks as round and red as a copper kettle you must think that it's Mina's face looking down at you. Mustn't he, my dear little god-child?"

When the rector had drunk three glasses of punch to the health of each set of lovers, and one to the health of the whole company, he was no longer to be restrained even by Kurz, but was determined to make a speech in spite of all opposition. He rose, picked up the tea-ladle, and the sugar-tongs which had been left on the table since coffee time, coughed twice to clear his throat, and then seeing that he had attracted every one's attention, and that Joseph watched each movement he made with curiosity and interest, he gazed thoughtfully at the spoon and the sugar-tongs. Suddenly thrusting the tea-ladle under Bräsig's nose, he asked: "Do you know this?" as emphatically as if Bräsig had stolen it and were now required to confess his guilt. "Yes," was the answer, "what do you mean?"--Upon which Baldrian held the sugar-tongs out to Kurz and asked if he knew them.--He acknowledged that he did, adding that they belonged to Joseph.--"Yes" the rector went on, "you know them, that is to say, you have an idea of them as sensible objects of knowledge; you can distinguish them from other objects by their colour, brightness and shape, but you do *not* know the moral teaching I derive from them."--Here he looked round upon them all as if to challenge anyone to dispute his assertion.--"No, you are ignorant of that, so I must make it known to you and explain it to you. Look, before long the careful mistress of this house will come, and taking these things which in appearance have no connection with each other, and will lay them side by side in the same tea-caddy; in thousands of households they are to be found in the same tea-caddy, and for thousands of years this has been the case. It is a custom sanctified by its antiquity, and what is joined together ought not to be put asunder. Adam"--holding up the sugar-tongs--"and Eve"--holding up the tea-ladle--"were joined together, for they were created for one another"--he held up both the tongs and the ladle--"and God Himself put them in the tea-caddy of paradise. And what did Noah do? He built an ark--or a tea-caddy, if you like to give it that name, dear friends--and called male and female, and they came at once in obedience to his call." He now made the sugar-tongs walk across the table, pressing the ends together and letting them out again as he did so, and then he made the tea-ladle follow close behind the tongs. "And went ....."--"Come in!" shouted Bräsig who heard a knock at the door, and in came Fred Triddelfitz. Hawermann had sent him to ask Mrs. Nüssler to lend him some rape-cloths, for the rape harvest was about to begin. This interruption obliged the rector to stop short in his harangue.--Joseph promised to give Hawermann what he required. Fred could not help wondering what had happened when he smelt the punch, and saw the rector standing up in the position he had been wont to assume in former times when Fred was a schoolboy, and the rector was about to cane him for some juvenile offence, so he crossed the room softly on tip-toe, and seated himself quietly. Then Joseph said; "Give Triddelfitz some punch, Mina."--Fred drank his glass of punch, and the rector continued to stand, ready to go on with his speech as soon as order was restored.--"Let us begin at the beginning," said Bräsig, "for Triddelfitz knows nothing of what has happened."--"We were talking ...." began the rector, but Kurz broke in impatiently: "About the sugar-tongs and the tea-ladle, and you told us that they both belonged to the tea-caddy," then taking the things out of his brother-in-law's hand and tossing them into their places in the tea-box, he went on: "There they are, male and female in Noah's ark, and now I think we may talk about our own affairs. You must know, Triddelfitz, that we are rejoicing over a double engagement, and that's the reason that the rector here wanted to preach us a sermon as a sort of ornament to the plain matter of our discourse. How is Hawermann?"--"Quite well, thank you," said Fred rising, then turning to the lovers he congratulated them, at first ceremoniously, but ended in an off-hand sort of way as if it were only a birthday, and the twins were betrothed every year.--The rector still remained standing, the better to seize his opportunity.

"Give your uncle Baldrian some punch, Lina," said Joseph, She did so, and the rector drank it. Instead of changing the current of his thoughts, it only made him more obstinately determined to finish his speech, but whenever he attempted to begin he was always interrupted by Joseph, Kurz, Bräsig or Fred, and when at last he brought up his heavy artillery in the shape of "thoughts upon the estate of matrimony," Bräsig said to him with the most innocent air in the world: "Yours has been a particularly happy marriage, hasn't it rector?" Upon which Baldrian subsided into his chair with a deep sigh, caused either by the thought of his own marriage, or by his inability to finish his speech. I think that the latter was the true reason of his sigh, for in my opinion it is much easier to meet with an example of a happy marriage, than with a good speech.

As it was now growing late, the rector, Kurz, and Triddelfitz said "good-bye," and Rudolph went with them, for Mrs. Nüssler and Bräsig were agreed that he must set to work at his new employment as soon as possible, as he had led an idle life long enough already. Joseph and Bräsig accompanied their friends a little way.

"How's your new squire getting on, Triddelfitz?" asked Bräsig.--"He's getting on uncommonly well, thank you, Mr. Bräsig. He made a speech to the labourers this morning which was really very good!"--"What!" cried Kurz. "Does he make speeches too?"--"What on earth had he to talk about?" asked, Bräsig.--"What did you say he had done?" asked Joseph.--"Made a speech," said Triddelfitz.--"I thought he was going to be a farmer," said Joseph.--"Of course," answered Triddelfitz. "But what's to prevent a farmer making a speech?"--Joseph could not get over it; a farmer make a speech! He had never heard of such a thing before, and pondered over it for the rest of the evening in silence, only saying the last thing before going to sleep: "He must be a very clever fellow!"--Bräsig's admiration was not so easily won, and he asked again: "What did he say? If he had any arrangements to make with the labourers, wasn't Hawermann there to receive his orders?"--"Mr. Bräsig," said the rector, "a good speech is never out of place. Cicero ...."--"Who was Cicero?"--"The most eloquent speaker of antiquity."--"I don't mean that. I want to know what his occupation was. Was he a farmer or a merchant; was he in a government-office, or was he a doctor? Or what?"--"He was, as I tell you, the most eloquent speaker of antiquity."--"Antiquity here, antiquity there! If he was nothing more than that, I don't think much of the word-monger. Every man ought to have some useful employment. And now, Rudolph, let me advise you never to be a speechifier. You may fish if you like, perch or trout, which ever you can get, but if once you get into the habit of making long speeches you'll never be good for much as a fisherman. Now good-night all of you. Come Joseph."--They then went back to Rexow. Fred also took leave of the others, and striking through the fields to the right took a short cut to Pümpelhagen.

He thought deeply as he went along the quiet field-path. He was not jealous, but still he had an uncomfortable feeling that his old school-fellows at Rahnstädt grammar-school had passed him in the race of life, for they were both engaged to be married while he was still free. However he soon comforted himself by the thought that *he* could never have engaged himself to a girl like either of the twins; that if Lina or Mina had been offered to him he would not have accepted the gift, and Louisa Hawermann was not good enough for him either. He would have been a fool if he had been contented with the first best plum he could reach, for such plums are always sour, no, he would wait till they were all ripe, and then he would take his choice. Till his choice was made, he had the pleasant feeling that, he could have any one he liked to honour with his regard, in the same way as before he bought his horse, he might have his choice of all horses. However he had made up his mind to buy Augustus Prebberow's mare Whalebone the very next day.

CHAPTER VII

A few weeks passed by, during which Alick, instead of going about the place and seeing how his estate was managed, shut himself up with Flegel, the carpenter, and busied himself in making a machine from the model he had formerly invented, that would act as harrow and clod-breaker at one and the same time. He wanted to complete it as soon as possible, for the benefit of himself, and the world at large. All the letters and accounts which ought to have been attended to regularly, and which form a portion of the necessary daily work of any one who has a large estate to manage, were pushed aside as matters of small moment. When Alick came home to dinner or supper he looked as grave and important as if he had been busy at the farm all day, and wished his wife to see how very necessary his presence was for the proper conduct of affairs. And who is so credulous as a young wife? Some one may say: a girl during her engagement. But that is a mistake, for her position is not so assured. She is always trying to know and understand her future husband better. But when once a woman thinks she knows a man's character, and has given him her hand, she follows him blindly until the bandage is torn rudely from her eyes. Then she strives against the truth, refuses to credit what she sees, and thinks it her duty to disbelieve the testimony of her own eyes. They were not wicked actions that he hid from her; they were only follies which he firmly believed would improve his affairs. But it was a pity that he did not know what he was doing, and that she did not see it. It never occurred to her that he could act differently with regard to his share of the duties of the estate, from what she did in her own domain of kitchen, larder and dairy, where she went about daily, looking carefully into everything, and learning all that she could, so as to be able to take the charge of everything into her own hands.

Nothing lasts more than a certain time, and as old Kopk, the shepherd, said: Puppies have their eyes opened on the ninth day.

Late one afternoon when Mrs. von Rambow was walking up and down the garden under the shade, of the high hedge which ran round the corner of the yard near the workshop, she heard an angry dialogue on the other side of it. "So--you don't like the looks of it! Do you think that I like it any better? Ugh! Get along with you! Get along with you, or ...."--Thud came something against the door. She wondered what was the matter and peeped through the hedge, but could only see the old carpenter Frederic Flegel. There was no one else there, and all the noise was made by the carpenter, who was quarrelling with his tools and his work. It is amusing to see a man in a rage with his own handiwork, and Mrs. von Rambow smilingly watched the old man: "Go to the devil! You're a deal more trouble than you're worth."--Thud! Thud! His foot-rule flew over the half-door, and when he had picked it up, he stood staring at the ground at his feet, muttering: "Confound the thing! It has nearly bothered me out of my life!"--"Good-evening, Flegel," said another voice, and Kegel, the labourer, coming up, leant upon his spade and asked: "What are you working at here? It's a holiday you know."--"Working at, did you say? There's enough to be done in all conscience! It'll be the death of me! Look. That's supposed to be a model! I can work from a model as well as any man, but devil a bit can I make head or tail of that thing."--"Is it the same machine that you were working at before?"--"Of course it is, and it won't be finished this summer either."--"He must be a clever fellow to be able to invent a thing like that."--"Do you think so? Then let me tell you that any fool can do that sort of inventing, but it takes a wise man to make a really useful machine. Look you, there are three kinds of people in the world. Those who understand how a thing ought to be, but can't make it themselves; those who can't understand, but can work under direction, and those who can neither understand how a thing should be made, nor are able to make it, and he belongs to the last class," so saying he flung his foot-rule at the door again, adding: "And what's to be done I don't know."--"Well, Flegel, I must say that I can't make out what he means. He said we were to go straight to him whenever we wanted anything, so I went and told him I required more potato-ground, and he said he didn't understand the rights of the case, and that he would ask Mr. Hawermann. And you see if it comes to that I've no chance, for he knows that the reason I ran short before was because I didn't hoe my potatoes properly."--"Mr. Hawermann's a great deal easier to work for though. He says to me: 'Flegel,' says he, 'make a handle for this hoe;' I do it, and then he says: 'Flegel, this wheel wants mending;' I mend it as he desires, and have no more trouble; but with him ..... Ah well, Kegel, mark my words, he'll come to grief, and so shall we before very long."--"You're right there," answered the labourer, "it's all of a piece with my potato-ground."--"Fair play's a jewel!" said Flegel as he locked the workshop-door and put on his blouse. "It's your own fault about the potatoes, remember. If you'd looked after them properly you'd have had enough."--"Yes," replied Kegel, shouldering his spade, and walking away with the carpenter, "but that doesn't help me to the garden, and it seems that I must just get on with what I have."

It is a true saying that even great and learned people are pleased when they hear the praises of those they love from the mouths of children or inferiors, and it is equally true that a harsh judgment coming from the same source hurts and saddens those who hear it. It was not much that she had heard. It was only village-gossip such as foolish men continually utter, but the smile had died out of the young wife's eyes, and a look of displeasure had taken its place. Circumstances had prevented her husband fulfilling the promises he had made in ignorance of all they implied; his kindness of heart had carried him further than he had intended.

Mrs. von Rambow was very silent when Alick came in to supper, and he on the contrary was more talkative than usual. "Now then, Frida dear," he began, "we are pretty well settled, and I think it's high time for us to make some calls on our neighbours."--"Very well Alick, but who do you mean?"--"I think," he said, "that we ought to begin with those who live within walking-distance of us."--"Then we should go to see our clergyman first."--"We'll go there of course--but not quite yet."--"Who else is there?" asked Frida thoughtfully. "Oh, Mr. Pomuchelskopp and Mr. Nüssler."--"Dear Frida," said Alick, looking a little grave, "surely you're joking when you speak of the Nüsslers. We can't admit tenant-farmers to our acquaintance."--"I don't quite agree with you there," answered his wife quietly. "I think more of what people are, than of their position. Your customs here may be different from ours in Prussia, but when I lived in my father's house we knew a great many families intimately, who only rented the land on which they lived. Mrs. Nüssler is said to be very nice."--"She is the sister of my bailiff. I can't call at her house; it wouldn't do."--"But Mr. Pomuchelskopp?"--"That's quite different. He is a land-owner, is rich, and is a justice of peace as well as myself ...."--"And has a bad name in the parish, and his wife still worse. No, Alick, I won't go there."--"My dear child ...."--"No, Alick; I don't think that you quite see all the bearings of the case. Supposing Mr. Nüssler had bought Gürlitz, would you have called on him?"--"That's supposing an impossibility. I will not call on the Nüsslers," he said angrily.--"Nor I on the Pomuchelskopps, I dislike them so much," said Mrs. von Rambow decidedly.--"Frida," began her husband.--"No, Alick," she said firmly, "I'll drive to Gürlitz with you to-morrow, but will get out at the parsonage."

That was the end of it. There was no quarrel, but both held to their own determination. Frida would gladly have given way to her husband, if it had not been for the disagreeable feeling left on her mind by what she had heard, which made her feel that Alick said and did things rashly without considering the consequences, and wanted firmness to carry out his intentions. Alick would gladly have given way to his wife had he not felt that Pomuchelskopp was a rich man, and that he might find it useful to be on friendly terms with him; and he would have liked to have gone to Rexow, had it not been that the foolish notions he had picked up in his regiment stuck in his throat.

It was all over now, and could not be altered. The beginning of strife had made its way into the house, and the door had remained ajar so that it might enter in and take up its abode there. Domestic strife may be likened to the tail of a kite, such as children play with, the string forming it is very long, and there are small bundles attached to it at regular intervals. Now though these bundles are only scraps of paper, still when once they get entangled it is long and weary work trying to straighten out the tail again, for there is neither beginning nor end to be found.

The next afternoon they started on foot for Gürlitz, as Alick had agreed to Frida's request to walk instead of driving. After taking her to the door of the parsonage Alick left her, and promising to call for her on his way home, set off for the manor-house.

They had just finished coffee at the Pomuchelskopps, and Phil, Tony and the other little ones were still hanging about the table like foals before the hayrack. They dipped bits of bread into the sugar at the bottom of the coffee-cups, and smeared their faces therewith. Then they mashed up the softened bread with tea-spoons and their fingers, and wrote their own beautiful name "Pomuchelskopp" on the table with spilt coffee and milk, glancing at their mother every now and then innocently, as much as to say, it wasn't me. Mrs. Pomuchelskopp was seated at the table, dressed in her old black gown, and watching the children to see that they were behaving themselves. Pomuchelskopp himself was lying on the sofa smoking, and looking at the picture of domestic happiness, sloppy bread and melted sugar before him. He had finished his coffee, for he always had a cup made particularly for himself, though he never got it, for Mally and Sally whose duty it was to make the coffee in turns used to drink half of the cup prepared for him, and then fill it up from the family coffee-pot. He lay back in the sofa-corner, his left leg crossed over his right according to the ordinance of Duke Adolphus of Cleves: "When a judge is sitting in the judgment-hall, let him always cross his left leg over his right," &c, and if he was not a judge, he was in point of fact more than that; he was a law-giver, and was busy thinking how absolutely necessary it was for him to attend the Mecklenburg parliament when it next met.

"Henny," he said, "I intend to go to the next parliament."--"Oh!" said his wife, "hav'n't you any other opportunity of spending money?"--"Why, chick, my position demands that I should show myself there, and it won't cost me much. The next parliament is to meet at Malchin, which isn't far from here, and if I take a basket ....."--"Then I suppose you expect me to put on your boots, and wade through the mud to see that the men are doing their work?"--"You needn't trouble to do that, my chick. Gus will look after everything of that sort, and if I'm wanted I can be home at an hour's notice."--"But father," said Mally, who was considered a great politician because she was the only one of the family who ever read the Rostock newspaper to such purpose as to know where their Serene Highnesses the Grand-Duke and Grand-Duchess were staying, for Pomuchelskopp looked at nothing but the state of the corn and money markets. "But father," she said, "you ought not to go unless you are prepared to try and bring about some reforms of great importance, such as allowing middle-class landowners to wear red coats, and then the convent question." She spoke as if she thought the convent question had reference to herself.--"What!" cried Pomuchelskopp, rising and pacing the room with long strides, "you surely don't think so meanly of your father as to imagine that he would go and give his votes and influence to the middle-class landowners and neglect the interests of his own family? No, if anything goes wrong here, write for me to come home. And as for the red coat, if I'm to have it I know the best way--Let everyone look out for himself--It'll redound more to my honour if I win it for myself *alone*, and not merely as one of a lot of poor wretches who have only a few hundred pounds to bless themselves with. When I come home and say: Mally, I alone have got it; you may be proud of your father." While saying this he crossed the room, and blew a cloud of tobacco smoke right in the face of his innocent child, making her look like one of the angels with a trumpet sitting in the clouds, and as if she had only to put the mouth piece of the trumpet to her lips to blow a blast in her father's honour.--"Are you crazy, Kopp?" asked his wife.--"Let me alone, Henny. We must keep up our dignity. Show me your friends and I'll tell you who you are. If I vote with the nobles and ....."--"I should have thought that you'd have had enough snubbing from the nobles already."--"Henny," remonstrated Pomuchelskopp, but was stopped by Sally who was seated at the window, exclaiming: "Law! Here's Mr. von Rambow coming across the court."--"Henny," said Pomuchelskopp again, turning his expressive eyes reproachfully on his wife, "you see that a nobleman is coming to my house! But now, clear out of this, will you," he went on, driving his younger olive branches out at the door. "Mally take away the coffee things. Sally bring a duster and be quick about it. And Henny go and put on another gown."--"What!" said his wife. "Is the young man coming to my house, or am I going to his? As he thinks fit to come here, he may just take me as he finds me."--"Henny," entreated Pomuchelskopp, "let me implore you to do as I ask, you'll spoil the whole visit if you appear in that old black dress."--"Are you a fool, Muchel?" she asked without moving. "Do you think that he is coming here for the sake of either of us? He's only coming because he needs our help, and so my dress is quite good enough."--Muchel begged her once more to do as he wanted, but in vain.--Mally and Sally hastened from the room to make themselves tidy, but their mother remained sitting on her chair as stiff and upright as a poker.

Alick entered and greeted the worthy couple, and it must be confessed that his politeness was as great to the lady in the old black dress as to the gentleman in the green checked trousers. He made himself so pleasant and talked so agreeably that Henny was charmed and called her husband Pöking; indeed before the end of the visit, even she came to the conclusion that the old gown looked too shabby to be worn any longer.--Mally then came into the room pretending that she had forgotten something, and she was soon afterwards followed by Sally, who pretended that she had come for something. Pomuchelskopp introduced them, and the meaningless chit chat of the earlier part of the visit was changed to a learned discussion about Sally's worsted-work, which in its turn gave place to a political conversation, when Mally took up the newspaper. Philip now came in and stationed himself in the corner behind his mother; he was followed by Tony, who joined him in his retreat, and then all the little ones came in singly and surrounded their mother, till Henny looked like an old black hen with all her chickens taking refuge under her wing when a hawk is overhead. And when she took the key of the linen press out of her basket--for she felt she could do no less--and left the room, she was followed by the whole brood, for they knew that the short-bread was kept there which Henny baked twice a year, and then kept for any important occasion. It cannot be denied that these cakes were uncommonly good at first, but in course of time they contracted a slight flavour of brown soap from their proximity to the linen; but that was no drawback in the estimation of the family at Gürlitz manor, they had been accustomed to the flavour from their infancy and would quite have missed it if it had not been there. If Alick had not been so deeply engaged talking to Pomuchelskopp he could not have helped hearing the begging and coaxing going on outside.--"Do give me some, mother"--"And me too, mother."--But Pomuchelskopp had taken him in hand and was determined to give his visitor a good impression of himself and his family. "Look here, Mr. von Rambow," he said, "you will find that ours is an extremely quiet family; I myself am a quiet man, and my wife," here he glanced round the room to make sure that his Henny was well out of hearing, "is also quiet, and so we have brought up our daughters and our other children very quietly. We make no show, and only care to live a simple family life. We don't desire to make many acquaintances, for I am thankful to say we are sufficient to ourselves, but," he added putting on a dignified patriarchal air, "everyone of us has some duty to perform; each of us has some necessary work which he or she *must*--I say *must* carry out after having once undertaken to perform it, and I am convinced that the blessing of God rests upon such work when it is conscientiously done."--Alick replied politely that these sentiments did him honour.--"Yes," said Pomuchelskopp taking Phil by his coat collar and drawing him forward with his mouth ninety eight per cent full of short bread and two per cent of brown soap, "Make a bow, Phil. Look at this little fellow, Mr. von Rambow. It's his duty to hunt for eggs, I mean for the eggs of those hens that may chance to lay out in the wood, he gets a ha'penny far every dozen he brings in, and the money is put in a savings-box for him. Phil, my boy, tell us how much you've made already by egg hunting?"--"One pound, four, and seven pence," answered Philip.--"You see then, my dear boy," said Pomuchelskopp patting his son on the head encouragingly, "that God's blessing always rests on the diligent. Then," he continued turning to Alick, "Tony gets so much a pound for all the old iron, nails and horse-shoes that he can find, while Polly, Harry and Steenie are allowed to sell all the apples, pears and plums--of course I only mean those that have fallen under the trees, most of them are mere trash, but still the townspeople are glad enough to buy them. So you see Mr. von Rambow that my children have each their own particular apartment"--Alick smothered a laugh at the last word, while Mally and Sally glanced to each other and then looked down and smiled at their father's mistake. Pomuchelskopp like Bräsig was sometimes guilty of mispronouncing or using a long word in the wrong place, but there was this difference between them, that Bräsig used long words from sheer love of them, and although he knew that he often made absurd mistakes he did not mind that a bit, while Pomuchelskopp who did it in self-glorification, took such accidents rather ill-humouredly. He knew that he had made some ridiculous blunder when he saw his daughters laughing at him, and was much relieved by his wife coming in with the cake and wine. She had taken the opportunity of changing her dress, and now wore a light yellow silk gown and a large mob-cab.--"Henny," said Pomuchelskopp, "not that wine. When we have such distinguished visitors let us always have the best we possess."--"Say what you want then," replied his wife shortly. He did so, and then went on with the thread of his discourse. "Even my two eldest daughters have their own particular lines. Sally is most interested in art, such as embroidery and music; while Mally delights in reading the newspaper and in studying politics." Alick was surprised to hear that, so few young ladies cared about such things, and Mally assured him that it was quite necessary for some member of a household to know what was going on at the seat of government, and her father did not read that part of the paper. She then went on to say that just as Mr. von Rambow arrived they had been agreeing that her father ought to attend the next meeting of parliament. "Yes, Mr. von Rambow," said Muchel, "I intend to go; not because of the changes my middle class colleagues want to bring about, I care nothing for them, and I know the difference between lords and commons perfectly. I'm only going because I wish to show those people what is the proper mode of action." Alick now enquired, for something to say, whether Mr. Pomuchelskopp had many acquaintances in the neighbourhood. "Who is there for me to know?" asked Pomuchelskopp. "Mr. Nüssler at Rexow? Why he's a fool. And as for the farm-bailiff that wouldn't quite do, and there's nobody else in the neighbourhood."--"Then I suppose that you are only intimate with the clergyman and his family?"--"No, not even with them. The parson's conduct has been such from the very first, that I could have nothing to do with him. He has friends whom I don't like; and besides that, he has adopted the daughter of your bailiff Hawermann, and I don't wish my girls to be thrown into such society."--"I thought that she seemed to be nice," said Alick.--"Oh yes, I've no doubt she is," replied Pomuchelskopp. "I've nothing to say against the girl. You see, Mr. von Rambow, I'm a quiet man. I used to know Hawermann long ago, and I won't say he deceived me, but ..... Besides that, I didn't like the way in which the girl was thrown with young Mr. von Rambow by her father and the people at the parsonage."--"With my cousin Frank?" asked Alick.--"Yes, his name was Frank. I mean the young gentleman who learnt farming with Hawermann. I don't know him myself, for he never entered my house, and I'm just as well pleased if what people tell me is true."--"He still writes to her," said Henny.--"No, mother," said Mally, "you can't say that, his letters are always addressed to Mr. Behrens. Our postman carries the parsonage letters too," she added, addressing Alick.--"It's all the same," said Henny, "which he writes to."--"This is the first time I've heard of it," said Alick looking down at the floor.--"Oh," said Pomuchelskopp, "the whole country-side knows it. She ran after him wherever he went, under pretext of visiting her father and your sisters, and if ever anything came between them Hawermann and the people at the parsonage made it all right again."--"No, father," cried Sally, "old Bräsig was the greatest match-maker amongst them, and he always carried their letters to each other."--"Who is this Bräsig?" asked Alick who was now very angry.--"He's a sly rogue," cried Henny.--"Yes, that's just what he is," said Pomuchelskopp disdainfully. "He has a small pension from Count .... and has nothing earthly to do but to go about making mischief. Besides that he's ....."--"No, father," interrupted Mally, "I'll tell. The old man is a democrat, Mr. von Rambow; an out and out de-mo-crat."--"You're right there," said Pomuchelskopp, interrupting Mally in his turn, "and I shouldn't be at all surprised if the scoundrel were also an incendiary."

Alick remembered that he had had that good-for-nothing fellow to dine with him at his own table, and that by Hawermann's fault. The conversation had irritated him so much, that he, not finding the shortbread a sufficient inducement to prolong his visit, took leave, and was accompanied by Pomuchelskopp as far as the gate of the court-yard. "Is what you have told me about my cousin quite true?" asked Alick as they crossed the yard.--"Mr. von Rambow," said Pomuchelskopp, "I'm a quiet old man, and people at my age don't trouble themselves about love stories. I only repeated what others had told me."--"Ah well, I suppose that it's a mere passing caprice; a case of 'out of sight, out of mind.'"--"No, I don't think so," replied Pomuchelskopp thoughtfully. "If I know Hawermann at all, he's a sly dog, and too wide awake to his own interest to let such a chance slip out of his fingers. Your cousin has fallen into his toils."--"The boy has only lost his head," said Alick, "and he'll soon learn more sense. Good-bye, Mr. Pomuchelskopp. Thank you for telling me about my cousin. I hope soon to have the pleasure of seeing you at my house. Good-bye," and with that he turned down the road to the right--"I beg your pardon," cried Pomuchelskopp. "You're going the wrong way. The Pümpelhagen road is to the left."--"I know," said Alick, "but I'm going to the parsonage to fetch my wife. Goodbye."

"Ah!" said Pomuchelskopp as he went back to the house. "This is charming, de-lightful! And why shouldn't she be there? It's quite proper for Mr. von Rambow to come to my house, but I'm not good enough for his wife to know! Children," he exclaimed as he entered the family sitting-room, "Mrs. von Rambow is at the parsonage. We ar'n't grand enough for her ladyship I suppose!"--"Well, Pöking," said his wife, "I congratulate you upon having been again taken in by an aristocrat."--"Is it possible!" cried Sally.--"It's an undoubted fact," said her father, giving Tony and Phil the remains of the short bread, and then added: "Now be off, you young rascals." After that he threw himself into the sofa corner and slashed at the flies, while his wife hovered about him, and made satirical remarks about grand acquaintances, beggars and aristocrats: "Sally," she said at last, "take that bottle of wine back to the cellar, there's enough of it remaining for your father to treat another of his grand friends on some future occasion."--After a long silence she exclaimed: "Come to the window, father. Look there. Your grand friend and his butterfly wife are passing, and do you see who they've got with them. Your incendiary old Bräsig."

It was quite true. Bräsig was walking along the Pümpelhagen road with the Rambows, and was so pleased with the young lady's gentle kindness, that he took no notice of Alick's short answers. He had met Mrs. von Rambow at the parsonage and thought her even prettier and nicer than on the memorable occasion of the dinner-party.

Well might he like and admire her; well might anybody like her who had seen her in the parsonage that day. When she entered the parlour she found the clergyman lying on the sofa weak and ill; he would have risen to receive her, but she would not allow him to do so. Then laying both hands on little Mrs. Behrens' shoulders she entreated the good old lady to help her in her new life, saying that she often needed good advice. After that she went to Bräsig and shook his hand warmly like an old friend.--When Louisa came in shortly afterwards, she greeted her also like an old friend, and could not help looking at her again and again, as if there were always something new to be read in her face, and as she did so she grew thoughtful like a person reading a beautiful book, who cannot turn to a new page before thoroughly understanding the preceding ones.

Mrs. von Rambow found that there were many pages of the book of human life for her to study in that quiet room. Mr. Behrens, with his long experience and loving sympathy for all men; Mrs. Behrens with her great housekeeping talents, her happy nature and true-heartedness; Louisa with her modesty and thoughtfulness, and her pleasure in making acquaintance with Mrs. von Rambow, who bore the same name as that she used to know so well, and which was so dear to her; and then there was Bräsig, who might be looked upon as forming a sort of commentary upon the others to make their meaning clearer, and Mrs. von Rambow read the commentary with as much pleasure as we young rogues used to do the Ass' Bridge ad modum Minellii in Cornelius Nepos. There was so much innocent mirth and affectionate sympathy amongst these people that Mrs. von Rambow felt almost as gay as if she were making one of a party of happy children dancing "kringel-kranz," with Louisa for their queen, round the bole of a shady old tree.

Alick at last joined the happy circle at the parsonage, but what he had just heard had made him too cross to be able to enter into the spirit of what was going on. He disliked the thought of his wife being in such company as he now found her, and was still more put out when Bräsig said: "How d'ye do, Lieutenant von Rambow." Instead of answering, he turned to the clergyman, and addressed a few words to him about his health and the weather, but his manner was so cold that his warm-hearted wife could not bear to see it, and hastily rose to take leave, that the friendliness with which she had been received might not be utterly chilled, and that Alick's manner might have no worse effect than a slight shower of hail on a summer-day.

They took their departure, but uncle Bräsig went with them. Mr. von Rambow's coldness made no impression on him, for he knew that he had done nothing to deserve it; his conscience was clear of offence. Another reason for his going with them was that he had a high opinion of his powers of conversation being able to charm any man out of a bad temper, and bring him back to a more cheerful view of life. He therefore walked on beside the young squire, and talked to him about this and that, but all his efforts were unavailing to change the short cold answers he received into more friendly ones. When Mr. von Rambow stopped at the end of the road leading to the church, and asked him which way he was going, it suddenly flashed upon the old man that his companion thought he wanted to thrust himself upon him.--"This takes me by surprise, Sir," he said, standing still in his turn. "Are you ashamed of walking with me in the public road? Well, let me assure you that it wasn't for your sake that I came with you, but entirely out of respect, for your wife, she has been so very kind to me. I won't incommodate you any further," then making a deep bow to Mrs. von Rambow, he went across the rape-stubble to where Hawermann was busy superintending the stacking of the rape-straw.

"Why were you so unkind to that good-natured old man, Alick," asked Frida.--"That good-natured old man, as you call him, is nothing better than a mischievous fellow and a match-maker."--"Do you really think so? And do you think that our Hawermann would be so fond of him if he were?"--"Why not, when he finds him useful?"--Frida looked at him anxiously: "What's the matter with you, Alick? You used to be so kind to every one, and so trustful. What can have set you against these two people? People who have always been friendly and honest in all their dealings with you."--"Friendly!--Well, why not? It's their interest to be so, I'm the owner of the estate. But honest?--Time will show. From all that I hear honesty isn't quite the term *I* should use."--"What have you heard? And from whom did you hear it?" cried Frida quickly. "Tell me, Alick. I am your wife."--"I've heard a good many things," answered Alick with a sneer. "I've heard that 'our' Hawermann, as you call him, was once bankrupt, and the best that I've heard is that he made use of the influence he had acquired as teacher to bring about a sort of engagement between my cousin Frank and his daughter. In this he was assisted by Mr. and Mrs. Behrens, and that old match-maker, Bräsig. And," he continued angrily, "the young fool has allowed himself to be caught in their snares."--Mrs. von Rambow felt her spirit rise against such a base libel. She knew how impossible it was for that innocent child Louisa Hawermann to have lent herself to such a scheme, and more than that, she resented the scandalous story as an insult to womanhood. Her eyes flashed, as laying her hand on her husband's arm, She made him stand still, and said: "You've been in very bad company, and have allowed yourself to be influenced by unworthy people." Then letting her hands fall to her side she went on sadly: "Oh, Alick, Alick, you are so good and true, how can you let such mean whispers affect your honest judgment?"--Alick was astonished at the zeal with which his wife took up the case, and would willingly have withdrawn what he had said, but he *had* said it, and he would have despised himself if he had not stuck to his opinion, so he asked: "What is the matter, Frida? It is a fact that my foolish cousin has got his name mixed up with that of the girl. It's the common talk of the neighbourhood."--"If you will change your way of putting it. If you will say that your cousin has fallen in love with the girl, I will believe it. I hardly know him, but I shall like him all the better if it is so."--"What? Do you think that my cousin who is rich and independent ought to marry my bailiff's daughter?"--"The advantage of being rich and independent is that a man is free to choose as he likes, and your cousin has not chosen unworthily."--"Then you think that it would be a pleasant thing for me to be connected by marriage with my farm-bailiff! And let the plotters win the day! No, I'll never consent to bear that silently."--"Why," cried Frida, "don't you see that the lie and calumny are in that part of your story. How can you believe such a wretched piece of scandal? How can you believe--putting aside the lovely innocent face of the girl--such ill of that unsophisticated old man, that loving father whose only joy is in his daughter's happiness; how can you think such wickedness possible in that dignified old clergyman or his true-hearted wife; or even in the good man who has just left us deeply wounded by your harshness to him, and whose uprightness and honesty are easily seen in spite of his mistaken use of long words? Do you really think it possible that these good people would make a mere speculation of their darling's beauty?"--"But," said Alick, "they only want to make her happy."--"Oh," answered Frida gravely and sadly, "then you and I have very different notions of happiness. Nobody can be made happy by such means."--"I'm not talking of my *own* idea of happiness," said Alick, struck by her reproachful tone. "I only mean what these kind of people think happiness."--"Don't deceive yourself, Alick. For God's sake, don't deceive yourself. A high worldly station may enable one to take a large view of human affairs, but believe me, in a less exalted position love influences the lives of men in a way that it unfortunately can seldom do those of higher rank. In short, we often have to do without it," she said slowly, and wiping a tear from her eyes as she thought of her motherless childhood passed in the society of a father whose life was spent in a hard struggle to keep up his position, and who found an unfailing comfort in every distress--in field-sports.

Then they went home. Alick in the goodness of his heart was kind and affectionate to his wife, and she took his kindness and affection as they were meant; thus peace was ratified between them--outwardly at least--for they each held to their own opinion.

Bräsig meanwhile made his way to where Hawermann was standing by the rape-stacks. He was angry, very angry. Such a thing had never happened to him before, except that once when Pomuchelskopp was rude to him, and he felt that the only way to get rid of his wrath was to expend a little of it on some labourer who might deserve it from his stupidity.-- "Good-day, Charles," he said, passing Hawermann with his head in the air, and his eyebrows raised as high as they would go. He walked round one of the stacks, and then placing himself in front of his friend, asked: "Are you trying to make a pancake?"--"Don't talk of it," said Hawermann, looking very much put out, "I've been angry enough about it as it is. I sent Triddelfitz to look after the stacking of the rape yesterday, and told him to make the stacks twenty feet broad and high in proportion, and he has only made them half what I told him. When I came out here I found the mischief done, and I hav'n't time to undo it all. It must just remain as it is--fortunately it's only straw, so that it won't hurt much if it should happen to rain before I can get it into the yard, but I hate to see such unworkmanlike stacks in one of my fields."--"Yes, Charles, and your neighbour Pomuchelskopp won't fail to draw attention to it."--"Let him! But what Triddelfitz means by it I can't make out. He has been neither to hold nor to bind since Mr. von Rambow promised him the horse."--"Have you spoken to him seriously?"--"What's the good of it? He can think of nothing but horses. He doesn't want my advice about that even, for Mr. von Rambow advised him to get an English mare, and has promised to buy all the foals. He won't listen to a word I say, and I'm sure he'll end by buying that wretched screw."--"Doesn't he want to get Augustus Prebberow's sorrel-mare Whalebone?"--"Yes, that's the very one he has set his heart on."--"Capital!" cried Bräsig. "Splendid! He'll ride about, and show himself off on that old mare when the Grand Duke makes his triump'ant entrance into Rahnstädt. Charles, that grey-hound of yours is a treasure."--"Yes," answered Hawermann drily, and glancing at his stacks, "you're about right there."--"Oh, I don't mean as a farmer, but as an amusing fellow, especially when he and your young squire get together."--"Bräsig," said Hawermann gravely, "don't speak in that way of my master before the labourers."--"Quite right, Charles, I oughtn't to have done so, but come away with me."--When they were, out of hearing of the work-people Bräsig stood still, and said slowly and emphatically: "Charles, that *young gentleman* was ashamed to be seen walking with me on the public road. What do you say to that? He gave me to understand as much in the presence of his lovely wife."--He then told all that had happened. Hawermann tried to talk him into a better humour, but did not quite succeed. Bräsig at last exclaimed with indignant emphasis: "It was his own folly that made him act as he did, but it was Samuel Pomuchelskopp who roused him to do it. He had just been calling at Gürlitz manor. And you may say what you like, Charles, your master's a fool, and when once you've been sent about your business, I'll amuse myself by coming over here, and standing on the top of this hill that I may see what a mess your master and your grey-hound make of the farm."--"Well," said Hawermann, "if you want to see something queer you needn't wait till then. Just look over there!" He pointed as he spoke over the thorn-bush behind which they happened to be standing, and down the road. Bräsig did as he was desired, and was so struck by amazement at what he saw, that he was unable to utter a word. At last he said: "Why, Charles, your grey-hound has gone crazy. Apothecaries often go mad, and I daresay their children inherit the disease from them."--It really seemed as if Bräsig was right. Fred was riding the famous sorrel-mare up the road at a foot's pace. He had taken off his hat, and was waving it violently, and shouting as loud as he could: "Hurrah! Hurrah!" and all apparently for his own edification, for he could not see the two old men behind the thorn-bush till they advanced towards him, and Hawermann asked whether he had gone mad.--"It's all a lie," said Fred.--"What's a lie?" asked Hawermann angrily.--"That the mare won't stand shouting," and with that he began to hurrah again.--"Look!" he said dismounting and tying his horse to a willow-branch, and then going to a little distance he shouted "hurrah!" once more. "You see she doesn't shy a bit. And you," turning to Bräsig who looked as if he were on the point of bursting out laughing, "told me she couldn't stand it, and you see it isn't true."--"I see," said Bräsig, shaking with laughter, "but still it's quite true. I said what I said, and it was this, that she couldn't *hear* it, and neither she can, for the creature's as deaf as a post, and has been so for all the five years that I've known her."--On hearing this Fred Triddelfitz, clever, quick-witted Fred Triddelfitz stood staring at the old man with the most sheepish expression in the world. "But," he stammered out at last, "Augustus Prebberow is a great friend of mine, and he never told me that"--"Ah," said Bräsig, "you'll soon find out that friendship counts for less than nothing in horse-dealing."--"Never mind, Triddelfitz," said Hawermann kindly, for he was sorry for the lad. "The mare may suit you very well though she's deaf; it's better to be deaf than tricky."--"Oh," said Fred, his spirits rising. "I know what to do. Look now--yes, that's spavin she has got, but still she's a thoroughbred. She's in foal by Hector. Mr. von Rambow has promised to buy all the foals, and when I've sold three or four ...."--"You'll buy a large estate," interrupted Bräsig. "We all know that. Now ride home quietly, and take care that you don't break your milk-jug on the way like that girl. You remember it Charles. In Gellert's Fables."

Fred rode off.--"The rascally grey-hound!" said Bräsig.--"I don't know why," said Hawermann, "but I can't help liking the lad. He is so sweet-tempered."--"That's because he's young, Charles."--"Perhaps so," answered Hawermann thoughtfully, "but just look at him, riding away on the deaf old mare as happy as a king."

CHAPTER VIII

And Fred was happy; he was the happiest creature at Pümpelhagen, for there was not much of that blessing to be found there, and the realities of life were discovered to be very different from what everybody had expected. Hawermann saw more distinctly every day that his old peaceful life was gone for ever, for the young squire was so full of plans he did not know how to execute, that he left but little time for the necessary work of the farm, which had to be hurried over anyhow. The labourers were kept in such a bustle that they got confused and made mistakes, and then when anything went wrong Hawermann had to bear the blame.--Neither was Mr. von Rambow happy, his debts weighed upon him and also the fact of their concealment from his wife. He was troubled by the letters he received from David and Slus'uhr, with whom he had made it a condition of his doing business with them, that they should never show their faces at Pümpelhagen, and they were only too glad to consent to this arrangement, for the more the affair was involved in secrecy, the better chance they had of fleecing him. When they got him into their clutches at Rahnstädt for a consultation, they could turn the screw on him to better purpose than at Pümpelhagen, where they had to treat him with more deference, as he was in his own house. But Alick had another reason besides this for his unhappiness. He wanted to be master, but had not the power, for before a man takes the reins of government into his own hands he ought to have a *practical* knowledge of the work to be done, not merely a *theoretical* knowledge such as he had, and which made him imagine he knew everything much better than anyone else. "The great point is to be able to do a thing yourself," old Flegel the carpenter used to say, and he was right. The most unfortunate of men is the one who undertakes to do what he knows nothing about.--And Frida?--She was not happy either; she saw that her husband did not confide in her; that they held opposite opinions on many important subjects; that he was totally ignorant of the work to which he was now to devote his life; that he threw the blame of his own mistakes on other people's shoulders, and more than that, she felt--what was harder than aught else for a clever woman to bear--that he made himself ridiculous. She was convinced that Pomuchelskopp, who, much to her distress, often came over to Pümpelhagen, must have other reasons for doing so than mere neighbourly civility, and that he must often laugh in his sleeve at the crude, ill-considered opinions propounded by her husband.--She made up her mind to try and discover the motive for his visits; but that determination did not tend to increase her happiness.

Fred Triddelfitz was the happiest creature in all Pümpelhagen, and if we except the twins, he might be called the happiest in the whole parish. But the twins must be excepted, for a girl who is engaged to a man she loves, is much happier than anyone else, even than her lover. Godfrey had taken a situation as tutor in the family of a good tempered enterprising landowner of the middle-class, whose sons he taught and flogged with cheerful conscientiousness. Rudolph was earning farming from Hilgendorf at Little-Tetzleben, where he had to superintend the spreading of manure over the fields till they were covered as though with a soft blanket, and on going to bed at night he used to whistle or sing merrily, but as he was very tired he always fell asleep before he had finished the first verse.--Happy as these two undoubtedly were, their happiness was not to be compared with that of the little twins who sat side by side sewing busily at their trousseaux, or making jokes with their father and mother, or telling Louisa all about it, or showing bits of their letters. No, no. Even Fred's joy in the possession of his new horse was not to be named in the same day with it.

But the boy was really very happy. His first act every morning was to go to the stable which his treasure shared with Mr. von Rainbow's two riding horses, and Hawermann's old hack. He fed his mare himself; he even stole the oats from under the noses of the other horses and gave them to her, indeed--little as he liked work in general--he rubbed her down with his own hands, for which Christian Däsel, who had charge of the riding horses, did not thank him.--On Sunday afternoon when there was nothing else to be done, he went into the stable, shut the door, and seating himself on the corn-bin stroked her gently, and looked on well pleased while his beloved mare eat her oats and chopped straw. When she could eat no more, he rose, passed his hand caressingly down her back and called her his "good old woman."--He never failed to visit her three times a day, and no one could blame him for it, for his future wealth depended upon the success of his speculation.

But there is no joy without a flaw.--In the first place he did not like his sorrel mare to be in the next stall to Hawermann's old horse, she was too good to be in such company; and secondly, he had a never ending battle with Christian Däsel about the food and cleaning of his favourite. "Mr. Triddelfitz," Christian said on one occasion when they were disputing about it. "I'll tell you something. I give each of the horses under my charge an equal quantity of food, and I rub them all down with equal care, but I've noticed that you always take away the oats intended for the bailiff's old horse and give them to your own. Don't take it ill of me, Mr. Triddelfitz, if I say that the one animal is every bit as good as the other, and that both must live. But what's the meaning of this," he asked, going, up to the rack. "Why, it's some of the calves' hay! How did it come here? I should get into no end of a scrape if the bailiff should happen to see it."--"I know nothing about it," said Fred, and it was quite true that he did not.--"I don't care," said Christian, "but I only give you fair warning that I'll break the legs of anyone I find bringing it. I won't have any such goings on here."

Christian Däsel set himself to watch for the person who smuggled the calves' hay into the stables, and before long he made a discovery. Who was it who broke the stable laws for the sake of Fred's sorrel-mare; who was it who was hard-hearted enough to deprive the innocent little calves of their provender for the sake of Fred's sorrel-mare; who was it who was so lost to every good feeling as to put Fred's sorrel-mare in danger of having her legs broken by Christian for having the hay at all? Who was it, I say? I shall have to tell who it was, for no one would guess. It was Mary Möller who brought Fred's "old woman" a handful of the sweet hay every time she left the young calves and went past the stable where the riding-horses were kept. Perhaps some one may exclaim: Stop, you're getting on too fast, how did there happen to be young calves so late in summer? To which I reply: My dear friend, surely I have a right to skip a few months if I like, and the fact is that I'm telling you what happened in the winter of 1844, about New-year's-time. And if I am asked: But how did Mary Möller come to do such a thing? I will answer, that that is as stupid a question as the one about the young calves. Havn't I as good a right to tell you about nice people who can forgive and forget, as about malicious wretches who go on nagging to all eternity? Mary Möller was a woman who was generous enough to be able to forgive and forget, and as she could no longer show her love for Fred in the old way, she contented herself with showing it to his horse by giving it the calves' hay. It was a touching incident, and Fred was much moved when he discovered, from finding his old sweetheart and Christian Däsel quarrelling at the stable-door, that it was she who had shown him this kindness in secret. He therefore made friends with her again and they once more entered into the old sausage and ham alliance.

Winter had come as I said before, and nothing of particular interest had happened in the neighbourhood, except that Pomuchelskopp had attended the parliament which met late in autumn, and had caused great excitement in his quiet family circle by his determination to do so. Henny rushed about the house, knocking everything about that there was no fear of breaking by such rough usage, and banging the doors; she did not even hesitate to say that her husband was mad. Mally and Sally took their father's part against her in secret, for they had heard that Mr. von Rambow, who was to command the guard round the parliament-house, drew a large part of his income from the grand ball given after the meeting of parliament was over, and to which he could give a ticket of admittance for the sum of eight and four pence. They had been to a Whitsun market ball at Rostock, and also to an agricultural meeting, but a parliament ball! That must be far more delightful than anything they had as yet experienced. They roused their father to summon up all his courage, and act in opposition to the will of his beloved wife. "My chick," he said, "I can't help it I promised Mr. von Rambow that I would go. He started yesterday and expects me to follow him."--"Oh, indeed!" said Henny. "Then I suppose that his grand lady wife expects me too?"--"She isn't going, my chuck. If I neglect this opportunity of showing myself, and of proving that I am a man in whom the nobility may trust, how can I expect them to raise me to their rank? I am going away in a black coat to-day, and I shall perhaps come back in a red one."--"You're sure to have it all your own way," answered his wife sarcastically as she left the room.--"I've as good a chance as any of the other noblemen," he muttered after her as she retreated.--"Good gracious, father," cried Sally running away, "I know ...." A few minutes afterwards she came back with a scarlet petticoat which she threw over her father's shoulders like a herald's mantle, and then she made him look at himself in the glass. Mr. Pomuchelskopp was turning, twisting and examining the effect of his decoration when his wife came back, and seeing what he was about exclaimed: "If you *will* make a fool of yourself, do it in the parliament house and not in my drawing-room."

Pomuchelskopp took this for a consent to his going to the parliament, and so he went. His discomforts began from the moment of his arrival at Malchin, for after he had taken a room at Voitel's Inn, he discovered that the nobility all patronised the Bull, and that no one went to Voitel's except the mayors of towns and middle-class landowners with whom he did not care to associate. He hung about the coffee-room for some time and got in everybody's way, for he did not know what to do with himself. At last he summoned courage to ask whether anyone had seen Mr. von Rambow of Pümpelhagen, as all his hopes rested on Alick. Nobody had seen him, but at last some one remembered that Mr. von Rambow had driven out to Brülow grange that afternoon with Mr. von Brülow to see a thoroughbred horse. It was a great disappointment to Mr. Pomuchelskopp for Alick was his mainstay, and was to introduce him to his noble friends, and now he had gone away to inspect a horse. He at last turned in his despair to a stout dignified looking man with a smiling face, but unfortunately for him he did not see the mischievous sparkle in the stranger's eyes which showed how thoroughly he enjoyed a joke, for if he had seen it he would have refrained from appealing to him: "Pardon me," he said, "I am Squire Pomuchelskopp of Gürlitz and have come here to attend parliament for the first time. You look so good-natured that I venture to ask you what I ought to do now."--"Ah," said the gentleman, taking a pinch of snuff and looking at him enquiringly. "You want to know what you have to do? You hav'n't anything particular to do; of course you've paid all the necessary visits of ceremony?"--"No," answered Pomuchelskopp.--"Then you must go and call on the government commissioner, the Chief of the constabulary, and High Sheriff at once. Good-evening, Langfeldt, where are you going?" he exclaimed, breaking off in his sentence and addressing a man who was leaving the inn with a lantern in his hand.--"To make those tiresome calls," and half turning round he added: "Shall I find you here when I come back, Brückner? I shan't be long."--"Well, make as much haste as you can," said the good-natured looking man, and addressing Pomuchelskopp again he went on: "Then you hav'n't paid those visits yet?"--"No," was the answer.--"I strongly advise you to get them over as soon as you can. The gentleman you saw with the lantern is going to make the same calls as you, so that all you have to do is follow him. Yes, that's a capital plan! But you must make haste."--Pomuchelskopp snatched his hat from the peg, hastened out of doors, and ran down the streets of Malchin in pursuit of the lantern as fast as his round-about figure and shortness of breath would allow him.--The good-natured looking man took a pinch of snuff smilingly, seated himself at one of the tables and said to himself with a chuckle of enjoyment: "I'd give a good deal to see Langfeldt now!"

And it would have been well worth the trouble! Langfeldt, who was mayor of Güstrow, having arrived at the house of the government commissioner from Shwerin, entered the hall, and, giving his lantern into the charge of a footman, was shown into an audience-chamber. Scarcely was this done when some one came puffing and blowing up the steps, and Pomuchelskopp made his appearance. He made a low bow to the footman and said: "Can you tell me, Sir, where I can ad the gentleman who has just come to call?"--The man opened a door and Pomuchelskopp entered the room, and made a series of deferential bows to Langfeldt, whom he mistook for the government commissioner; mistake for which he might the more readily be pardoned, that the worshipful mayor of the border town of Güstrow was in the habit of holding his head so high, that it looked as if it would go through the ceiling, and that was quite what might be expected of a Mecklenburg government commissioner. He however met Pomuchelskopp right by showing him the real man, and then, as his own business was finished, he went way taking his lantern with him. Pomuchelskopp, in deadly fear of losing sight of him, made a bow to the commissioner and hurried after Langfeldt and his lantern. The same thing took place at the house of the Chief of the constabulary forces. The mayor had just begun to make a polite speech when Pomuchelskopp panted into the room after him.--"What brings that fellow here, I wonder," he asked himself, and at once taking leave hoped to make good his escape; but Pomuchelskopp was wary and the lantern was his only guide, so off he steered again in its wake.--They met once more at the house of the High Sheriff of the Wendish district and Langfeldt lost his temper at the intrusion. As he knew the High Sheriff well, indeed they were members of the same select committee, he was determined to come to the bottom of the affair, and enquired sternly: "Sir, may I ask why you are pursuing me?"--"I--I," stammered Pomuchelskopp, "I have as good a right as you to make calls."--"Then make them by yourself," cried the mayor.--The High Sheriff tried to smooth over matters, and Pomuchelskopp began to put on a look of clownish stupidity, but no sooner did the mayor get out of doors than he again started in pursuit.--Langfeldt became still more angry and turning round in the street, said: "Sir, why are you running after me?"--And Pomuchelskopp had now lost the shyness which the High Sheriff's presence had made him feel, and knew that it was only a mayor he had to deal with, so he answered loftily: "Sir, I am every bit as much the Grand Duke's pheasant as you are!"--He meant to have said "vassal," but used the word pheasant by mistake.[3]--However angry a man may be he is certain to be amused by a ludicrous blunder such as Pomuchelskopp had made, and as the mayor happened to be a good tempered fellow in the main, he burst out laughing, and said: "All right then. Come away. I see what sort of man you are."--"And," cried Pomuchelskopp furiously, for he bitterly resented being laughed at, "let me tell you, I've got every bit as good a right to go to these places as you have!" Having said that he set off once more in pursuit of the lantern. But he might have spared himself the trouble, for Langfeldt had finished paying his visits, and was now on his way back to his inn. Arrived there, he took his key off the nail and went to get some money to pay his stakes at ombre. On looking round he found that Pomuchelskopp had followed him into the room.--The mayor put his lantern on the table, and as the affair amused him, he said laughingly: "Pray tell me what you want?"--"I tell you that I've every bit as much right to pay visits as you have," said Pomuchelskopp, who was boiling over with rage at finding himself made a laughing-stock.--"But whom do you want to see here?"--"What's that to you?" said Pomuchelskopp, "the gentleman I have come to visit will soon be in," and he seated himself on a chair with a flop.--"This is as good as a play!" said the mayor, and going to the door he called out: "Sophia, bring candles." When the servant brought the candles he asked: "Did you ever see a pheasant, Sophia?--Look there," pointing to

Pomuchelskopp, "that's a pheasant, one of the Grand Duke's pheasants!"--Sophia ran away in fits of laughter. A few minutes afterwards the landlord came in to have a look at the pheasant, and he was soon followed by his children, who showed their amusement so openly that Pomuchelskopp was not long in finding out whom he was visiting. He went away in a rage and the mayor followed him lantern in hand.

The good-natured looking gentleman said to his friend smilingly as he entered the coffee-room at Voitel's: "Well, Langfeldt, have you finished your calls?" "To be sure!" exclaimed the mayor, "I understand it all now, I wonder that I didn't guess at once that you had sent that idiot after me."--Then he told the whole story, and as even members of parliament like a little fun, Pomuchelskopp was known ever after by the nick-name of the "pheasant," and Alick, whose footsteps he was continually dogging, was called the "game-keeper," while Mally and Sally who came to the ball in splendid attire were talked of as the "chickens." On one occasion when Pomuchelskopp had to record his vote in favour of a motion, he wrote "yeaws" instead of "yes," so a wit, who saw what he had done, proposed that he should be called the "parliamentary-donkey," but nobody was inclined to adopt the new name, and the old one of "pheasant" carried the day.

Pomuchelskopp cannot be said to have had much enjoyment during the time he attended the sitting of parliament, for even the nobles to whom he paid court, and with whom he voted, would have nothing to do with him for fear of making themselves ridiculous, and when he was at home again his wife made him even more uncomfortable by her compassionate "Pöking." He was ill at ease, and yet neither Mally nor Sally came to his rescue, for they had had no dancing on the evening of the parliamentary ball, but had been left sitting as motionless as if they had been hatching eggs. The womenkind all united in stabbing the poor quiet man and law-giver with their sharp words as he sat cowering in his sofa-corner, till the sight of his misery would have softened a heart of stone.--"Well, Pöking, were you much thought of at the parliament?"--And: "Will they soon make you a nobleman, father?"--And: "What do people do, Pöking, when they are up at the parliament-house?"--"How can I tell?" he said. "They're always fighting."--"What was settled about the nunneries, father?"--"I can't tell. You'll know soon enough from the Rostock newspaper."--Then he rose and went to the barn, where he got rid of some of his ill-temper by abusing the farm-servants.

CHAPTER IX

The new year 1844 had come and winter was gone. Spring was waiting at the door till the Lord of the house gave him permission to enter, and re-clothe the earth with her garment of leaves, grass and flowers. When the ice and snow melted all hearts at Pümpelhagen grew lighter as though awakened to new life by the sunshine. Even old Hawermann was happier as he worked away in the fields, and while he sowed the corn-seed in the dark soil, God sowed the seed of hope in his sad heart. As Mr. and Mrs. von Rambow had gone to visit some of their relations he was able to get on quicker with the work of the farm, and also to see more of his daughter than during the winter. He had seen and spoken to her that morning at church, and he was now spending the Sunday afternoon quietly in his sitting-room thinking over the past. No one interrupted him for a long time, as Fred was in the stable with his mare, and that was a great comfort to the old man, for he could now find his pupil at a moment's notice if he wanted him, which was not always the case before.

Bräsig came in: "How-d'ye-do, Charles," he said.--"What?" cried Hawermann, starting up, "I thought you were laid up with gout, and was just meditating paying you a visit, but the difficulty was that Mr. von Rambow is from home, and Triddelfitz isn't to be trusted just now."--"Why, what's the matter with him?"--"Oh, his old mare is going to foal very soon."--"Ha, ha, ha!" laughed Bräsig. "The thoroughbred foal that he's going to sell to the squire."--"Yes. But tell me, hav'n't you had another attack of gout?"--"Well, Charles, it's very difficult to tell whether one has had the real thing or not. But it comes to much the same thing in the long run, for one's suff'ring is quite as severe in the one case as in the other. The only great difference is in the *cause*. You see *real* gout is brought on by good eating and drinking, and what I had wasn't quite the right kind, for it was caused by wearing wretched thin-soled patent leather boots."--"What on earth makes you wear such things then?"--"I had them when I was in the Count's service, and I can't throw them away. But what I wanted to say was this: have you seen the parson today?"--"Yes."--"Well, how is he?"--"He looks ill, and is very weak; when he got into the pulpit the perspiration stood in great beads on his forehead from the exertion, and he had to rest quietly on the sofa for some time after he went home."--"Hm! Hm!" sighed Bräsig, shaking his head. "I'm sorry to hear that, Charles, but we must remember that he's an old man now."--"Yes, that's true," said Hawermann thoughtfully.--"How's your little girl?" asked Bräsig.--"She's very well, thank you, Zachariah. She was here last week, but I had no time to speak to her, as I had to go and see to the sowing of the corn. Mrs. von Rambow saw her though, and called her into the house where she kept her till the evening."--"Charles," said Bräsig, and getting up from his chair he walked up und down the room, biting the mouth-piece of his pipe so hard in his excitement that the knob broke short off, "believe me, your squire's wife is a capital product of humanity."--Hawermann also rose and paced the room. Every time the old friends passed each other in their walk they gave their pipes a vehement puff, and Bräsig said: "Well, Charles, am I not right?" and Hawermann answered: "Quite right, Zachariah."--Who knows how long they would have gone on repeating this question and answer, if a carriage had not driven up to the door, and Kurz and the rector made their appearance.

"How-d'ye-do! How-d'ye-do!" cried Kurz as he entered the parlour. "Oh, I see, you're here too, Mr. Bräsig. How are you, old friend? I've come to speak to you about the clover-seed, Hawermann."--"Good-day!" said Baldrian to Bräsig, drawing out the word "day" till one would have thought he wanted that day to last to all eternity, "how are you my worthy friend?"--"Pretty bobbish," replied Bräsig.--"Hawermann," interrupted Kurz, "isn't it splendid seed?"--"Well, Kurz," said Hawermann, "I've seen worse seed and I've seen better. I put a little of it on a hot shovel, and as you know, if it's good seed it ought to jump off the shovel with a skip like a flea, but a good many of the grains never moved at all."--"You don't look quite so blooming, my dear Sir," continued the rector, "as on that memorable occasion when we met round the punch-bowl to celebrate the betrothals at Rexow."--"There's a good reason for that," said Hawermann, laying his hand affectionately on Bräsig's shoulder, "my dear old friend has been suffering from gout."--"I see," laughed the rector, trying to be witty,

> "'Vinum, der Vater,
> Und cœna, die Mutter,
> Und Venus, die Hebamm,
> Die machen podagram.'"[4]

"The seed is splendid," cried Kurz again, "you won't see finer between Grimmen and Greifswald."--"Take care, Kurz!" said Hawermann, "don't crow too loud, remember the proverb!"--"Listen!" Bräsig exclaimed, at the same moment addressing the rector. "Don't talk French to me! I can't understand you. But what do you mean by talking of Fenus? What have I and my gout to do with Fenus?"--"My honoured friend," said the rector with a deep bow, "permit me to inform you that Venus was the name given in ancient times to the goddess of love."--"I don't care about that," answered Bräsig, "she may have been anything you like, but now-a-days every stupid shepherd's dog is called Venus."--"No, Hawermann," exclaimed Kurz eagerly, "I assure you that when clover has the real purply red colour it ....."--"Yes, Kurz," was the answer, "but yours wasn't like that."--"My good friend," said the rector to Bräsig, "Venus was a goddess, as I told you before, and how a shepherd's dog ...."--"But," interrupted Bräsig, "you make a mistake in saying she was a goddess, for a Fenus was a kind of bird. Now, Charles, us'n't we to hear of a bird called the Fenus when we were children?"--"Ah, I see what you mean now," said the rector, who had received a new light on the subject. "You're thinking of the Arabian bird, the Phœnix, which builds its nest of costly spices ..."--"Humbug!" interposed Kurz. "How is it possible for any bird to build a nest with cloves, pepper, cummin and nutmegs."--"My dear brother-in-law, are you not aware that it is an old saga?"--"Then," said Bräsig, "the saga tells what isn't true, and besides that, you don't pronounce the word rightly. It isn't Phœnix but Ponix, and they aren't birds at all, but small horses that come from Sweden and Ireland, and not from Arabia, as you say. The Countess always used to drive two of these ponixes in her carriage."--The rector was going to put his friend right, but Kurz stopped him: "No, brother-in-law," he said, "just let it alone. We're all willing to admit that you're much better up in learned subjects than Bräsig."--"Let him say what he will," said Bräsig, standing before the rector, and looking quite ready to fight out the point.--"No, no," cried Kurz, "we didn't come here to quarrel about Venuses or clover-seed, but to have a good game at Boston."--"That's much better," said Hawermann, beginning to prepare the table.--"Stop, Charles," said Bräsig, "that isn't proper work for you to do; the apprentice ought to do it for you."--He then put his head out at the window and shouted "Triddelfitz" across the court. Fred came running to see why he was wanted. "We're going to play at Boston, Triddelfitz, so please put the table in order for us, and get a dish of some kind for the pool, then you can fill our pipes and make a handful of matches."--As soon as Fred had done this they sat down to play, but could not begin at once, as they had first to determine what the stakes were to be. Kurz wanted to do things grandly when he was about it, and proposed penny points, but he was always of a reckless disposition, and the others agreed with Bräsig that the stake was too high, as they were not playing for the pleasured of winning other people's money. At last Hawermann got them to fix on a smaller sum, and to begin.--"Diamond begins," said the rector.--"Kurz deals," said Bräsig. They might have begun now, but the rector laid his hand upon the cards, and said as he looked round upon the circle: "What a strange thing it is! We are all sensible men, and yet we are playing at a game, which, if old tales are true, was invented for the amusement of a mad king. King Charles of France ....."--"No, no, good people," said Kurz, pulling the cards from under the rector's hand, "if we're going to play let us play, and if we're going to talk let us talk."--"Fire away!" said Bräsig, and Kurz began to deal, but in his haste, he misdealt. "Try again!" This time it was all right, and they could begin.--"I pass," said Hawermann. It was now the rector's turn, and they had all to wait till he had arranged his cards, for he had a superstitious fancy for picking up his cards singly, thinking it would bring him better luck, and as he was very conscientious in all his actions he was careful to arrange them in regular order, placing the sevens and fives in such a way that he could see the centre mark on each card, and so distinguish between them and the sixes and fours.--Kurz meanwhile laid his cards on the table, folded his hands and sighed.--"I pass," said the rector.--"I knew that," said Kurz, who was quite aware that it would be very odd play if his brother-in-law were to declare anything, but still he was always frightened, lest Baldrian should return the lead when he himself had declared anything, and when in consequence he had nothing more, or else should not lead up to him when he ought.--"Pass," said Bräsig whose turn it now was.--"Boston grandissimo," said Kurz.--"Who can follow?"--"Pass," said Hawermann.--"Dear brother-in-law," said the rector, "I--I--one trick, two tricks--this'll be the third. I follow."--"Oh," said Kurz, "but remember, we're not going to pay together, we're each to pay for ourselves."--"Then, Charles," said Bräsig, "if that's the way *of* it we'll have to give them a double beating."--"No talking," said Kurz.--"Certainly not," answered Hawermann, laying the ten of hearts on the table; "'Archduke Michael fell on the land.'"--"'Cœur, Mr. Bräsig," said the rector throwing down the knave of hearts.--"'Hug me (Herze mich), and kiss me, but don't crumple my collar,'" said Bräsig playing the queen.--"The lady must have a husband," said Kurz putting down the king and taking the trick. He then played a small club; "clubs."--"Quick, snap it up," cried Bräsig to Hawermann.--"Hush!" said Kurz, "no talking allowed."--"Of course not," said Hawermann playing a small club.--"Well done our side," said the rector playing the nine.--"I've conquered with a club and a lady," said Bräsig taking the trick with the queen.--"What the mischief!" cried Kurz. "He has no more clubs. I wonder what he has!"--"Keep a bright look out, Charles, we're going to begin," cried Bräsig; "Sir," he went on turning to Kurz, "this is Whist. The ace of spades leads the way," and he threw down the ace. The king followed: "Long live the king!" and then the queen: "Give place to the ladies!"--"Hang it!" cried Kurz laying his cards on the table and staring at the rector; "what *can* he have? He has no spades either!"--"Dear brother-in-law," said the rector, "I'll do my part afterwards."--"And then it'll be too late," said Kurz taking up his cards again with as deep a sigh as if the rector had been ill-treating him and he was determined to bear it with the resignation of a Christian--"Charles," asked Bräsig, "how many tricks have we altogether?"--"Four," answered Hawermann.--"Hush," said Kurz. "That's not the game. No talking allowed."--"I wasn't giving any hints," said Bräsig. "I was only asking a question. Now, Charles, do your best. I can make *one* more trick, and so if you make another we'll do."--"*I* shall make one," said Kurz positively.--"And so shall I," said the rector.--After a couple of rounds, Kurz laid his hand over his tricks and said: "I've got mine now."--Diamonds were led. Baldrian recklessly played his queen, and Bräsig threw down the king, exclaiming: "Where are you going to, my pretty maid?" so the poor old rector was out-done, and he muttered confusedly: "I don't understand how that happened."--"Because you don't know the rules of Whist," cried Kurz.--"Charles," said Bräsig, "if you had only been paying proper attention to the game you might have got another of their good cards."--"Might I? Well, you made a mistake too, you ought to have returned my lead that time I led hearts."--"Now, Charles, how could I when I had none. I had nothing but the king."--"Well, brother-in-law," exclaimed Kurz, "you threw away the game. Why did you play the nine of trumps when you had the king. If you hadn't done that the game would have been ours."--"Faugh!" said Bräsig with great contempt, "you boy, you savage! How can you say that, when you remember what a strong hand I had in spades, to say nothing of my other cards. What do you mean by it?"--"Sir, do you think that when I agreed to play at Boston I should be afraid of your stupid grumbling?" said the rector.--"Don't let's talk about it any more," said Hawermann beginning a new deal. "It's always unpleasant to play a game over again."

They began to play once more with the firm determination to get the better of their adversaries.--The rector won as was right and proper, for, as is well known, the one who loses the first game is sure to win the second.--Kurz looked gloomy for a time, but afterwards brightened up: "Ten grandissimo," he said. Everybody was astonished, and so was he. He looked at his cards again, and repeated: "Ten grandissimo," laid the cards on the table and began to walk up and down the room: "That's the way they play in Venice and in other great towns," he said in conclusion.

Fred Triddelfitz entered the parlour at the moment when Kurz was triumphant and the others hardly knew what to do next. He looked pale and frightened: "Mr. Hawermann," he said, "do please come with me."--"What's the matter?" asked Hawermann starting up, but Kurz forced him back into his chair, saying: "You mustn't go till you've finished the game. The same thing happened to me once before, at the time of the great fire, I had just laid a grandissimo on the table when everyone ran away."--"Confound it," cried Hawermann freeing himself from Kurz, "can't you tell me what it is. Is there a fire?"--"No," stammered Fred, "it's--it's--it's only something that has happened to me."--"What has happened to you?" asked Bräsig sharply across the table.--"My mare has got a foal," said Fred.--"Is that all?" said Bräsig, "she has often had one before and I don't see what's to frighten you in that. Such an event is always a subject of rejoicing."--"I know," said Fred, "but--but--it looks so very odd. You must come, Mr. Hawermann."--"Is the foal dead?" asked Hawermann.--"No," answered Fred. "It's quite well, it only looks so odd ..... Christian Däsel says it's a young camel."--"Bless me!" cried Hawermann. "We'll put off the game till another time. Will you all come with me?"--And in spite of Kurz's expostulations they all followed Fred to the stable.--"I never saw a foal like it," said Fred while they were on their way there, "its ears are so long," and he showed them his arm from his elbow upwards.

When they came to the stable they found Christian Däsel in the stall, where the sorrel-mare was making much of her foal, which was trying to skip about merrily though rather staggeringly. He turned to Bräsig and said with a shake of his head: "Please, Sir, what in all the world is it?"--Bräsig looked at Hawermann and said emphatically: "Yes, I know what it is, Charles, this thorough-bred foal is neither more nor less than a mule."--"You're right," said Hawermann.--"A mule?" cried Fred, rushing into the stall and, notwithstanding the mother's displeasure, succeeding in getting hold of the foal's head and examining its face, eyes and ears with anxious scrutiny. As soon as he was convinced of the dreadful truth, he exclaimed angrily: "I'd like to strangle the creature, as I can't get at Augustus Prebberow."--"For shame, Triddelfitz!" said Hawermann gravely. "Don't you see how pleased its mother is with it although it isn't a thoroughbred?"--"Yes," said Bräsig, "and she's 'the nearest' to it, as Mrs. Behrens would say. You may strangle Augustus Prebberow though for all I care; he's a thrice distilled contraband rascal!"--"Nay," said Fred, whose wrath had given place to sadness, "how is it possible? He was my best friend, and yet he cheated me into buying a deaf mare and a mule. I'll prosecute him."--"I tell you that friendship and honesty are nowhere in horse-dealing," said Bräsig, taking Fred by the arm and leading him out of the stable, "but I'm *very* sorry for your disappointment. You've paid dearly for your experience in horse-dealing, but that's what everyone has to do. You mustn't go to law about it, for a law-suit is an endless thing; it'll still be going on long after the mule is dead. Look here," he said, making Fred walk up and down the yard with him, "I'll tell you a story as a warning. Old Rütebusch of Swensen sold his own brother-in-law, who was bailiff here before Hawermann, a regular porcupine of a riding-horse. Well, or as you always say, 'Bong,' three days afterwards the bailiff wished to try his new inquisition. He climbed into the saddle, and it was really climbing, I can tell you, for the horse, which had very short legs, had poked up its back till it looked more like a rainbow than anything else. No sooner was he mounted than the beast ran away with him, and never stopped till it had got deep into the village pond, right up to the neck in fact, and there was no inducing it to move either one way or the other. That was a blessing though in one sense, both for the horse and the bailiff, as they would otherwise most likely have been drowned. The bailiff shouted for help. The water was too deep to allow him to wade ashore, and he couldn't swim, so at last old Flegel the carpenter had to save him in a boat. Then there was a law-suit, for the bailiff said the horse was incurably mad, or as we farmers call it 'witless,' and Rütebusch must take it back, as madness when proved was sufficient cause to dissolve any bargain. Rütebusch refused, and the brothers-in-law became on such bad terms that they couldn't see each other three miles off without getting into a rage. The law-suit went on. All the Swensen people were called upon to swear that the horse was in full possession of its senses, and the Pümpelhagen people had to swear to the contrary. The law-suit went on for five years, and during that time the horse was left quietly in the stable eating his oats comfortably, for the bailiff had never ridden him since the first day, as he looked upon him as a dangerous wretch that had sold his soul to the devil, and he didn't dare to kill the beast because he was what is called the *corpus delictus* of the whole affair. The most learned vetinairy surgeons, six in number, were brought to look at the horse, but no good came of that, for they didn't agree. Three of them said he was all there, and the other three pronounced him mad. The lawsuit went on, and a number of other law-suits branched out of it, for the learned horse-doctors accused each other of being malicious and rude, and ended by going to law. Then a famous professor of vetinairy surgery in Berlin was applied to, and he wrote to desire them to cut off the horse's head and send it to him, as he must examine the brain before he could pronounce judgment. It's very difficult to say of any reasonable human being whether he is witless or wise, and how much more difficult is it to speak decidedly of an unreasoning animal. The bailiff determined to do as the professor wished, but old Rütebusch and his legal advisers wouldn't consent, so the law-suit went on as before. At last Rütebusch died, and six months later his brother-in-law died also. They hadn't made up their quarrel at the time of their death and each of them went into eternity clinging to his own opinion; the one that the horse was in his right senses and the other that he was mad. The law-suit was then suspendicated and three weeks afterwards the old horse died of fat and idleness. The head was nicely pickled and was sent to the learned professor at Berlin, who wrote clearly and decidedly that the horse had never been mad in all its life; that in point of fact it had been every bit as sane as he was himself, and that he only wished for the sake of the rival litigants that their brains had been in as perfect a condition as that of the horse. And he was right, for the rascally boy who had saddled the bailiff's horse, confessed to me afterwards when he was in my service, that he had tied a burning sponge under the poor beast's tail out of revenge, because the bailiff had thrashed him the day before. Now I ask you as a reasonable mortal, didn't the horse show his wisdom by running into the pond and so putting out the fire? The great law-suit was at an end, but the little ones between the farriers are still going on. And now I'll tell you something; Hawermann is a great friend of old Prebberow, the father of your roguish friend, and he will try to make an arrangement for you and see that you have fair play. You may go now, but don't be unkind to the innocent little foal or its mother, for they are not to blame for your having been cheated, indeed the mother was as much cheated as you were." Bräsig then went to join his friends and they all resumed their places at the card-table.

"All right!" said Kurz, "well it was ten grandissimo, and my turn to play."--"Charles," said Bräsig, "you must have a talk with old Prebberow some time or other, and try to make better terms for that confounded grey-hound of yours."--"I'll see to it, Zachariah, and it'll all come right. I'm heartily sorry for the poor boy having his pleasure spoilt like this--a mule of all things in the world!"--"I perceive," said the rector, laying down the cards which he had just finished arranging, "that you all talk of that little new born foal as a mule, and mule is the term used in natural history....."--"Don't drive us mad with your natural history!" cried Kurz who had been sitting on thorns in fear of a long harangue. "Are we playing at natural history or at cards? Look, there's the ace of diamonds lying on the table."--They went on with their game and Kurz won. He was never tired of talking of his ten grandissimo during the next few weeks.

They played in the most friendly manner, till the rector who had arranged his money in a half circle, found out that he had won ten shillings, and then seeing that fortune was beginning to go against him, determined to stop playing; he therefore rose, and complaining of his feet having grown very cold, put his winnings in his pocket.--"If you suffer from cold feet," said Bräsig, "I'll tell you an excellent cure; take a pinch of snuff every morning before you have eaten anything and that'll prevent your ever having cold feet."--"Nonsense!" cried Kurz, who had been winning, "what's to make his feet cold?"--"Why," said the rector, defending himself, "can't I have cold feet as well as you? Don't you always complain of having cold feet at the club when you've been winning?" And so Baldrian succeeded in keeping his right to cold feet and to what he had won. After a little further talk the two town's people drove away taking Bräsig with them as far as their roads went in the same direction.

Just as Hawermann was going to bed he heard loud talking and scolding outside his door, and immediately afterwards Fred Triddelfitz and Christian Däsel came into the room.--"Good evening, Sir," said Christian, "and I don't care a bit."--"What's the matter?" asked Hawermann.--"Well, Sir," said Fred, "you know--how--how disappointed I was about the--the mule, and now Christian won't let the poor thing remain in the stable."--"Why not," asked Hawermann.--"You see, Sir," answered Christian, "I don't mind anything else, but I can't consent to that. My work lies amongst horses and foals, and I never set up to undertake camels and mules. And why? If I did Mr. Triddelfitz would be for bringing apes and bears into my stable next."--"But if I tell you that the mule is to stay there, and that you're to treat it as you would any other foal?"--"Nay then, of course I must do it if you tell me that, and it's all right now. Well, goodnight, Sir, I hope you'll not take it ill of me saying what I did," and so saying he went away.--"Mr. Hawermann," asked Fred, "what do you think that Mr. von Rambow will say when he hears what has happened, and Mrs. von Rambow too?"--"Don't distress yourself, they won't trouble themselves about it"--"Ah," sighed Fred as he left the room, "I'm awfully sorry that this has happened."

When the squire came home he was told the whole story of the sorrel-mare by Christian, and as he was a good-natured fellow at heart, and really liked Fred, whom he felt to be somewhat like himself in disposition, he spoke kindly and comfortingly to the lad, saying: "Never mind! Our little traffic in thorough-bred foals has come to nothing as the mare had made a mésalliance. We'll soon put her and her foal out into the field, and you'll see that things will turn out better than you expect"--Every one took an interest in the little mule, which soon became a general favourite. When the village children were passing through the field on Sunday afternoons they went to the enclosure where the foals were kept and looking at the mule used to say: "Look, Josy, that's it."--"Yes, that's the one. Just look how he's waggling his ears."--"I say, he's kicking like a donkey."--And when the young women who worked on the farm trooped past the enclosure, they also stood still, saying: "Look, Stina, that's Mr. Triddelfitz's mule."--"Come, Sophie, let's go a little nearer."--"No, I'd rather not. What an ugly beast it is to be sure."--"You've no right to say so. You don't dislike him so much, for he always gives you the easiest bits of work."--The sorrel-mare, the mule and Fred became well known in all the country side, and wherever the latter showed himself, he was asked how the mule was getting on, much to his chagrin. The little mule was happy and careless of all the remarks made about him, he ran and jumped about the paddock with the other well-born, high-bred foals, and when one of them tried to bully him he was quite able to take his own part.

CHAPTER X

Everything went on well at Pümpelhagen that year. The harvest was plenteous, and the price of corn was high. Alick von Rambow saw a way opening before him of getting out of his difficulties; he did up his accounts over and over again, and saw clearly that if he sold the rape for so much, the sheep for so much, and the cattle for so much, that all this, with what he got for the wheat would be amply sufficient to pay off the last farthing of his debts. The devil himself must take part against him, if he failed to do so. He thought that the reason of his good fortune this year was that he himself was at Pümpelhagen, and was therefore able to look after things with his own eyes. The eye of the master is to a farm what the sun is to the world, everything ripens under it, and the tender blades of grass grow green under his footstep. So thinking, it was not long before Alick quite forgot that these blessings were the gift of God, and began to look upon them as the result of his own efforts, and even the high price of corn seemed to him to be a piece of well merited good fortune.

He rode his high horse without fear, and even when the farming and household expenses of the moment ran away with all the bank-notes with which David and Slus'uhr had provided him, and his small change began to run short, he congratulated himself on his excellent farming which gave him such unlimited credit in the neighbourhood, that Pomuchelskopp had offered to lend him various small sums from time to time. He had accepted loans from Pomuchelskopp without fear, in order to get rid of David for the time being, so that he paid David and Slus'uhr with Pomuchelskopp's money, and they paid it back to Pomuchelskopp, and he again lent it to Alick, thus the money was kept continually going round and round in a circle. It would altogether have been a very pleasant little arrangement, if Pomuchelskopp had not been obliged to take the trouble of removing the marks from the bills for fear of Alick's finding out that it was always his own money that he got back. It could not be helped however if Pomuchelskopp still wished to keep his plans for gaining the Pümpelhagen acres a profound secret from his victim, and indeed he enjoyed the sense of power which came of his rapid intimacy with Alick far too much to grudge the trouble he had to take.

Alick was also perfectly satisfied with the course events were taking, for he was always well supplied with money to ward off the attacks of the usurers, and at what seemed to him a very small price, for he never thought of adding up at the end of the year how much the total came to, and he was firmly convinced that his affairs were better attended to now that he lived at Pümpelhagen than they had ever been before. It was the old story over again. When a young squire who knows nothing whatever of farming wants to make improvements, he always begins with the live-stock. And why is this the case? Well, I imagine it is because young gentlemen think this subject the easiest to understand. All that they have to do is to buy a new bull, and a ram or two of some new fashioned breed, and then, as the laws of cattle-breeding are still sufficiently indefinite to allow of much theorising, even the stupidest of them has no difficulty in speaking learnedly on the subject. They have only to pass over as of no account, all that the old men around them have learnt from the experience of years, and they do not find it hard to do; after that these youthful farmers are as worthy of being listened to, in their own opinion at least, as those whose hair has grown grey at the work.

There was a dairy of Breitenburg cows at Pümpelhagen, which the old squire had bought by Hawermann's advice and with Hawermann's assistance. This dairy must now be improved, so Alick went to Sommersdorf in Pommerania where there was a great cattle-show, and bought a splendid Ayrshire bull by Pomuchelskopp's advice. He bought this bull because he was handsome, because he came from Scotland, and because he was something new. There was a flock of Negretti sheep which produced a great quantity of wool, and were of a high market-value, but as Pomuchelskopp *said* he had got four and sixpence a stone more for his wool, the young squire was induced to buy a couple of Electoral rams from his worthy neighbour, for which he was obliged to pay ready money. It never occurred to Alick to set the sum he made by the large quantity of wool given by his sheep, against that gained by Pomuchelskopp for the smaller quantity of finer wool; had he done so he might have found the result to be in his own favour, but unfortunately for him he had enough to do adding up other sums on a different subject.

Hawermann defended himself from the new arrangements as well as he could, but his efforts were vain. His master looked upon him as an old man who clung to the traditions of his youth too vehemently to be able to advance with the age, and when the old man's reasons against the introduction of some new method were unanswerable, he always said impatiently: "Hang it! Let's try how it does at all events," and it never entered his head to remember that experiments run away with more money than anything else. The bailiff could do nothing, and only thanked God that the squire had not yet really thought of breeding thorough-bred horses, though he spoke of doing it every now and then. Mrs. von Rambow could do nothing, for she was not aware of the way in which her husband put off the evil day of paying his debts, and in ordinary matters she was obliged to be contented with the result of what she saw, and that was that Alick was apparently satisfied with the course of events, and was looking forward to a golden future.

The Pomuchelskopps at Gürlitz manor were also happy; I do not mean that they enjoyed great domestic happiness, they were too modest to expect such a thing? but they were satisfied with their financial condition, and looked forward to still greater wealth coming to them in a short time, for the boundary between Pümpelhagen and Gürlitz was growing more shadowy every day. Pomuchelskopp's only difficulty after any new business-transaction with Alick was to keep his Henny quiet, for in her ardour for possession she was anxious to cross the boundary, and seize upon Pümpelhagen without further delay.

There was great contentment in Joseph Nüssler's house, and much looking forward to a golden future of the ideal sort, such as poets mean when they try to describe the "golden glory of the dawn," not that they think the brilliance of gold an exact representation of that wonderful light in the eastern sky, but because they know nothing more beautiful, they so seldom get a glimpse of it. Godfrey gradually got rid of his long hair, and began to look upon the world with other eyes than before. He no longer used the mental blue spectacles they had provided him with at Erlangen or elsewhere, and much to Bräsig's delight he even went so far as to play at Boston, though it must be confessed that he did it very badly; on another occasion he had got on horse-back, and had managed to fall off without hurting himself, and he had appeared at Joseph Nüssler's Harvest Home. He did not dance, that is to say before all the rest, but he enjoyed a quiet turn with Lina in the next room, and at the end of the evening he sang "Vivallera!" clearly but wretchedly ill. And Rudolph? It is sufficient to repeat what Hilgendorf said to Bräsig about him: "He'll do, Bräsig. He's just such another youngster as I was myself; there's no tiring him; he's as strong as a horse. He has only to glance at a thing, and he knows how to do it at once, and it was just the same with me. And as for books? He never opens one! And that's like me again."--Mrs. Nüssler rejoiced in her children's happiness; and young Joseph and young Bolster sat quietly by the hour together, gazing straight before them, and saying nothing, they were thinking of the time when they would each have a new heir to their dignities, young Joseph in Rudolph, and young Bolster in young Bolster the seventh. Theirs could not be called a looking forward to a golden dawn, but to contented natures like Joseph and Bolster the evening-sky has likewise its golden light.

Every house in the parish had its share of happiness, each of them after its kind, but one house formed an exception to this rule, although it used to have its full share. In winter round the fire-side, and in summer under the great lime-tree, or in the arbour in the garden there always used to be a calm peaceful happiness, in which the child Louisa as she played about the old house and grounds, and little Mrs. Behrens, who ruled all things duster in hand, had had part, and also the good old clergyman, who had now done with all earthly things for ever. Peace had taken leave of the house, and had gone forth calmly to the place from whence she came, and during that time of illness, care and sorrow had taken up their abode there, deepening with the growing weakness of the good old man. He did not lie long in bed, and had no particular illness, so that Dr. Strump of Rahnstädt could not find amongst all the three thousand, seven hundred and seventy seven diseases of which he knew, one that suited the present case. Peace seemed to have laid her hand on the old man's head in blessing, and to have said to him: "I am going to leave thee, but only for a short time, I shall afterwards return to thy Regina. Thou needest me no more, because thou hast had me in thy heart during all the long years thou hast fought the good fight of faith. Now sleep softly, thou must needs be tired."

And he was tired, very tired. His wife had laid him on the sofa under the pictures, that he might look out at the window as much as he liked, Louisa had covered him comfortably with rugs and shawls, and then they had both left the room softly that he might rest undisturbed. Out of doors the first flakes of snow were falling slowly, slowly from the sky; it was as quiet and still outside as within his heart, and he felt as if the blessing of Christ were resting upon him. No one saw it, but his Regina was the first to find it out--he rose, and, pushing the large arm-chair up to the cupboard, opened the door, and sitting down, began to examine the treasures that he had kept as relics of the past. Some of them had belonged to his father, and some to his mother, they were all reminiscences of what he had loved.

This cupboard was the place where he had stowed away whatever reminded him of all the chief events of his life, and they had become relics the sight of which did him good when he was down-hearted. They were not preserved in crystal vessels or in embroidered cases, but were simply placed on the shelf, and kept there to be looked at whenever he wanted to see them. When he felt low and sad it did him good to take out these relics, and to live over again in thought the happy days of which they reminded him, and he never closed the cupboard-door without gaining strength and courage, or without thanking God silently for his many blessings. There lay the Bible his father had given him when he was a boy; the beautiful glass vase his old college-friend had sent him; the pocket-book his Regina had worked for him during their engagement; the shell which a sailor had sent him in token of his gratitude for having been shown the way to become a better man; the pieces of paper on which Louisa, Mina and Lina had written their Christmas and New Year's-day messages of affection, as also some of their earlier bits of handiwork; the withered myrtle wreath his wife had worn on her wedding-day; the large pictorial Bible with the silver-clasps that Hawermann had given him on his seventieth birthday, and the silver-mounted meerschaum that Bräsig had given him on the same occasion, and down below on the lowest shelf were three pairs of shoes, the shoes that Louisa, Regina and he had worn when they first entered the parsonage.

Old shoes are not beautiful in themselves, but the memories attached to these made them beautiful in his eyes, so he took them out of the cupboard, and laid them down by his side, and then placing his first Bible on his knee, he opened it at our Lord's Sermon on the Mount, and began to read. No one saw him, but that was not necessary, and his Regina knew it when it was all over. He grew very tired, and resting his head in the corner of the great chair fell asleep like a little child.

And so they found him when they came back. Mrs. Behrens seated herself on the arm of his chair, clasped him in her arms, closed his eyes, and then resting her head against his, wept silently. Louisa knelt at his feet, and laying her folded hands on his knee, looked with tearful eyes at the two quiet faces that were so dear to her. Then Mrs. Behrens rose, and folding down the leaf of the Bible, drew it softly out of her husband's hand, and Louisa also rose and threw her arms round her foster-mother's neck. They both wept long and passionately, till at last when it was growing dusk Mrs. Behrens replaced the shoes in the cupboard, saying as she did so: "I bless the day when we came to this house together," and while laying Louisa's little shoes beside them, she added: "and I bless the day when the child came to us." She then closed the cupboard-door.

The good old clergyman was buried three days later in the piece of ground he had long ago sought out for his last resting-place, and any one standing by the grave, which was lighted by the earliest rays of the morning-sun, might easily see into the parlour in the parsonage-house.

The people who had been at the funeral were all gone home, and Hawermann had also been obliged to go, but uncle Bräsig, who had spent the day at the parsonage helping his friends in every possible way, had announced his intention of remaining for the night. Seeing the two women standing arm in arm at the window buried in sad thought, he slipped quietly upstairs to his bed-room, and going to the window looked sorrowfully down into the church-yard, where the newly made grave showed distinctly against the white snow surrounding it. He thought of the good man who lay there, who had so often helped him with kindness and advice, and he swore to himself that he would be a faithful friend to Mrs. Behrens.--Down-stairs the two sad-hearted women were gazing at the same grave, and silently vowing to show each other all the love and tenderness that he who was gone from them had been wont to bestow. Little Mrs. Behrens thanked God and her husband for the comforter she had in her adopted daughter whom she held in her arms, and whose smooth hair she stroked, as she kissed her lovingly. Louisa prayed that God would bless the lessons she had learnt from her foster-father, and would give her strength to be a good and faithful daughter to the kind woman who had been as a mother to her. New-made graves may be likened to flower-beds in which the gardener puts his rarest and most beautiful plants; but alas, ill-weeds sometimes take root there also.

Two people were standing in one of the windows at Gürlitz manor on the same evening, and gazing out in the dusk, but not towards the church-yard and parsonage; no, they were looking covetously at the glebe-lands, and Pomuchelskopp said to his Henny that they were sure to fall into their hands soon, for he would be the first to propose to take a lease of them when the new clergyman came to the parish.--"Muchel," answered his wife, "the Pümpelhagen people will never stand that; they'll take very good care not to let the land slip through their fingers."--"Through *their* fingers did you say, Henny? Why, don't you know that their very fate is in my hands?"--"That's quite true as far as it goes, but perhaps a young clergyman may come who would like to farm his own glebe."--"Chuck, Chuck, you're not as clever as you used to be. We have to choose the new parson, and we'll choose a methodist. Those clergymen who are never to be seen without a Bible and hymn-book are the kind we want, for they have no time to farm."--"You ar'n't the only patron, remember. Pümpelhagen, Rexow, and Warnitz have votes as well as you."--"But, my Chick, don't you know that Warnitz and Rexow have no chance if they vote against Pümpelhagen. If the Pümpelhagen people and mine only vote together ....."--"Don't trust to your people, Kopp, they've no particular love for you. Mrs. Behrens will be against you, and all the villagers will do her bidding to a man."--"I shall get rid of her as soon as possible. She must leave the village at once. There's no house in the neighbourhood for a parson's widow to live in, and I'm not going to build one. No, no, Mrs. Behrens must go away, and the sooner the better in my opinion."--"What a fool you are, Kopp! Don't you know that she has a right to remain at the parsonage until the new clergyman is elected?" And with that Henny walked away.--"Chuck," Pomuchelskopp called after her, "I'll manage it, dear Chuck."

Many an evil weed flourished upon that quiet grave, and covetous hands were stretched out to seize the place left vacant by the good old man, but harm always comes sooner or later to him who with greedy joy uses the misfortunes of the widow and orphan for his own advantage, and makes capital for himself of his neighbour's necessities.

CHAPTER XI

Bräsig remained a week at the parsonage, and did everything that was necessary to be done at such a time. He made the inventory, wrote a large bundle of letters announcing the sad news of Mr. Behrens' death, and took them to the post-office himself in spite of snow, cold and gout, settled accounts with the Rahnstädt tradesmen, and was now seated at the breakfast-table with Mrs. Behrens and Louisa on the Monday after the funeral, taking his last meal before leaving them, when a carriage stopped at the door, and Frank von Rambow getting out of it entered the room with joyful impetuosity. But on seeing the deep mourning worn by both the women, he stood still and exclaimed: "What has happened? Where is Mr. Behrens?"--The widow rose from her arm-chair, and going to the young man shook hands with him, and said with difficulty: "My pastor is gone. He has gone home, and wished to be remembered to all, to all ...." Here she broke down, and covering her face with her pocket-handkerchief, continued: "To all he loved, and you were one of those."--Louisa now went and shook hands with him, but without speaking. When he entered the room the blood had rushed to her face, but she had had time to regain self-command. Bräsig then welcomed the new-comer, and began to talk of this or that to change the current of his friends' thoughts, which had gone back to the time when they first knew of their bereavement; but Frank did not hear a word that he said, and stood as motionless as if he had been struck by lightning, the news he had just heard had shattered his joyful anticipations so completely.

He had been at the agricultural school at Eldena for the last two years, where he had worked hard, and had learnt all that was needed to make him a good farmer; the practical part of his business he had been taught by Hawermann, and so now that he was of age he was fitted to take possession of his estate, and even to take a wife if he felt inclined. The prudent advice of Mr. Behrens had prevented him hurrying on to such a consummation too quickly. His disposition was neither cold nor calculating, and his heart beat as warmly in his breast as that of any other young man who was very much in love, but he had been obliged to think for himself while so young that he had grown cautious, and had accustomed himself to think twice before doing anything of importance--some people said that he was too cautious--but it is a fault on the right side. In this instance he was right to consider well the step he proposed taking, for it was the most important of his life. He had buried the sweet dream of happiness deep in his heart in the same way as the kernel of the acorn is hidden by its hard shell; he had not pleased himself with building up images of ideal bliss, but had waited patiently till the proper time came for the seed to sprout out of which was to grow the stately tree under whose shade he and his Louisa might sit in peace. Whenever he had longed to go and see her, he struggled against the temptation, for he did not wish to speak to her then, he wanted to leave her free, and to give her plenty of time to make up her mind unharassed by opposition. And when his heart bled at the thought that he must not see her, he used to strengthen himself by saying: "Be still. This is no game of chance. I must learn to be worthy of her. And then if I win her, success will be all the sweeter."

He was now of age and was able to take his place in the world as a man. The time was come where pride and honour no longer stood in the way and he might tell his love to her whom he deemed the noblest, sweetest girl on the face of the earth. The seed had begun to sprout, the tender green shoot was showing above the soil, and the time was come to tend it that it might grow into a tree; not only was it time to do so, it was his duty. So at last yielding to the dictates of his warm heart, and putting aside all further deliberation, he got into a carriage and set out for Gürlitz parsonage.

Now that he had arrived there, the song of joy his heart had been singing on the journey was hushed, and he stood between the two black-robed women feeling more sorrowful than he had ever done before. The object of his journey must remain unknown, for his own feelings, respect for the grief he saw in his friends, and his own sorrow for the true and good man who had passed away from them, all combined to keep him silent, at the cost of much pain to himself.--Love is selfish and cares nothing for the feelings of others is a common saying, and often a true one. It has a world of its own, and goes it own way as though the fate of others were nothing to it; but when it comes from God, its course is determined by the eternal laws of right and goodness, and its influence on sad hearts is sweet and calm as the light of the evening star.

Such was the character of Frank's love, it could neither hurt nor annoy the people with whom he had to do, on the contrary it comforted and did good to all. He said nothing of the errand that had brought him to Gürlitz, and when he took leave of his friends he felt like the traveller, who, towards the end of a long and toilsome journey, sees a church-spire rising in the distance and walks on cheerily, thinking that his destination will soon be reached, but who is undeceived by the sight of the first houses of the village, and finds that he has yet further to go.

It was a beautiful winter-day when Frank set out to walk from the parsonage to Pümpelhagen, letting the carriage follow slowly. Bräsig went with him. The young man was busily engaged with his own thoughts, while Bräsig was not at all inclined to be silent so that they were by no means suitable companions. Bräsig might certainly have held his tongue and have kept all the stories that came into his head to himself, but it was one of his peculiarities never to see when he was not wanted. He could not help seeing at last that he received no answer to his remarks, and then he stood still, curiously enough, nearly on the same spot where Alick had given him to understand that he did not want his company any further, and asked: "Perhaps my presence is disagreeable to you. It was just about this very place that your cousin Mr. von Rambow told me that he did not wish me to walk with him, if that is the case with you, I can easily leave you alone."--"Dear Mr. Bräsig," said Frank; taking the old man's hand, "don't be angry with me, but I can't help thinking about the death of the good old clergyman, and the sad change that has taken place in the parsonage."--"If that is it," answered Bräsig pressing his hand, "I quite understand, and only think the better of you for it. I have always told Mrs. Behrens and little Louisa that you are one of the cultivated farmers such as one meets with in books, for you have a deal of humanity in you and yet you are quite able to keep order amongst those confounded farm-lads; I tell Rudolph that he can't do better than follow your ensample."--He then went on to tell Frank about Rudolph and Mina, Godfrey and Lina, and from them he passed to other people living in the parish; Frank forced himself to listen attentively, so that by the time they reached Pümpelhagen he knew all that had been going on during his absence, even to the doings of Pomuchelskopp and his Henny.--"Well," said Bräsig in conclusion as they entered the court-yard at Pümpelhagen, "you're going to see your cousin, I suppose, and I'm going to Hawermann, but there is one request that I want to make you; let what I have told you about Pomuchelskopp and his projections remain a secret between us, and you may trust me to have my eye upon him and to put a spoke in his wheel whenever I can."

But Frank did not go to the manor-house, he hastened to the bailiff's quicker than Bräsig could follow, rushed into the parlour where he had spent so many quiet hours alone with Hawermann, and fell upon his neck. The old man's eyes were moist, and the cheeks of the youth were flushed, as if age had given his best gift, the dew of his blessing, and the young heart on receiving it were revived and strengthened.--It should always be so.--Frank then went up to Fred Triddelfitz, and holding out his hand, said: "How d'ye do, Fred."--But Fred was proud, with a true middle-class pride; and he had also a desire for revenge which was born on the evening he had been caught in the field-ditch near the parsonage, so he said quietly: "How d'ye do, Mr. von Rambow."--"What's the matter, Fred?" asked Frank turning him round, and letting him stand as if Fred were some inexplicable note of interrogation to which he must find an answer, then shaking hands with the two old gentlemen, he went to his cousin's house.--"Charles," said Bräsig, seating himself by the table on which dinner was laid, "that young Mr. von Rambow is really a most capital fellow. Ah, what a splendid roast of pork! It's an age since I saw roast pork."

Alick welcomed his cousin heartily, for he was really pleased to see him. He and Frank were the last male descendants of their race. Frida, who had only met Frank once before, on the occasion of her marriage, was glad to renew her acquaintance with him, and did all in her power to make his visit a pleasant one. When Hawermann was crossing the yard after dinner, on his return from seeing Bräsig part of the way home, she sent out, and invited him to come to coffee, because she knew that Frank would like it. Then it came out that Frank had gone to the bailiff's before appearing at the manor-house, which made Alick rather angry; he frowned with displeasure and Frida saw that his manner changed and became haughty. That would not have mattered much, however, if he had not been so foolish and unjust as to revenge Frank's mistake, if mistake it were, on Hawermann by the coldness of his demeanour.

The company were therefore not on such easy terms as they might have been, and every friendly word which Hawermann and Frank exchanged added to Alick's wrath; he grew stiffer and colder every moment, so that in spite of the sunshine of Mrs. von Rambow's kindness, the conversation was in danger of dying away, when suddenly Hawermann jumped up, looked out at the window and then hastened from the room.--Alick's face flushed with anger: "What very extraordinary conduct! Most improper!" he said. "My bailiff seems to think that he may dispense with the commonest rules of politeness."--"Something of great importance must have happened," answered Frida going to the window. "What can he be saying to that labourer?"--"It's Regel," said Frank who had also gone to the window.--"Regel? Regel?" asked Alick starting up. "That's the messenger I sent to Rostock yesterday with three hundred pounds in gold, he surely can't have got back already."--"What can it be," cried Frank, "I never saw the old man so excited. Look, he has seized hold of the labourer," and with that he rushed out of the house, followed by Alick.

When they reached the yard, they saw that the old bailiff had caught the strong young labourer by the collar, and was shaking him so violently that his hat fell off and rolled into the snow: "That's a lie," he exclaimed, "a mean, wicked lie! Mr. von Rambow," he said, "this fellow says that he has lost the money!"--"No, it was taken away from me," cried the labourer who was deadly pale.--Alick also changed colour. He had long owed the three hundred pounds to some people in Rostock, and had put off paying the debt till he could put it off no longer; Pomuchelskopp had lent him the money to pay it--and now it was gone.--"It's a lie!" cried Hawermann. "I know the fellow. He isn't one to allow the money to be taken from him by force. He could and would keep any ten men at bay who only wanted to steal a little tobacco from him," and he shook the man again.--"Wait!" said Frank, separating them. "Let the man explain the whole affair quietly. What's all this about the money?"--"They took it away from me," said Regel. "When I got to Gallin wood on the other side of Rahnstädt this morning, two men came up to me, and one of them asked me to give him a light for his pipe. I refused, and so the other caught me by the waist and knocked me down. They then took the black parcel out of my pocket and ran away with it into Gallin wood, and I ran after them but couldn't catch them."--"But," interrupted Alick, "how does it happen that you just reached Gallin wood this morning, it's only a couple of miles on the other side of Rahnstädt. Didn't I tell you plainly to get a passport from the mayor of Rahnstädt, and to walk all night so as to be able to pay over the money in Rostock at twelve o'clock to-day?"--(If the money were not paid at that hour proceedings were to be instituted against him.)--"Yes, Sir," said the labourer, "and I did get the passport. Here it is," pulling it out of the lining of his hat, "but I really couldn't walk a whole winter's night, so I remained with my friends in Rahnstädt, and thought that I'd be sure to get to Rostock in time."--"Christian Däsel," cried Hawermann, who had grown quite calm again, his previous excitement having been caused by the conviction that the labourer was telling him a lie.--"Mr. von Rambow," he asked, as soon as Christian came, "will you not send for a magistrate?" and when Alick had consented, he said: "Christian, harness two of the carriage horses into the dog-cart, and go for the mayor of Rahnstädt; I'll have a letter for you to take by the time you're ready to start. Now, Regel, come with me, and I'll put you in a quiet place where you'll have time to come to your senses," he then took the labourer away to his house and locked him up in one of the rooms.

When Alick went back to the house with his cousin, he had a good opportunity for consulting him about his affairs, but he did not do it although he knew that Frank was both able and willing to help him. It is a true saying that the real spendthrift turns for help much more readily to a hard-hearted usurer than to his friends and relations.--He is too proud to confess his debts and sins, but not too proud to humble himself by begging and borrowing from disreputable Jews. Such conduct however cannot, in the true sense of the word, be said to arise from pride, but from a miserable insensate cowardice, a fear of the kind and sensible advice of friends and relations.

Alick was silent, and Walked restlessly up and down the room while his wife and cousin talked over what had occurred. He felt himself to be in a very disagreeable position, for unless the money was paid, his creditor, perhaps all his creditors, would go to law with him. He could bear it no longer, and though it was rapidly growing dark, ordered his horse, and went out for what he called a ride--in reality it was to see Mr. Pomuchelskopp.

Pomuchelskopp listened sympathetically to Mr. von Rambow's story, and loudly bewailed the wickedness of mankind, adding that in his opinion when Mr. von Rambow went to the expense of having a bailiff, that bailiff ought to be able to choose a trustworthy man to send on an errand of such importance. He did not want to say more at present, but still he must confess that he thought Hawermann always acted too much on his own judgment; for instance with regard to the glebe lands; he had persuaded the late squire to rent the fields for his own benefit, and he, Pomuchelskopp would prove clearly that the lease of the glebe had been injurious to the interests of Pümpelhagen. He then went on to tell Alick a long winded tale, which he could not understand, because he was a very poor arithmetician, and besides that, could think of nothing but his lost money at the moment. He therefore said "yes" to everything his companion told him, and at last forced himself to ask Pomuchelskopp to lend him another three hundred pounds. Pomuchelskopp at first looked doubtful, scratched his ear, and then said, "yes" in his turn, but only on condition that Alick should not rent the glebe from the new clergyman.--Mr. von Rambow might have turned restive at this condition being annexed to the bargain, but Pomuchelskopp showed once more by figures that Pümpelhagen and Gürlitz would both gain by the arrangement. Alick only half heard what was said to him, and at length agreed to give a written consent to the plan proposed; his debts were pressing, and he must rid himself of the worst claims at any cost. He was just the kind of man who would cut the throat of his only milch cow in hopes of making money by the sale of its skin.

Everything was settled now. Alick signed the paper given him. Pomuchelskopp packed up the parcel of three hundred pounds and sent his own groom with it to the Rahnstädt post office. This was much the wisest thing to do, for thus no one at Pümpelhagen got to know anything of the affair. Alick told himself two things so often during his ride home that he ended by believing them: the first was, that the loss of the money was entirely Hawermann's fault; and the second was, that he was glad to have got rid of the glebe lands on such terms.

CHAPTER XII

In the meantime the mayor of Rahnstädt, who was chief-magistrate in Alick's district, had arrived at Pümpelhagen, bringing Slus'uhr with him as clerk. The mayor had made good use of his time; before starting he had sent a detective to all the public houses and shops which farm-labourers were wont to frequent, to find out whether the labourer Regel from Pümpelhagen had been there, and thus he had discovered enough to assist him in his enquiry. Regel had come to his office about four o'clock on the previous afternoon, had got a passport from him, and had showed him the parcel of money, which was sewed up in a piece of black wax-cloth, and he had seen that the seal on the packet was still intact. The man--who was of a very talkative disposition--had told him, he was to walk all night, and that considering the time of year was a good deal to require of any one, but still the fellow was very strong and healthy looking; there was no fear of its being too dark for a traveller to see his way, the snow covering the ground made it so light; he had advised the man to set out at once, but he had not started till nearly midnight. Regel had gone into a public house, and had bought a glass of schnaps; at nine o'clock he was seen standing in front of a shop drinking brandy, giving himself airs, and talking of the money he was carrying, he even went so far as to show the parcel to one of the shopmen. Where he had gone next the mayor did not yet know, but looked upon it as an undoubted fact that the man had got very drunk, and asked Alick and Hawermann whether he was in the habit of drinking.--"I don't know," answered Alick, "my bailiff can answer that question better than I."--The squire's tone was so peculiar that Hawermann looked at him enquiringly, and seemed as though about to say something, but changing his mind he merely said to the mayor, that he had never noticed anything of the kind in the man, nor yet had he ever heard of his being drunk; he had little to say against any of the Pümpelhagen labourers in that respect, and least of all against Regel.--"That may be," said the mayor, "but the man was drunk for all that. Once is the first time, as we say--he was certainly drunk when he came to my office. Will you send for his wife."

His wife came. She was a young and nice-looking woman; but a very few years ago she had been the prettiest girl in the village, neat, trim, and frank, like every Mecklenburg country-maiden, now children and housework had stolen away all the roses from her cheeks, and had made her thin and angular--married women soon grow old in our country-districts. She also looked sad and anxious. Hawermann was very sorry for her, so he went to her, and said: "Don't be afraid, Dame Regel. Tell the truth, and all will be well."--"Lawk a daisy! Mr. Hawermann, what is it? What's the matter? What has my husband done?"--"Tell me, Dame Regel, does your husband often drink more brandy than is good for him?" asked the mayor.--"No, Sir, he was never known to have done such a thing in his life. He never drinks brandy, we have none in the house; the only time he ever tastes it, is during the harvest when he gets it from the farm the same as the other men."--"Had he not had some brandy yesterday before he left home?" asked the mayor again.--"No, Sir. He had his dinner, and then went away about half-past two. No, Sir .... but stop. I didn't see it, but still .... I remember now! Yesterday evening when I looked into the cupboard, I found the brandy-bottle empty."--"But I thought you told me you had no brandy in the house?" asked the mayor.--"Neither we have; that was the remains of the brandy used at the funeral; we buried our eldest little girl last Friday, and some of the brandy was left. Ah, how miserable he was! How very miserable he was!"--"You think that your husband drank it?"--"Yes, Sir, who else could have done it?"

The case was made out so far, and Dame Regel was allowed to go.--"We've got out the story of the brandy," whispered Slus'uhr to Alick, winking and blinking slyly at the mayor, "I only hope that we'll make out as much about the missing money."--"Take down the examination, clerk," said the mayor quietly, pointing to a seat. "Let the labourer Regel be sent for, and put upon oath."--"Mr. Mayor," cried Alick, springing to his feet, "I don't understand what the brandy has got to do with my money. The fellow has stolen it!"--"That's just what I want to find out," replied the mayor calmly. "Has he stolen it, or has he been acting for some one else, or was he in a condition to carry out either of these actions," and going up to the young squire, he said kindly but decidedly: "Mr. von Rambow, a man who had made up his mind to steal three hundred pounds wouldn't go and get drunk first. And then I must remind you that it is my duty as a magistrate to look after the interests of the accused, as much as after yours."

Regel was now brought into the room. He was deadly pale, but had lost all the nervousness he had shown in the morning when the old bailiff was questioning him, and looked as stern and hard as if his figure had been hewn out of granite. He confessed that he had drunk all the brandy that had been left in the cupboard at home; that he had had more at Rahnstädt; that he had been still in the wine-shop at nine o'clock; that he had spent the night with his friends, and had set out on his journey again about six in the morning;

but he remained true to his first story, and maintained that two men had taken the money from him by force in Gallin wood. Whilst this last part of the deposition was being taken down, the door opened, and Dame Regel, rushing up to her husband, threw herself into his arms. In Mecklenburg courts of justice strict formality is not considered necessary, so there are no police to prevent the occurrence of incidents of this kind.--"Joe! Joe! Have you made your wife and children miserable for ever?"--"Oh, Molly, Molly, I didn't do it. My hands are clean. Did you ever know me steal?"--"Tell these gentlemen the whole truth, Joe."--The labourer hesitated, turned dusky red and then pale again, looking shyly and uncertainly at his wife: "Mary, did I ever take what was not my own?"--Dame Regel let her hands fall from his shoulders: "No, Joe, you never did that. You never did that. But you have told lies; you have often told me a lie." She hid her face in her apron, and went out; Hawermann followed her. The labourer was removed.

The mayor had not disturbed the meeting between the husband and wife, it was against rules, but it might furnish him with a clue, and show the truth. Alick started, and began to walk rapidly up and down the room when he heard Dame Regel say: "You have told lies, you have often told me a lie." His conscience reproached him, he hardly knew why on this evening of all others, but he felt that he too had never stolen anything, and that he too had *lied*. But like every man who is not upright in heart, the moment his conscience pricked him, he lied to himself again, and denied the accusation his conscience had brought against him. He and the labourer were very different; he had only told a *fib* for his wife's sake, to save her uneasiness, while the labourer had *lied* for his own sake.

Ah, Mr. von Rambow, if you remain as you are, the devil will yet reap a goodly harvest in your soul!

Slus'uhr, having finished, slipped up to Alick, and whispered: "Yes, Mr. von Rambow, the man who lies will also steal."--Alick shivered at the words; partly because of the turmoil in his own heart, and partly because he knew how very like stealing Slus'uhr's business was; he was not merely astonished, he was horrified at the impudence of the man. He would not have been so startled however, if he had only heard the stories people told of the attorney.

Nothing more could be done for the moment, as all the witnesses, including the labourer's friends, were in Rahnstädt, the mayor therefore ordered that the prisoner should remain at Pümpelhagen that night, locked up in some secure place, and that he should be brought to Rahnstädt on the next day.--"Then let him be put in the front-cellar of the manor-house," said Alick to Hawermann who had come back.--"Wouldn't it be better, Sir, to leave him in the room where I put him before, in the farm-house, as the window is barred with iron ....."--"No," answered Alick sharply, "the cellar-windows are also grated, and I wish to prevent his having the opportunity of speaking to his friends which he might have at the farm."--"I'm a light sleeper, Mr. von Rambow, and if you want to make sure, a trustworthy man might guard the door."--"I have already told you what I desire you to do. The matter is far too important for me to trust to your light sleep, or to the guard that a comrade of that rascal would keep."--Hawermann looked at him in surprise, said, "as you will," and left the room.

It was about ten o'clock in the evening, supper had long been on the table, Mary Möller had groaned and moaned over everything being spoilt, and Frida was rather cross because of having to wait so long for news, and because of the supper; the only thing that kept her patient was talking to Frank. At length the gentlemen came back, and Frida went to the mayor, and asked: "He didn't steal the money, did he? I hope not."--"No, Madam," answered the mayor calmly and decidedly, "the labourer didn't steal the money; it was stolen from him, or he lost it."--"Thank God!" she said from the bottom of her heart, "I'm so glad that the man isn't a thief. I should hate the thought of there being dishonest people in the village."--"Surely you don't imagine that our people are better than those in other places. They're the same everywhere," said Alick.--"Mr. von Rambow," said Hawermann, who had come to supper, "our people are perfectly honest; I have been here long enough to be convinced of that. There hasn't been a single case of theft known in all the years that I've been at Pümpelhagen."--"Ah! That's what you've always told me, and now--yes now, you see that my foolish credulity has made me lose three hundred pounds. If you really know the people so well, what induced you to recommend me to use that man of all others as my messenger?"--Hawermann stared at him: "It seems to me," he said, "that you want to make out that the loss of the money is my fault, but I cannot acknowledge that to be the case. It is true," he went on, his face reddening with anger, "that I advised you to send Regel to Rostock, but my only reason for doing so, was that you have always hitherto used him as a messenger in your money transactions; he has been more than ten times at Gürlitz for you, and attorney Slus'uhr can bear witness to how often you have sent to him by that man."--Frida looked quickly at Slus'uhr when she heard this, and the attorney returned her gaze; neither of them spoke, and different as their thoughts were, it seemed that each could read the other's soul. Frida saw in the sly sinister expression of the attorney's eyes, that he was a man who would not scruple to use his power over her husband to the uttermost, while the attorney on his side read in the clear thoughtful eyes of the lady of the house, that she was the person he had to fear most in the prosecution of his designs. Alick stifled a hasty answer to what the bailiff had said, when he saw the old man's grave determined face, and Frida's look of enquiry. Slus'uhr was also silent, but watched anxiously lest his prey should escape him. Thus Frank and the mayor were the only people at table who were unaware that Hawermann's words had touched a sore subject, and they were the only ones who were able to keep up a conversation. The party separated as soon as supper was over; the mayor spent the night at the manor-house.

Everyone at Pümpelhagen was sound asleep with the exception of two pairs of married people. These were Mr. and Mrs. von Rambow, and the labourer and his wife. Alick and Frida were sitting at their own fire side, he longing to tell his wife all that weighed upon him and made him miserable; to tell the whole truth for once. But he could not. She entreating him to confide in her now that she knew so much, now that she knew of his money difficulties; she said that she would economise, but begged him to give up all transactions with Pomuchelskopp and Slus'uhr, and to consult Hawermann who would be able to advise him what to do. Alick always did things by halves; he never told a downright lie, and yet he did not tell the truth. He did not deny his present need of three hundred pounds, but said that no one could help his means being straightened after having met with so considerable a loss. He had not had time to consider what was best to be done, and could not yet see what he should sell to meet the claim--but he never said that he had already sold some fine wheat and had got the money for it too. He assured her that his business relations with Pomuchelskopp and Slus'uhr--he never spoke of David--could do him no harm; it was an old story now with both of them--he did not tell her of his new dealings with Pomuchelskopp--and he had found both very civil in their treatment of him, "but," he said in conclusion, "you know it would never do for me to talk to Hawermann about money matters, it wouldn't be fitting."--Alick's untruths were more a suppression of the truth than direct falsehoods, and indeed when putting his arm round his wife's waist, he assured her that his affairs would soon be in good order; he was merely saying what he, for the moment, fully believed.--Frida was sad at heart when she left him.

The other husband and wife were not in a warm room like these; the labourer was confined in a cold cellar, while his wife knelt at the window of his prison unheeding the cold drizzling November rain which was wetting her to the skin, they were not sitting side by side, but were separated by an iron grating.--"Joe," she whispered through the grating, "tell the truth."--"They stole it from me," was the answer.--"Who stole it, Joe?"--"How can I tell?" he said, and it was the truth; he did not know the name of the woman who had taken the black pocket-book out of his waistcoat pocket in the full light of day, when he was reeling along the Gallin road only half conscious of what he was doing after his potations of the night before, to say nothing of the two gills of brandy he had taken that morning on an empty stomach. He could not tell the truth; how could he acknowledge that he, a young strong man, had allowed a woman to steal three hundred pounds from him on the public road? He could not do it even to save his life.--"You're telling me a lie, Joe! If you can't tell me the truth, won't you tell it to our old bailiff?"--It was impossible, he could not tell him of all people; especially when he remembered how solemnly he had once promised Hawermann that he would never again tell a lie. He could not do it.--"Bring me my file, Mary, and any silver you have"--"What do you mean, Joe?"--"I'm going to run away."--"Oh, Joe, Joe, will you really leave me and the babies all alone?"--"I must go, Molly. I'll never get on here now."--"Only tell the truth, Joe, and all will be well."--"If you don't bring me the file and some money, I'll kill myself to-night."--There was much entreaty of her husband here also, as upstairs in the sitting-room, but the truth remained unspoken, and this wife left her husband with as sad a heart as the other had done.

Next morning there was great excitement at Pümpelhagen when it became known that the labourer had escaped. The mayor made arrangements for his apprehension, and then drove home with the attorney. Alick was furious, no one knew exactly with whom, but probably with himself, for it was by his orders that Regel had been locked up in the cellar.

Pomuchelskopp arrived at breakfast time to ask what had really happened, for, as he said, he had only heard a vague rumour of what had taken place. Frank received him coldly and stiffly; Alick on the contrary welcomed him warmly. Pomuchelskopp told many stories of the shameful way in which the magistrates were befriending the common people, and of the extreme kindness the mayor of Rahnstädt had always shown any rogues he had to deal with. He told of thefts which had been perpetrated on himself or his friends, and ended by saying that he believed with Hawermann that the labourer had not committed the theft, "I mean," he said in conclusion, "that he didn't do it for himself; but was employed by some one else; no labourer would dare to steal such a large sum as three hundred pounds; the deed would become known too soon. And so, Mr. von Rambow, I advise you to keep your eye on those who may have assisted the labourer in his flight, or who even take his part."--Alick's mind was so restless and upset by anger and anxiety that it was ready to receive the seeds of suspicion which Pomuchelskopp was trying to sow. He walked up and down the room, thinking: Yes, Pomuchelskopp was right, he was well up to things of the kind and therefore was sure to know best; but who was it who had helped Regel to escape? He knew no one. Who had taken Regel's part? Why

Hawermann, to be sure, when he said so decidedly that the man must have lost the money. But when he first heard what had happened he had seized the fellow by the collar? That might have been all pretence though. And why did he want to have the man put into the room next his own? Perhaps that he might speak to him; perhaps that he might help him to run away?

These would have been foolish thoughts for a wise man to have had; but the devil is "cunning," he does not choose the wise and the strong as his instruments, but the foolish and weak.

"What is your bailiff saying to that woman, I wonder?" said Pomuchelskopp, who was looking out at the window.--"It's Dame Regel," said Frank, who was standing beside him.--"Yes," said Alick hastily, "what can he be saying to her? I'd like to know very much."--"It's an odd thing certainly," remarked Pomuchelskopp.

Hawermann and the labourer's wife were standing in the yard, and he seemed to be talking earnestly to her; she appeared to be unwilling to do as he wanted, but at last gave way and followed him to the manor-house. They entered the room.--"Mr. von Rambow," said Hawermann, "Dame Regel has just confessed that it was she who helped her husband to escape last night."--"Yes, Sir," said the woman, moving her hands and feet about restlessly, "I did. I did, but I couldn't help it, for he said he'd kill himself if I didn't get him away;" the tears rolled down her cheeks, and she hid her face in her apron.--"A nice story," said Alick harshly. "There seems to have been a regular plot!"--Frank went to the woman and making her sit down, asked: "Didn't he tell you where he had spent the night with the money?"--"No, Sir, he told me nothing, and I know that all he did tell me were lies; the only thing I know for certain is that he didn't steal the money."--Alick now turned upon Hawermann and asked: "What made you give the woman an audience without orders?"--Hawermann was startled at the words, but still more at the tone of this question: "I thought," he answered calmly, "that it would be a good thing to find out when and how the man escaped, and so perhaps discover some indication of his whereabouts."--"Or perhaps to *give* an indication," cried Alick, and then he turned away hastily as though afraid of the consequences of what he had said.--Hawermann had not understood the sense of the words, but the tone in which they were uttered hurt him: "I don't know what you mean," he said gravely, "but I wish you to know that I will not stand being spoken to as you have been doing both last night and this morning. I took no notice of it yesterday out of consideration for Mrs. von Rambow, but in the present company"--here he glanced at Pomuchelskopp--"there is no need for such forbearance on my part," as soon as he had done speaking he went away and the labourer's wife followed him. Alick was going after him, but was stopped by Frank:

"What are you going to do, Alick? Just think of what you said. Your words were even crueller to the old man than he imagined."--"That was a strong measure," said Pomuchelskopp, as if he were talking to himself, "a very strong measure for a bailiff; but it's time for me to go home now," and putting his head out at the window, he called for his horse. He felt that everything was going on as he wished at Pümpelhagen.

The horse was brought round. Alick accompanied his neighbour to the door, and Frank remained in the room.--"Your cousin seems to be a most excellent young man," said Pomuchelskopp, "but he knows nothing of the world, he appears to be ignorant of what is suitable conduct in master and servant." So saying, he rode away.

Alick rejoined his cousin, and tossing the cap he had put on to go to the door, as a protection against the cold morning air, into a corner of the sofa, exclaimed: "A d--d rascally story! The devil take the whole business! There's no one to be trusted."--"Alick," said Frank gently, as he went up to him, "you are doing your people a grievous wrong, you are doing yourself wrong, dear cousin, by nursing such unjust suspicious in your kind heart."--"Unjust? What do you mean? I've been robbed of three hundred pounds"--"The money has been lost, Alick, by the thoughtlessness and folly of a labourer."--"*Lost*, did you say? Are you going to repeat the tale my bailiff has thought fit to tell me?"--"Everyone is of the same opinion, Alick; the mayor himself says ....."--"Don't talk to me about what that old fool said. If I had only conducted the examination myself I should have discovered something before now; if I had even spoken to the woman first this morning she'd have told a different story; but now ... It's nothing more nor less than bribery!"--"Stop, Alick!" cried Frank sternly. "You've hinted at that already this morning but fortunately were not understood. You are now making an open accusation, and I must know what your grounds are for making such a charge."--"I have good reasons for doing so."--"Just consider for a moment. You are accusing an honest old man; you are unjustly and hastily casting a slur on a man who has lived for sixty years in the world and whose honour in unblemished."--Alick grew calmer and tried to excuse himself: "I never said that he had done it, only that he might have done it."--"It's just as bad to suspect him of perhaps doing such a thing; the suspicion hurts you as much as it does the old man. Only think, Alick," he went on laying his hand affectionately on his cousin's shoulder, "how long and faithfully Hawermann has looked after your father's and your own interests. To me," he added in a low tone, "he has been more than that, he has been a true friend and a painstaking teacher."

Alick walked up and down the room. He felt he was wrong--at least for the moment--but he was too much of a moral coward to acknowledge that he wanted to throw the blame of his own faults and follies on Hawermann's shoulders, so taking refuge in the mode of action commonly employed by weak souls when in a difficulty such as the present, he determined to carry the war into the enemy's country. He once more shut his heart to the pure unvarnished truth, selling it, as it were, for a piece of silver.

"Of course," he said, "Hawermann is much more to you than he is to me."--"What do you mean?" asked Frank looking at him quickly.--"Nothing," said Alick. "I only meant that you will soon call him, 'father.'" The worst of this speech was the intention he showed in it to wound the man who had cared for him enough to tell him the truth. He had used the gossip he had heard from Pomuchelskopp because it was the only weapon he knew of that would answer the purpose.--Frank reddened. The secret he had deemed so holy was dragged into the common light of day at such a time and in such a way as to make the intended insult the more apparent. The blood rushed to his face, he struggled to command himself, and said: "That has nothing to do with what we are speaking about."--"How do you make that out?" asked Alick. "To my mind it fully explains the warmth with which you defend Mr. Hawermann."--"He needs no defence. His whole life is his best defence."--"To say nothing of his beautiful daughter," said Alick striding up and down the room, and congratulating himself upon the success of his last remark.--Frank was very angry, but he forced himself to say quietly: "Do you know her?"--"Yes; no; that is, I've seen her. I met her at the parsonage, and she often comes to see my wife. She's a very pretty girl upon my honour. I first noticed her when she was quite a child at my father's funeral."--"Did you not try to become better acquainted with her when you found that I loved her?"--"No, Frank, no. Because I knew that nothing could come of such a love affair."--"Then you knew more than I did."--"I know even more than that. I know how you have been hunted and caught, and how they tried to make sure of you."--"Who told you that? But why do I ask? Such scandalous gossip can only proceed from one house in this neighbourhood--now that we are talking on this subject I will tell you frankly that I intend to marry the girl if she will have me."--"She won't say no! She'll take good care not to say no!" cried Alick angrily. "And so you are really going to be such a fool? You seriously intend to bring this disgrace on our family?"--"Take care what you say, Alick!" said Frank passionately. "I don't see, however, how the matter affects you."--"What? *I* am the head of our old family, and do you think that it is nothing to me when a younger member of our race disgraces himself by a mésalliance?"--Again Frank commanded himself, and said: "You yourself married for love, and nothing else."--"That was different," said Alick, who thought he was now getting the best of the argument. "My wife is my equal in birth; she is the daughter of an old and noble house, while the girl you love is only the daughter of my bailiff, and was brought up by the clergyman and his wife out of charity."--"For shame!" cried Frank. "How dare you treat misfortune as if it were a crime."--"I don't care," stormed Alick. "I tell you once for all that I'll never call my bailiff's daughter, cousin; the wench shall never cross this threshold."--Frank turned deadly pale, and said with a voice that trembled from suppressed emotion: "That is enough. You need say no more, we must part. Louisa shall never cross your threshold, nor I either." With that he went away. Frida met him at the door, she had heard the loud voices in the next room and had come to see what was the matter: "Frank, Frank, what is it?" she asked.--"Good-bye, Frida," he said quickly and went out across the yard towards the bailiff's house.

"Alick," cried Frida going up to her husband, "what have you been doing? What have you been doing?"--Alick walked proudly up and down the room as if conscious of having put the whole world right and of having shown it the way it ought to go: "I've been showing a young man," he said, "a young rustic, who has made a fool of himself for the sake of a fair face, what he is about. I made his position clear to him."--"Did you dare to do that?" said Frida, sinking into a chair pale and trembling. She fixed her great clear eyes on her husband as he continued his triumphal march and went on: "Did you *dare* to thrust your petty pride of birth between two noble and loving souls?"--"Frida," said Alick, whose conscience told him he had done wrong, but who refused to acknowledge it, "I believe that I have done my duty."--It is a curious fact that those people who never do their duty, pride themselves most upon doing it.--"Oh," cried Frida, starting to her feet, "you have wounded a true and noble heart most sorely. Alick," she entreated, laying her clasped hands upon his shoulder, "Frank has gone to the bailiff's house, won't you follow him and say that you are sorry for having hurt him, and bring him back again to us?"--"Am I to beg his pardon before my bailiff? No thank you, I'd rather not do that! It is too good a joke," he said working himself into a rage, "I've been robbed of three hundred pounds, my bailiff orders me about, my cousin takes his beloved father-in-law's part, and now my own wife joins with them against me!"--Frida stared at him, let her hands fall, drew her shawl round her, and said: "If you won't go, I will."--As she left the room he called after her: "Go, go, but the old scoundrel shall leave my service."

When she crossed the yard the horses were being put into Frank's carriage, and as she entered the parlour Hawermann had just said: "You'll forget it in time, Mr. von Rambow. Your life has hitherto been spent in a narrow circle of friends; you should travel--I think that you ought to do so--and then you'll soon change your mind. But, dear Frank," the old man added familiarly in memory of old times, "let me entreat of you not to bring unrest to my child by telling her of this."--"No, Hawermann, I promise," said Frank, and then Frida came in.--"Bless me!" cried Hawermann. "I quite forgot. Excuse me, Madam," and he left the room.

"He's always so thoughtful, so very thoughtful," said Frida.--"Indeed he is," answered Frank looking after the old man. The carriage drove up to the door, but had to wait there for a long time, Mrs. von Rambow and Frank had so much to say to each other, and when they parted Frida's eyes were red with weeping, and Frank looked much moved: "Say goodbye to the good old man for me," he said, and then added in a lower voice, "and to Alick too." He shook hands with her once more. The carriage drove away.

CHAPTER XIII

Young Joseph was sitting in his usual place by the fire-side, smoking. Young Bolster was lying under his chair with his head stretched out far enough to be able to see his master. Young Joseph looked back at him but said nothing, and Bolster was also silent. It was very still and quiet in Rexow farm-house on that December afternoon, the only noise that was to be heard came from Mrs. Nüssler's basket-chair upon which she was sitting in the window; every time she made a stitch in her knitting it creaked out a remark upon it, a circumstance not to be so much wondered at, when it is remembered that Mrs. Nüssler had now become what might be called rather a stout lady. The old chair was creaking even more than usual to-day, for she had knitted herself into a deep reverie, and the more she became immersed in her own thoughts the louder her chair creaked in unison with her every movement.--"Ah me!" she said, laying her knitting down in her lap. "What a strange thing it is that the sorrow of one human being is often the cause of happiness for another. Do you know what I was thinking of, Joseph?"--"No," said young Joseph, looking at young Bolster, but Bolster could not help him to guess.--"Joseph," she asked, "how do you think it would do for Godfrey to offer himself as a candidate for the Gürlitz living? I know that Godfrey's but a poor rush-light in comparison with the old parson; but a man of his kind is likely enough to get the living, and why shouldn't he as well as another?"--Joseph said nothing.--"Even if Pomuchelskopp were against him, our people and those at Warnitz would vote for him, so that it all depends upon what the squire of Pümpelhagen does, whether the election goes against him or not. What do you say Joseph?"--"Oh," said Joseph, "it all depends upon circumstances," and then because he was very much taken with the idea, he added, "What's to be done now?"--"Oh, dear," said Mrs. Nüssler, "what's the use of talking to you about it. I wish that Bräsig were here, he would and could tell us what to do." And then she took up her work, and began to knit vehemently.

Half an hour later Mrs. Nüssler exclaimed: "'Speak of an angel, and you see his wings.' Here's Bräsig driving into the yard. Who's that with him? Rudolph--just fancy, Rudolph! I wonder why Rudolph has come to-day? Now, Joseph do me a favour--the lad does everything so nicely--don't overwhelm him with talk." Then she hastened from the room to receive her guests.

She had put off too much time, and she was not the first, for there was Mina clasped in Rudolph's arms. "Goodness gracious me!" cried Mrs. Nüssler, "what are you doing here, Mina?" She then took Rudolph into the parlour with her.--"Well," said Joseph. "Sit down, Bräsig. Sit down, Rudolph."--But they were not ready to do that yet, Rudolph had too much to say to Mina and Lina to be able to sit down quietly, and Bräsig's head felt as if it were going round and round like the hands of a clock, so he walked quickly up and down the room making his legs act pendulum, and thus working off some of his excitement. "Have you heard the news, young Joseph?" he asked. "They hav'n't caught him after all."--"Who?" asked Joseph. "Preserve us all, Joseph," said Mrs. Nüssler, "can't you let Bräsig go on? You always interrupt people so suddenly; *do* let him finish his story! Who is it that they hav'n't caught, Bräsig?--"Regel," said Bräsig. "They traced him as far as Wismar where they found that their prey had escaped them. He had sailed out into the Baltic eight days before in a Swedish trading-vessel."--"Oh, dear," cried Mrs. Nüssler, "What a misfortune that may be for my brother Charles."--"You're right, Mrs. Nüssler. Charles is hardly to be known for the same person he used to be, he has insulated himself entirely, and looks very miserable. He feels the misfortune bitterly--not for his own sake--but for his master's, for as you will see, the young squire will sooner or later have to declare himself insolvent."--"That would be the death of Charles," said Mrs. Nüssler.--"What help is there?" continued Bräsig. "The young man has ruined himself with open eyes. His latest fad is the breeding of thorough-bred horses. Old Prebberow told me that he had got into Lichtwarte's hands, and that he had sold him a thorough-bred horse which has a ruptured muscle, spavin, and string-halt, and a variety of other diseases; as soon as he was in possession of this beautiful creature Mr. von Rambow bought, with a great flourish of trumpets, a thorough-bred mare, and now, I'm told, he has serious thoughts of taking Triddelfitz's deaf old mare off his hands, and so setting up a hospital for sick horses in Mecklenburg. The little mule is to be thrown into the bargain, and I'm glad of that, for it's the only healthy member of the stud."--"Let him be, Bräsig; he must fight his own battles," said Mrs. Nüssler. "Joseph and I were talking of young Mr..... Mina, you and Rudolph may go into the garden for a little, and Lina you'd better go with them;" as soon as they were gone, she said: "It's about the Gürlitz living. I wish that Godfrey could get it."--"Mrs. Nüssler," said Bräsig, standing before her and looking important, "what you have just said may be called an idea, and no one in the whole world is so quick in seizing an idea as a woman. How did you manage to get hold of this idea though?"--"It is my own thought entirely," she answered, "for Joseph never agrees with me now-a-days. He has always some objection to everything I propose."--"Joseph, be quiet," said Bräsig, "you were wrong to oppose your wife, for her idea is a good one. I'll answer for Warnitz, the Count and Countess will, I know, agree to let the people vote as I wish them. You, young Joseph, must see to Rexow. Pomuchelskopp will be against us from love of opposition, but that doesn't matter. Pümpelhagen is the only difficulty. Who's to speak to Mr. von Rambow? Hawermann? Nothing could be less *apropos* at this moment. Myself? Impossible, for he has insulted me. Young Joseph? I can't trust young Joseph, he'd content himself with using some of his favourite forms of speech. Godfrey? He's a good fellow, but too slow. Who else is there? Rudolph? He is a clever lad, as Hilgendorf tells me. Yes, Rudolph must go, and you, Mrs. Nüssler, must go with him, because of family circumstances, and that the young man may be more at ease."--"Good gracious!" cried Mrs. Nüssler. "Do you mean that *I* am to go and see Mr. von Rambow?"--"No," said Zachariah Bräsig, "you are to go to Mrs. von Rambow, and Rudolph to the squire. Where's Rudolph. He must come in at once."

Rudolph was quite ready to go to Pümpelhagen for his cousin's sake, and so it was settled that he and his aunt should drive over there on the following day.

When the deputation arrived at Pümpelhagen, Mr. von Rambow was out riding, but when their coming was announced to his wife, she received them very kindly.--"Madam," said Mrs. Nüssler, going frankly up to Mrs. von Rambow, and beginning to speak to the point without much loss of time, "Madam, I hope that you will not be offended with me if I talk to you in the dialect I'm accustomed to; I can speak better, but it's very difficult. We keep up old customs at Rexow, and I always say that I'd rather have bright shining tin plates, than silver ones that are dull from want of rubbing."-- Frida took off the good woman's shawl, made her sit down on the sofa, and signed to Rudolph to take a chair; just as she was about to seat herself, Mrs. Nüssler rose and said confidentially: "You see, Madam, this is my nephew and future son-in-law. He's the son of Kurz, the shopkeeper in Rahnstädt, from whom you also get your things."--Rudolph bowed, and now Mrs. von Rambow at last persuaded her visitor to seat herself, and took her place beside her. "He has been to college," Mrs. Nüssler went on, "but didn't do much there. Now that he has turned farmer, however, he does very well, as Hilgendorf tells Bräsig."--Although what she said was all in Rudolph's praise, he found it rather embarrassing, and said: "But, my dear aunt, we hadn't come here to talk of me, but of Godfrey"--"Yes, Madam, he's quite right. You see I've got another nephew who also wants to be my son-in-law, I mean the son of rector Baldrian in Rahnstädt. He has passed all his examinations, and knows everything he needs to know. He's quite fit to be a clergyman any day. Now that our good old parson has gone from us--and oh, Madam, what an excellent man he was--you won't think ill of me for saying that I'd like to keep my Lina near me, and to have Godfrey at Gürlitz parsonage."--"No, dear Mrs. Nüssler," said Frida, "I think that it is quite natural in you to wish it, and if I had anything to do with it, your son-in-law should certainly get the living. I've heard so much good of you and your daughters."--"Have you really," said Mrs. Nüssler, looking pleased, "well, they *are* dear children."

At this moment foot-steps were heard approaching, and Mr. von Rambow, who had returned from his ride, entered the room. His wife introduced her visitors to him, and Alick, when he heard their names, made rather a long face. Rudolph would not allow himself to be put out by this reception, he held a trump-card that he thought would soon change the aspect of affairs, so he said: "May I speak to you alone for a moment, Mr. von Rambow?"--Alick took him into the next room.

"I understand, Mr. von Rambow," said Rudolph, "that you were robbed of three hundred pounds the week before last. The money, I think you said, was in Danish double Louis d'ors. From what I hear there is no chance of your catching the labourer, but the police are busy tracing the money."--"What?" cried Alick. "How do you know that?"--"I understand that the detective, employed by the mayor of Rahnstädt, found clear traces of the money yesterday afternoon. I was in my father's shop when a woman, a weaver's wife, who with her husband is trying to get a decree of divorce, came in and asked for change for a Danish double Louis d'or. I know the woman to be in abject poverty, and the mayor knows it also from the proceedings in the divorce case. My father and I made the circumstance known to the authorities, and after examination it was discovered that she had more money than the gold piece she had shown. She could give no account of how she had become possessed of the money, and--this is the most damaging part of the whole evidence--it has been proved that she went along the same road as your messenger on the same morning."--"Is it possible!" cried Alick. "Then the labourer didn't steal the money after all."--"It seems," said Rudolph, "as if he had been robbed. The mayor has committed the woman to prison for sundry small thefts that have been proved against her, and has forbidden my father and me to tell any one what we know, but when he heard that I was coming into this neighbourhood, he desired me to let you know what has been done. You will no doubt have a letter from him to-night on the subject."--"Thank you, Mr. Kurz," said Alick, "for having come here to tell this news," and he shook hands heartily with the young man.--Rudolph smiled, and said: "I should certainly have come even if that had been the only object of my visit which it was not. You saw my aunt in the drawing-room, she has come to see you about something she has much at heart."--"If I can be of any use ...." said Alick courteously.--"I will explain. One of my cousins, who is a theological student, offers himself, through my aunt, as a candidate for the living of Gürlitz."--"A cousin? Are you not a theological student?"--"I was, Mr. von Rambow," answered Rudolph brightly, "but I don't think I was, what people call, highly organised enough to be a clergyman, so I became a farmer, and I can assure you," looking laughingly at Alick as he spoke, "I never was so happy in my life as I am now."--In spite of Alick's faults and foibles, he was too good hearted not to be pleased and touched by the freshness of the other, so he said heartily: "That's right! That's right! I've taken to it too. The life of a Mecklenburg farmer is the happiest of all. Where are you living just now, Mr. Kurz?"--"With the greatest farmer of the century," laughed Rudolph, "with Hilgendorf at Little Tetzleben."--"A most admirable man," cried Alick, "and thorough-bred! I mean has thorough-bred horses."--And now they began to praise Grey Momus, Herodotus, and Black Overshire, &c., and to praise Hilgendorf's management, and when Rudolph at last rose to take leave, Mr. von Rambow shook hands with him warmly, and said: "You may rely upon your cousin having my vote, Mr. Kurz."

When they went into the drawing-room, Mrs. Nüssler rose, and said to her hostess: "He'll do all that he can for you and the squire," then going up to Mr. von Rambow she said: "You'll give us your vote, won't you, Mr. von Rambow? How happy I shall be to be able to keep my Lina so near me."--Alick disliked this free way of speaking, and--without any particular reason for it, disliked the Nüssler manner, but being pleased at the prospect of recovering his money, and having had his heart further opened by his horsey talk with Rudolph, he was on this occasion able to see the sterling qualities of Mrs. Nüssler under her somewhat unpolished manner. He went to his wife and said: "Dear Frida, we have some hope now of recovering our three hundred pounds."--"Thank God!" said Mrs. Nüssler, "Rudolph, did you speak to Mr. von Rambow?"--"Yes," answered Alick. "And it's all settled, I promise to give your nephew my vote; but--I should like to see him first."--"That's only right and proper," said Mrs. Nüssler. "No one cares to buy a pig in a poke! You'll see when he comes to preach that he's quite up to the mark. But, goodness gracious me! This is folly. Like every other man, he has his own little ways, I can't deny that."

Then they drove away. Godfrey had a good chance of the living. "Everything promises well," said Bräsig, "but Godfrey must manage with Pomuchelskopp himself. Let the iron be struck while it is hot, and as neither God nor man can help him with Samuel Pomuchelskopp the sooner he tries his fate with him the better." This advice was considered good, so Godfrey was written to and told what had already been done for him, at the same time he was ordered to make his appearance at Rexow on the following day, there to receive further instructions.

He arrived, and when Bräsig had explained everything to him shortly, he consented to make the difficult visit. Christian, the coachman, drove the "phantom" round to the door; Lina put in a foot-stool, cloaks and shawls, and wrapped up her future husband warmly. "That's right, Lina," said Bräsig, "wrap him up well that he mayn't catch cold, and that his lovely voice mayn't be lost in this frightful weather."--Suddenly Joseph rose from his corner by the stove, and said: "Mina, my cloak."--"The world's coming to an end!" cried Bräsig.--"Joseph, what are you about?" cried Mrs. Nüssler.--"Mother," said Joseph, "you went with Rudolph, and I intend to go with Godfrey. I shall do my part." And as he said this he nodded his head so decidedly, and looked round at them all with such determination that Bräsig exclaimed: "As sure as your nose is in the middle of your face, I never in all my life saw anything like this."--"Ah, Bräsig," said Mrs. Nüssler, "he's quite changed of late, but let him go quietly, no talking will prevent it."--So Joseph was allowed to go. Lina went straight upstairs to her little garret-room and prayed as passionately for Godfrey's success in his difficult interview as if he had been going to his execution.

Joseph and Godfrey drove through the deep lane silently; neither spoke, for each was buried in his own thoughts, the only remark made during the drive was when Christian, turning his head over his shoulder, said: "This would just be the place for an upset, Sir, if one were driving in a dark night."--It was about three o'clock in the afternoon when they arrived at Gürlitz manor.

Pomuchelskopp was lying on the sofa looking unhappy and rubbing his eyes, for Gustavus had disturbed him in his after dinner sleep by choosing a plate to take to the loft, for it was Saturday and he wanted to make up an account of the measurement of the grain, "Gus," he cried angrily, "you'll be a fool all your life, a regular ninny! You nincompoop! I'll put you on a pedestal to let all the people see what an ass you are."--"But, father ....."--"Father here, father there! How often have I told you never to make a clatter with the plates when I'm asleep! What carriage is that driving into the yard?"--"My eye!" cried Gustavus. "It's our neighbour Nüssler and another gentleman."--"Idiot!" said Pomuchelskopp. "Hav'n't I often told you not to call every Jack and Tom 'neighbour'? Brinkmann the labourer, is my neighbour in the sense that he lives close to my garden. I won't be every man's neighbour," and when he had said that he went out to see what was going on.

Joseph and Godfrey had got out of the carriage by this time, and Joseph now came forward, saying: "How-d'ye-do, neighbour."--Pomuchelskopp made him one of the very low bows he had learnt to make when he was attending parliament, and signed to him to go into the parlour. The silence in the parlour was so intense that the only sound to be heard was a faint creak from one of the chairs when it was moved. Godfrey thought that Joseph ought to speak, Joseph thought that Godfrey ought to speak, and Pomuchelskopp would not speak for fear of compromising his interests in some way. At last, however, Godfrey began: "Mr. Pomuchelskopp," he said, "good old parson Behrens has gone to his rest, and though it may seem hard and unchristian to make an application for the living so soon after his death, I do not think that in doing so I am really sinning against proper feeling, or true Christianity, for I am only acting in accordance with the advice of my own parents and of those of my future wife."--Godfrey had now opened the proceedings to the best of his ability; but still Pomuchelskopp was quite justified in drawing himself up a little and saying: That might be all very well, but he wanted to know with whom he had the honour to be talking. Joseph signed to Godfrey to answer, and Godfrey said that he was the son of rector Baldrian, and a theological student. As soon as this information had been given Joseph leant back in his chair comfortably, as though he had nothing more to do and might have a quiet pipe. But as Muchel did not ask him to smoke, he was obliged to content himself with making a fruitless movement with his lips as if he were doing so, which made him look exactly like a Bohemian carp, gasping for air.--"Sir," said Pomuchelskopp, "a good many of your sort have already called upon me, and asked for my vote,"--that was a lie, but it was the only way he knew of making a bargain, for he looked upon a living as a species of merchandise, and chaffered as much about it as he would have done with a butcher who came to buy his fat pigs,--"but," he went on, "I sent them all away for the present without an answer, for there is only one thing that I care about in the whole business."--"And that is?" asked Godfrey. "My examina ....."--"I don't care a pin about that," said Mr. Pomuchelskopp. "I mean the glebe lands. If you will promise to give me a lease of the glebe--of course I should give you a good rent, a very good rent,--you shall have my vote, but not otherwise."--"I think I heard," said Godfrey, "that the glebe is let to Mr. von Rambow, and I should not like ...."--"You need have no scruple on that head," said Pomuchelskopp decidedly.--Joseph said nothing, but looked at his future son-in-law as much as to say: "What have you to say to that, my boy?"--Godfrey was very much taken aback, for he was ignorant of worldly matters, but after a moment's thought his whole honest soul revolted against such a bargain, so he answered frankly: "I cannot and will not make you such a promise, I do not wish to gain the living by these means. There is plenty of time to settle matters of this kind, and they had better be left alone until I am in office."--"That's the way, is it?" said Pomuchelskopp with a cunning smile. "Then let me tell you that the fox is not to be trapped; 'a bird in the hand', &c; if Mr. von Rambow does not want the glebe, you may perhaps let it to your father-in-law. Is it not so, to your father-in-law?"

That was a horrible idea Pomuchelskopp had promulgated.--Joseph take a lease of the glebe! Joseph, who already found the burden of his daily work more than he could bear! He sprang to his feet and said: "Neighbour, when a man does what he can, he can't do more than he can; and what am I to do now? If the squire of Pümpelhagen won't have the glebe, I won't have it either, I've enough to do without."--"Mr. Nüssler," said Pomuchelskopp slyly, "will you give me your promise in black and white that you won't take a lease of the glebe?"--"Yes," cried Joseph from the bottom of his heart; he then reseated himself and resumed his former occupation of pretending to smoke.--Pomuchelskopp began to walk up and down the room, and as he did so thought within himself: Mr. von Rambow was not going to renew his lease, and Joseph wouldn't take it if it were offered him, so that all danger from without was guarded against, for the glebe was too small for anyone to rent by itself. The only remaining fear was lest Godfrey should wish to farm the land himself, and Pomuchelskopp was determined to find out. Now God has created many different kinds of men, each of whom has his own special capacity; there was one thing that was completely wanting in Godfrey's composition, and that was all comprehension of agricultural subjects. Bräsig had given himself no end of trouble to teach Godfrey a few of the rudiments of the subject, but all his efforts were vain. It is impossible to get from any man that which he does not possess. Godfrey did not know the difference between oats and barley, he could not tell a cow from a bull, and his ignorance was altogether so dense that Bräsig said to himself at last: "God bless my soul! I don't see how the poor lad is ever to get through the world!"

Pomuchelskopp was not long in discovering this weak point in Godfrey's composition, and he rejoiced greatly thereat: "He'll never be a farmer," he said to himself, "and so he's just the man for me. But, I mustn't let him see that."--"Sir," he said aloud, "I am satisfied with you so far, for you seem to be a very large-minded sort of person, and also a man of morality"--he thought that a particularly good word for the occasion--"you will not grant my request--good!--neither shall I grant yours. But if Mr. Nüssler will sign a written document to the effect that he will not take a lease of the glebe, I am willing to have a further conversation with you on this subject, for, as I said, I am satisfied with you so far."

Young Joseph signed the paper as he was asked, and then he and his nephew drove away from Gürlitz manor perfectly contented with what they had done. They had gained nothing from their visit, but an indefinite promise from Pomuchelskopp, for which Joseph had had to put his name to a paper; but still they were pleased with the result of their application. Joseph was convinced that his signature had been the ultimate cause of their good luck, and had secured the living to his future son-in-law.

Joseph and Godfrey wanted to go to the parsonage, but Christian, the coachman, refused point blank to take them there, for, as he said, it was getting as dark as pitch; so the "phantom" floated back to Rexow like a ghostly shadow in the mist and gloom. Now sleep is the almost inevitable consequence of a long drive through the mist and darkness of night, therefore it was not wonderful that Joseph sank into a peaceful slumber shortly after leaving Gürlitz, and soon afterwards Christian followed his example and though he seemed to be driving, the horses really went of their own accord; had it been daylight this would of course have been discovered, but as it was, no one saw it. Godfrey was the last to fall asleep, and when he did so his dreams were all of Lina, his election sermon, and the first sermon he should preach after he had been chosen minister of the parish. When they reached the spot where Christian had made the remark that it was a good place for an upset, and when Godfrey was dreaming of his election papers, the carriage began to sway from side to side in a terrible manner; then the fore wheel rose in the air, and the hind wheel on Godfrey's side sank in a deep hole--and the next moment--they were all tumbled into the ditch.

I have seen many Grand Ducal chamberlains get out of their carriages at my neighbour, Mrs. Laurence's inn, but never in all my life did I see anything so perfect as the way in which Joseph was shot out of the phaeton; he fell on the top of Godfrey into the muddy ditch, and Christian, not to be behindhand with his master, tumbled from the box in such a manner as to lie side by side in the ditch with him.--"Faugh! Oh! Just stay where you are, Sir," cried the honest old fellow. "The horses are standing quite still!"--"You idiot!" said Joseph.--"Thank God!" said Christian rising, "none of my bones are broken. But stay where you are, Sir, I'll catch the horses."--"You idiot!" cried Joseph once more as he struggled to his feet, while Godfrey was coughing and choking in the deep mud bed in which he was lying, "what on earth made you upset us?"--"It all depends upon circumstances," answered Christian, who had learnt to make use of his master's favourite expressions during his long years of service at Rexow, "what was to be done on such a road in a pitch dark night?"--Joseph did not know what else to say, now that the very words were taken out of his mouth, so he contented himself with asking: "Are any of your bones broken, Godfrey?"--"No, uncle," said the divinity student, "and yours?"--"No, I'm all right except my nose, which I think has been knocked off my face altogether."--Meanwhile the carriage had been raised, and when Joseph and Godfrey had resumed their seats in it, Christian once more turned round on the box, and said: "Didn't I tell you so this very afternoon? This is the exact place."--"Idiot!" said Joseph rubbing his nose energetically, "you had gone to sleep."--"To sleep, Sir, to sleep? It doesn't much matter in such pitch darkness whether one's asleep or awake; I told you before. I know the road by heart and I warned you." And whenever he told the story afterwards to the other servants, he always added: "but I told him how it would be beforehand," and made out that Joseph was a regular daredevil who had no fear of risking his life.

They drove home, and Godfrey was the first to get out of the carriage. Lina had long been uneasy about their absence, and was listening anxiously for every sound that should bring her certainty of the good or evil fate of her father and lover. There was a noise outside. They are coming!--It was only the sighing of the wind in the poplars.--But now!--Yes, it was a carriage, it same nearer, it drove up to the door. She sprang up and rushed out of the room, but had to stop a moment with her hand pressed to her side to still the beating of her heart, which was torn by the conflicting emotions of hope and fear. Would Godfrey bring her good news or had he failed in his attempt? She ran out into the porch. "Don't come near me!" cried Godfrey, but his warning came too late, for Lina, although she was the eldest of the family, was still very thoughtless, and she had thrown herself into his arms as soon as she saw him. But suddenly she felt her hands and arms quite damp and cold, it almost felt as if she were embracing a frog, and letting him go, she exclaimed: "Good gracious! what's the matter?"--"The carriage was upset," said Godfrey; "the carriage was upset by the Providence of God; I mean that Christian upset the carriage, and God has providentially shielded us from all harm."--"What objects you look, to be sure!" said Bräsig, who just then came into the porch with a candle in his hand, and saw Joseph behind Godfrey.--"Yes, Bräsig," said Joseph, "it's just as it is. We've had an accident."--"How did you manage it," asked Bräsig. "I don't see how any reasonable mortal can get himself upset on his own roads; a man of your age too! You must have gone to sleep, Joseph."--"Merciful Heaven!" cried Mrs. Nüssler, "what a sight you've made of yourself, Joseph!" and she turned him round before the candle, as if he were a roast she was turning on a spit-

-"Mercy! Joseph, look at your nose!"--"His Reverence is in a nice mess too," said Bräsig, examining Godfrey from head to foot. "Hollo," he cried, "just look at Lina! Why, Lina, were you in the upset too? Mrs. Nüssler, do you see that she has got half the road from here to Gürlitz sticking to her clothes."

Lina blushed deeply, and Mina at once began to rub her down, while Mrs. Nüssler did the same kind office to her husband: "My goodness, Joseph, what a state you're in, to be sure. And your beautiful new cloak!"--Joseph had bought the cloak twenty years before, when he was engaged to be married.--"This'ill never do," he said, "I must change my clothes, and then to-morrow they can all be put in the oven, and thoroughly dried."--They all agreed that it was the only thing to be done, and soon afterwards uncle and nephew were able to join the rest of the family in the parlour. Mrs. Nüssler now caught sight of her Joseph's nose in the bright light, and exclaimed: "Joseph, look at your nose!"--"You said so before," said Joseph.--"Well," said Bräsig, "I should be telling a downright lie if I were to say that I had ever thought your nose a particularly handsome one; but keep this nose! and what a nose it is!"--"For shame, Bräsig. Why do you wish him to keep this nose. Preserve us all! it's growing thicker every moment! What's to be done?"--"Mrs. Nüssler," said Bräsig, "he must go to the water-cure."--"What!" cried Mrs. Nüssler, "my Joseph go to a water-cure because he has given his nose a little bit of a knock."--"Please, understand me," said Bräsig, "I don't mean him to try the water-cure on his whole body, on his legs and arms; no, I only mean him to put a cold plaget on his nose. Or, Joseph, what do you say to bleeding your nose a little. It would cool it down nicely if you did."--Joseph could not agree to the last proposal, so they determined to try the effect of cold water. At last he settled down in his chair with stately composure, a wet linen rag on his nose, and his pipe in his mouth.

"But now," said Bräsig, "none of us have heard what arrangements you made with Samuel Pomuchelskopp."--"Yes," said Lina, "what did you do Godfrey?"--Godfrey then described their interview with the squire of Gürlitz, and when he had done, Joseph said: "It's all right. I signed a paper."--"And what paper did you sign?" asked Bräsig angrily.--"A promise not to take a lease of the glebe."--"That was a very foolish thing to do. Oh the Jesuit! He wants the land himself. Nightingale, I hear you, you want to get it all your own way! That's your aim and object! But--but"--here Bräsig sprang to his feet and began to pace the room with long strides--"I'll catch you in your own net. Don't count your chickens before they're hatched! Samuel Pomuchelskopp, we've not done with each other yet. What did the celebrated poet say of David and Goliath? I look upon myself as David, and upon him as Goliath. 'He took the sling in his hand and struck him on the forehead, and so did for him.' And how beautifully the celebrated poet ends the story by saying: 'Thus it is with all boasters, when they think they stand, they are sure to have a fall.'--And so it shall be with you, Samuel. I've been in a passion, Mrs. Nüssler, so I can't eat any supper, and will say 'good-night' now as I've a good many things to think about."--He took his candle and went to his room, and the others followed his example soon after supper was finished. Lina lay awake for a long time in anxious thought, listening to the wind in the trees by her window, and to uncle Bräsig walking about in his room, which was below hers.

CHAPTER XIV

The year 1845 had come, and the earth had completed another of its old crooked courses. Day and night, joy and sorrow had changed places again and again, just as they used to do in the old time, just as they have done since the Lord God created day and night, placed man in the Garden of Eden, and then drove him out again. How many days and nights, and how much joy and sorrow have come into the world since then! The day shines for every man, and the night closes over every man; there is no respect of persons. But is it the same with joy and sorrow? Are they meted out to every one with equal justice? I think so. God stretches His hand over each individual, and happiness and grief, consolation and care are equally spread over the world, and each has his share in them; but man does not see clearly, he often changes what is meant for his happiness into sorrow, and thrusts the cup of consolation away from him as if it contained gall, and then laughs away his care.

The men and women whose history I am relating in this book were no better than the rest of their kind, and acted in the same way as their neighbours would have done. Two things that God has sent into the world especially form our joy and sorrow; in the first there is no gall mixed, and our feelings about the other cannot be laughed away; these are Birth and Death, the Beginning and the End. And in the little world of which I am writing there was also Beginning and End, Birth and Death. A beautiful young wife was sitting in the manor-house at Pümpelhagen with to little daughter on her knee, and the child had reopened the doors of the mother's heart, so that she was able to feel the sunshine of God's goodness. The dark shadowy figures which had surrounded Frida ha vanished in the clear light of day, and she was happy, very happy.--Close by Gürlitz parsonage was a grave often visited by two women clothed in deep mourning, who, when spring came on, planted flowers upon it, and who later in the season, when the old lime-tree came into leaf, sat side by side on the bench beneath it, as in the old days when Mrs. Behrens and her little Louisa had been wrapped in the folds of the same shawl. But now it was Louisa who sheltered her foster-mother, and wrapped her own shawl round her. Thus the two women sat silently blessing the memory of him who was gone from them; they were often joined by Hawermann, and then the three mourners would sit together till the shades of evening fell; none of them thrust aside the cup of consolation which had been given them, and so when they separated they felt comforted and refreshed.

The first violence of grief was over at the parsonage, but its traces were still to be seen in the look of chastened sorrow, the Angel of Death had imprinted on the faces of those who remained, after he had taken their husband and father from them. The Angel had kissed Louisa's forehead as he went and had left her graver, higher thoughts than she had ever had before; he had clasped little Mrs. Behrens in his arms, and after that embrace her old lively impetuosity had died away leaving in its place a calm gentle determination to dedicate her future life to the carrying out of her pastor's wishes. She only lived in her memory of him, everything must remain as he had been used to see it. His arm-chair was placed before his study-table on which his last sermon was lying with the pen beside it, and his old Bible was kept open at the place where his hand had ruffled the leaves when he was dying. The first thing she did every morning was to go to his study with her duster and put everything in good order for the day, and when this was done she would often look round at the door as though she expected him to come in and say: "Thank you, dear Regina," as in the old time. At dinner Louisa always prepared for three people, and the pastor's chair was kept in its old place because her foster-mother liked it to be so, and it seemed to her as if he must needs come in as usual with some cheerful greeting. She took care not to indulge in the luxury of woe, but always tried to make the meal pass as pleasantly as it used to do, and never despised any consoling thought that came to her. This state of things could not go on for ever. Some new clergyman must have the living sooner or later, and then Mrs. Behrens would be obliged to leave the house and even the village, for there was no house for her to go to. She must go away from her husband's grave, for Pomuchelskopp, who alone had power to let her stay, had determined that she should go. She watched the fruit-trees her husband had planted blossom for the last time. She sat under the flowering palm-willow where she had so often sat by his side for the last time. She had seen the spring come and wind his leafy garlands round her old home for the last time. Now summer was showering his golden glory over the world. She said to Louisa one day with a sad smile: "When the swallows take their flight in autumn, Louisa, we shall have to go too." As she spoke she felt the full bitterness of death had come to her.

Hawermann was her most untiring friend and she allowed herself to be guided by him in all things. With the best will in the world to spare her, he could not save her from having to leave the parish; but at least he could make the parting as easy as possible for her. Kurz the shopkeeper had a house adjoining the one in which he himself lived, which he wanted to let with its back garden, and this house Hawermann arranged as much as he could in the style of the parsonage. He took Louisa into his confidence and got her to measure the size of the parsonage rooms, after which, Schulz the cabinet maker was ordered to furnish the rooms in the new house according to Louisa's measurements and description; but he utterly refused to do so, "for," he said, "I can't do it. Women always measure by their belts or apron strings and I can't do anything from that sort of measurement. All the same, plans are plans, and I don't like drawn plans; I get on much better when I carry my plans in my head."--Kurz was of opinion that the more the new house differed from the old one, the better it would be, but Hawermann was not to be dissuaded, and Schulz seeing how determined he was, said: "If you will have it so, I'll go out to the parsonage and make all the measurements myself."--So one morning early while Mrs. Behrens was asleep, Schulz appeared and made all the necessary measurements. When he was doing so he might have been heard muttering: "Seven--seven--five and twenty--five and twenty--Kurz--Hawermann--Kurz--Hawermann--bother--a mistake here would have put it all wrong--too great a space--a beam across--Ah, yes--all right--yes, yes, done, done!" After that was done he went out, and getting into his tax-cart drove his lazy brown pony home, and as he jogged along the road he matured his plan. The furnishing was now begun, and Hawermann was very well pleased with the result of Schulz's plan upon the whole, although he would have liked a few little things to have been different, however the cabinetmaker was so pleased with the look of the house that he would change nothing, and Hawermann was obliged to be satisfied with things as they were. Kurz helped as much as he could, by giving a ready consent to all their wishes.

As I said before, there was great joy at Pümpelhagen. Frida's clear eyes were turned lovingly on her little daughter, and motherly love had woven an invisible veil with which to cover their clear-sightedness, and hide the impending gloom from her for the time being. It had never been the case before in her active life, but now she indulged in one dream after another of the future happiness of her husband and child, especially when she held the baby out for its father to look at. Alick's heart was also full of joy. He came out and in continually to look at his wife and child, but still there was one drop of bitterness in his cup: he had hoped for a son to carry on his old and noble race, and he was disappointed. It is a sad thing for an innocent little girl to come into the world when she is not wanted, and to have to suffer because of the disappointed hopes of other people. Alick would have been angry if any one had said that to him, for he had really rejoiced in spite of his disappointment. He had at once announced the "good news" to all his acquaintances, not excepting the horse-dealers he employed, and Pomuchelskopp; he had only forgotten to announce the event to three people: to his cousin Frank--"the young fool"--to Mrs. Behrens--"the matchmaker"--and to Mrs. Nüssler--"the under-bred old woman." When he laid the envelopes containing the announcements on his wife's bed and she expressed her surprise that he had omitted these three people, he answered coldly, that he did not care to have anything to do with such persons, and that if she wished to send them announcements she must do it herself. She did so.

A few days later Louisa called to congratulate Mrs. von Rambow in Mrs. Behrens' name. While she was there, Alick came into the room, but as soon as he saw her, he bowed and went away again, saying: "Ah, Miss Hawermann. Pray excuse me."--A couple of days after that Mrs. Nüssler drove up to the door in the "phantom," and Alick seeing her arrival went off into the fields. When he came back he heard from Daniel that Mrs. Nüssler was still with Mrs. von Rambow, and exclaimed angrily: "I can't understand what pleasure my wife can find in the society of such uneducated people!" This was a very uncalled for remark on Alick's part; for only a few weeks earlier he had spent an evening in the society of some horse-breeders of the same quality as his friend, Mr. von Brülow, who was pronounced by some of the people present to be a man of vast knowledge. A young doctor, who happened to be one of the party, had then remarked that he did not think the knowledge Mr. von Brülow had displayed was so very great after all, upon which Alick had risen and glancing over his shoulder at the overbold young man, had said, that any one who had met with Mr. von Brülow's success in rearing foals and keeping up a good stock of thoroughbreds must assuredly be looked upon as a man of vast knowledge and experience. And now forsooth he regarded good Mrs. Nüssler as an ignorant old woman, although she was giving his wife the benefit of her experience, together with sensible and practical advice as to the best way of rearing his little child. Pomuchelskopp came in his turn, dressed in his blue coat and brass buttons, seated in his carriage with the coat-of-arms on the panels and drawn by four horses. That pleased Alick better. His ways were so much more high-bred! The young squire received Pomuchelskopp heartily, and made him stay to supper; after which he showed his visitor his thoroughbred mare and foal, with both of which Pomuchelskopp seemed to be much pleased. At last laying his hand on the young man's arm, Pomuchelskopp said: "This is very good, Mr. von Rambow, very good indeed for a beginning; but if you really intend to make money by horse-breeding you must set up a paddock, for as you know fresh air is a necessity when you want to bring up young creatures of any kind. Freedom, freedom, Mr. von Rambow. That's one of the most indispensable requisites to ensure success. And you could manage it so easily here. You might make the land behind the park into four paddocks, one for each of your four mares. Look, I mean the land over there stretching up to the top of the hill; you'd only have to sow it with grass and clover seed instead of with corn, and then you see how conveniently the brook flows through the field. You couldn't have a better place. Naturally," he went on after a pause during which Alick had been thinking silently, "your bailiff wouldn't approve of that plan."--"My bailiff has to obey orders," said Alick hastily.--"Of course," answered Pomuchelskopp soothingly, "and besides that he doesn't understand horses."--"The space you propose wouldn't be large enough for corn if I left out the best bit of ground," said Alick.--"Ah," replied Pomuchelskopp, glancing over his shoulder, "but you'll have to alter the fences at any rate, for you have always had the glebe hitherto, and now you're going to give it up. Taking in a little more or less can make no difference."--"True," said Alick shortly, for the promise he had given in his time of need was weighing heavily upon him, and he had as great a dislike as any other man to give up an advantageous possession in which he had taken pride. But Pomuchelskopp was so true and honest in his desire for his welfare, and gave him such good advice, that--as he thought--he could not want for much when he had such a friend at his side; and when they parted, Alick shook his neighbour heartily by the hand and then retired to his room, his head full of the new paddocks.

Hawermann came across the yard, and Alick seeing him, put his head out at the window, and called: "Mr. Hawermann." When the old man had come up to the window, he said: "How far have you got on with sowing the barley behind the park?"--"I think that we shall be finished by the day after to-morrow; we're going to begin the bit beyond the brook to-morrow."--"Good. It goes to the top of the hill--I will tell you the particulars afterwards--be sure you sow Timothy, rye-grass and white clover with the barley. Send Triddelfitz to Rahnstädt to-morrow for the seed; he had better get it from David."--"But no one ever lays down grass immediately after barley."--"Did you not hear me *tell* you to sow grass in that field? I intend to make paddocks there for the mares and foals."--"Paddocks? Paddocks?" questioned the old man, as if he could not believe what he had heard.--"Yes, paddocks," said Alick, preparing to shut the window.--"Mr. von Rambow," entreated Hawermann, laying his hand on the window sill, "that bit of ground is the best in the whole field, and if you separate it from the rest the field will be too small. That was the reason the late squire took a lease of Gürlitz glebe." The bailiff said exactly what Alick had himself said a short time before, and Alick knew that he was right; but what master likes to confess that a dependent is right!--"I don't intend to renew my lease of the glebe," said the squire.--The old man's hands sank to his side: "Give up the glebe," he murmured. "Sir, that land has brought us .... I have it all written down and ...."--"I don't care. I'll tell you, I don't intend to keep it."--"Mr. von Rambow, it is impossible ....."--"Didn't you hear me say that *I don't intend to take a new lease of the glebe.*"--"Oh, Sir, let me entreat you to consider ....."--"What do you mean?" cried Alick, slamming down the window and muttering as he turned away: "A troublesome old fool! A self-important old humbug!" He then threw himself into a chair and thought about the paddocks he was going to set up; but the brilliant pictures of success his imagination had painted but a short time before, would not return at his call, and at last he put aside the thought for the moment with a vague sense of ill-usage.

And the old man? He went back to the field feeling pained and sad at heart. He found it very difficult, in spite of all his love and gratitude for the kindness of the old squire, to bear the unkindness of his benefactor's only son. And what was the use of it all? What good did his remaining at Pümpelhagen do? How could he help the young squire? In nothing. Step by step, Mr. von Rambow was approaching the edge of the precipice, and when he put out his hand to save him, he was thrust back; and though his heart was full of love and good-will to his young master and his whole house, he was treated like an unfaithful servant, who cared for nothing but his wages.--"Triddelfitz," he said when he got to the barley field, "the squire wants this part of the field near the brook and up to the top of the hill sowed down with grass. He will explain what he wishes to be done more particularly when he comes out. You'd better sow the barley rather thinner here."--"What's he going to do with it?" asked Fred.--"He'll tell you himself if he thinks fit. There he is coming out of the garden," added the bailiff as he turned to go away.

"Triddelfitz," said Mr. von Rambow when he came up, "I want to have this piece of ground up to the top of the hill sowed with grass, and so you must get the seed for it from David to-morrow. I intend to turn this part of the field into paddocks."--"Capital!" cried Fred. "I wondered whether we shouldn't have to set up something of the kind before long."--"Yes, it's quite necessary."--"Of course it is. Quite necessary," said Fred in a tone of the utmost conviction. Let no one think that he was merely swimming with the stream; he meant every word that he said thoroughly, and if he had had the slightest notion of the expense and misery these paddocks were to cause, he would never have said a word in their favour, but--as I said before--he was honestly of the same opinion as his master in all matters of this description.--"Have you a measuring pole here?" asked Alick.--"A measuring pole? No," said Fred with a slightly contemptuous and at the same time modest and conscious laugh. "I have invented a new instrument for measuring. If you'll allow me, I'll get it and show it to you," and then he hastened to the nearest ditch, out of which he pulled an enormous wooden hoop that originally had been round a barrel. A piece of rope was woven and twisted about the hoop, and into the centre of this rope, he thrust the end of his walking stick, as if through the nave of a wheel, thus making the hoop roll round. "The circumference of the hoop is exactly the same as the length of one of those measuring poles," he explained, "and whenever the hoop has turned completely round this hammer strikes that board, so you see we have only to count the number of times it goes round to be able to measure the land exactly."--"Let me see! Let me see!" cried Alick with all his old love of invention awake within him. "Was it entirely your own thought?"--"Yes, it's quite my own invention," replied Fred; but he ought to have said that he owed the discovery to his own laziness, for he did not like making his long body stoop.--"Well, measure that bit of land for me," said Alick. And then he went home, and as he went he said to himself: Triddelfitz will make me a capital farm-bailiff. He's wide-awake, and it's much easier to work with him than with Hawermann.

After a short time the old bailiff came back, and said angrily to Fred: "What are you about, Triddelfitz? You're sowing the barley much too thick."--"I don't see how that can be the case," said Fred, "I held the machine as you told me, and I measured the land myself."--"Impossible!" cried Hawermann. "My eyes can't deceive me so completely. Where's the measuring pole?"--"I hav'n't a measuring pole," said Fred, "and I don't require one," he added defiantly, for the squire's recognition of this discovery was too pleasant to be forgotten. "I measure everything with my instrument," he said, pointing to his invention which was lying at his feet--"What?" cried Hawermann, "What on earth is that?"--"An invention of mine," answered Fred, with as much pride as if he had invented the first steam engine.--"Oh, that's it, is it?" said Hawermann. "Take your hoop and measure me off ten poles length along there."--Fred lifted up his invention, and set it rolling; Hawermann walked by his side pacing the ground: "How much is that?" he asked.--"Ten poles," answered Fred.--"I only make it nine, and two feet," said the bailiff.--"That's impossible," answered Fred, "you must have miscounted, for my hoop goes quite right."--"Five of my steps make a Mecklenburg pole," said the bailiff, "but you see that you're mismanaging the whole piece of ground because you're too stupid to set to work properly. How could you expect a machine like that to answer on a hill-side, when it would require very smooth and even ground before it could possibly do at all? It's nothing but laziness--laziness! Go and get a proper measuring pole at once!" Then opening his pocket-knife he cut Fred's invention into small pieces, and after that he re-arranged the sowing-machine.

Fred stood still gazing blankly at his invention which was being chopped to bits before his eyes. It is a dreadful blow to anyone who thinks he has made a discovery that will benefit the world, when he suddenly finds that he has failed to realize his idea. Fred had meant so well--to himself first of all--and then to his colleagues, and to all land-measurers throughout the province of Mecklenburg; he had wanted to save them the trouble of stooping, and now his invention was lying at his feet an utter wreck. "I'll get the measuring pole," he said to himself, "it's no good trying now. I'd rather a thousand times work with the squire than with old Hawermann." During his walk home to get the pole, he felt very bitter against the bailiff, and quite forgot that he had ever wished to give him the best rooms in his house, and to keep a pair of carriage horses and a hack for his use. On his arrival at the farm he had a few minutes talk with Mary Möller, with whom he was on as friendly terms as ever. She told him of the squire's interview with Hawermann at the window, and he was much comforted when he heard of it. As he went back to the field with the measuring pole over his shoulder, and a nice little bit of sausage in his hand, he said to himself: "Poor old fellow, I'm not a bit angry with him now. He's old, and can't take in new ideas."

CHAPTER XV

So the seed-time passed away, and summer came in its turn. Mrs. von Rambow no longer went about the farm as much as before, and the old bailiff had to do without the comfort of her kindly smile and friendly words of greeting, which used to give him encouragement to persevere. She had other and pleasanter occupations now, which fully engrossed her attention. She was so much taken up with hopes, wishes, and plans for the little child she rocked in her arms, that she rather neglected outside duties. Alick had also changed a good deal since the birth of the baby. He took a vaguely gloomy view of his responsibility as the father of a family, and instead of going about his estate as formerly, and seeing how matters were going on, in the same manner as a field-marshal looks after what is under his charge, he now inspected each farming-detail as carefully as a corporal does those regimental matters which lie in his department. He put his finger into every pie, not excepting the feeding-troughs in the cattle-sheds. He might always have done that if he had liked, and it is delightful to see a squire interesting himself in such things, but he had better not have meddled with the existing regulations, for he did not understand how to improve them. He would give foolishly ignorant orders, alter all the arrangements the bailiff had made, and then when he had got everything at sixes and sevens, he would go home and say grumblingly: "That old man is of no use whatever. He's far too old. I can't stand it much longer."--Christian Segel said one day to Derrick Snäsel: "What's to be done now, I wonder; the squire tells me to do one thing, and the bailiff tells me to do another."--"Well, lad," said Derrick, "if the squire says ...."--"But it's such a stupid thing to do."--"You needn't be in too great a hurry, and if the squire desires you to do it, it can't be helped."

Harvest had begun, and the grain was falling under the mower's scythes. The rye was all cut, and the sheaves had been standing in the fields for three days.--"Mr. Hawermann," cried Alick out at the window, and as soon as the bailiff had come up he went on: "I want you to lead in the rye to-morrow."--"It's too soon, Sir. The weather has been so damp and heavy both yesterday and to-day, that the corn hasn't dried properly; besides that it's still quite soft, and some of the ears are rather green yet."--"It'll do all right. Where shall you begin to lead in?"--"If we are to do it, we should begin below the village, and have two sets of carts going, one to take the rye to the great barn, and the other to the barn where we usually store the barley."--"What? Below the village? Two sets of carts? Why?"--"Because the nearer the village we begin the more we shall be able to save in the day, and it looks rather like rain. The reason I proposed having two sets of carts was to prevent the people and the waggons getting into each other's way."--"H'm!" said Alick, "I shall take what you have said into consideration," and then he shut the window. After due consideration he made up his mind that he would get in the rye alone, with Fred Triddelfitz's help. Hawermann should have nothing whatever to do with it, and in order to show him that he was of no use, the rye should be taken from the field to the barn with *one* set of carts. Alick did not quite understand what one set or two sets of carts meant, but that was of no consequence, as of course it was only one of the old bailiff's antiquated notions with which he would have nothing to do.

At five o'clock next morning he was up and about. Finding the bailiff in the yard, he went up to him, and said with a friendly smile: "I've been thinking it over, Mr. Hawermann, and--don't be angry with me--would so much like to manage this all by myself with young Triddelfitz to help me"--The old man stood before him in speechless amazement. At last he said slowly and sadly: "And I am only to look on then, Sir. You'd rather have the assistance of a foolish young apprentice than have mine." Then grasping his walking-stick more firmly, he gazed at Mr. von Rambow with sparkling eyes that looked quite youthful in the old face. He continued: "You were a little boy, Sir, when I entered your good father's service, and devoted myself to him. He thanked me on his death-bed, thanked me. But you--you have made my life hard to me, and now you want to insult me."--He walked away, and Alick followed him, saying: "Indeed, Mr. Hawermann, I never meant to do that, I assure you. I only wished to try ....."--But he had meant it so; he knew very well that he had meant it so; he wanted to rid himself of the old man, for he knew too much of his affairs, and often made him feel ashamed.

The bailiff went to his room, shut his door, and sat down to think, but it was long before he could make up his mind to any course of action. Meanwhile there was much shouting and talking going on in the yard. "Triddelfitz."--"Mr. von Rambow."--"Where are you going, Joseph?"--"I don't know, I've had no orders."--"What are you going to do with that harrow, Fred Päsel?"--"How can I tell, I'm going to harrow the ploughed land."--"What a fool you are," cried Fred Triddelfitz, "we're going to lead in the rye."--"I'm sure I don't care, what isn't to be, isn't to be," pulling the harrow out of the cart, "I shall do whatever the bailiff tells me."--"Flegel," shouted the squire.--"Fred Flegel," repeated Triddelfitz.--"What do you want," shouted a gruff voice from the hay-loft.--"Where are the boards to heighten the waggons?" asked Fred Triddelfitz.--"There, just as they were," was the answer, "no one told me, they'd be required to-day."--"What's to be done now?" asked the labourer Näsel.--"God alone knows," answered Pegel, "we've received no orders."--"Flegel," cried Fred, "we're going to lead in the rye, and the waggon-wheels must be greased."--"You may do it for all I care," shouted Flegel from the loft. "Here's the tub if you want it"--"Where's Hawermann, Mr. von Rambow, mayn't I call him?"--"No," answered Alick lowly as he turned away.--"Well then," said Fred, who was growing rather anxious, "we won't get any of the rye in this morning."--"That doesn't matter. We can begin this afternoon."--"But what are the labourers to do till then?" "Confound the labourers," said Alick petulantly and turning to go, "it's always the labourers. They can make themselves useful here in the yard until they are wanted. Stop a moment," he added looking back, "they can help to grease the waggon-wheels."

Meantime the old bailiff was sitting at his desk, thinking how best he could write something that it nearly broke his heart to have to write. He was about to sever the tie that bound him to the place where the late squire had been so good to him. He heard some of the foolish talk that was going on in the yard, and started to the window to put things right, but no sooner had he got there than he drew back again, remembering that he had nothing more to do with it. He crumpled up the letter he had begun, and tried to write another, which gave him as little satisfaction as the first. He put all his writing things together and shut his desk. What was he to do now? What was there for him to do? Nothing! He was supposed to be beyond work. He threw himself into the corner of the sofa, and thought and thought.

Everything was ready for leading in the rye by the afternoon, thanks to the exertions of the old carpenter, and of two or three of the steadiest of the old labourers. So the work began. Alick got on horseback, and took command of the whole affair, and Fred, not to be outdone by his master, must needs ride also. As his deaf mare was lame he mounted a spirited old thoroughbred, and acted as adjutant. They set off. Six pairs of horses were taken out, and a pair of these was harnessed into each of the six harvest-waggons, which were then driven out of the yard in a row. Order was of more importance than anything else. On one side were the forkers, and the men who standing in the waggons arranged the sheaves on them, then others went to the barns to be ready to receive the loaded waggons, and the field-workers got into the waggons, and set off for the corn-field preceded by Alick and Fred on horseback. Such an arrangement was never known before at Pümpelhagen as on that lovely afternoon; but order must be maintained. The old carpenter, Frederic Flegel, stood at the barn-door and watched the harvesters set out: "Wonders will never cease," he muttered, scratching his head, "however it's no business of mine," and as he went back to his work, he said: "What has become of our old bailiff?"

Hawermann was still sitting quietly in his room thinking. His first anger had passed away, and he was able to write calmly, so he rose and wrote a few lines giving up his situation at Christmas, and asking for leave of absence during harvest, for he knew that he could be of no use there. Having done this he took his hat and stick, and went out; he felt that he must have fresh air; he was stifling in the house. He seated himself on a stone wall under the shade of an elder-bush, and gazed down the Warnitz road to see if the waggons were coming; but there were no waggons to be seen; the only moving object he could descry was Bräsig, who was coming towards them along the Warnitz road.--"As sure as your nose is in the middle of your face, I can't understand you, Charles! Why are you leading in the rye so soon? It's as green as grass! And what do you mean by letting six waggons follow one another in a row? And why are the loaded waggons stopping on the road?"--"I don't know, Bräsig. You must ask the squire and Triddelfitz."--"What?"--"I've nothing more to say, Bräsig"--"How? Why? What do you mean?" asked Bräsig, raising his eyebrows as high as he could in his astonishment.--"I've nothing more to say," repeated the old man with quiet sadness, "I am put on one side; the squire thinks me too old to be of any use."--"Charles," said Bräsig, laying his hand on his friend's shoulder, "what's the matter? Tell me."--And so Hawermann told him all that had happened. When Bräsig knew the whole story he turned round, and clenched his teeth savagely, looking as if he wished the beautiful world, at which he was glaring so angrily, were a hazel-nut that he might grind it between his teeth. Then he growled passionately as he looked down the Warnitz road: "The Jesuits! The beastly Jesuits!" and turning again to Hawermann, he said: "Triddelfitz is another serpent you have warmed in your bosom, Charles."--"How do you make that out, Bräsig? He must do as he is told."--"Here he comes at a gallop, and all the six waggons after him! Will they ever keep up, I wonder--just look how top-heavy they are! It's a comedy, an agricultural comedy! Mark my words! There'll be an upset at the old bridge!" cried uncle Bräsig, dancing as vehemently on his poor gouty legs, as if he wished to make them pay the penalty of all the mischief that had been done that day. I am sorry to have to confess it, but it is nevertheless true that Bräsig was full of delight at the thought that the returning harvesters were almost certain to meet with an accident, which he thought would only serve them right after what had happened that morning. "There it is, as flat as a flounder!" he exclaimed joyfully when the first overloaded waggon reached the turn of the bridge, and then upset.-

-"Wo!" was shouted from the bridge. "Confound it! won't you stop! Wo, can't you!" Fred looked round about him, what was to be done? He did not know what to do. Suddenly he caught sight of Hawermann and Bräsig, seated on the wall, galloped up to them, and said: "Oh, Mr. Hawermann ....."--"Sir, you've made your bed, and must lie upon it!" interrupted Bräsig.--"Oh, Mr. Hawermann, what are we to do? The first waggon is lying right across the bridge, and the others can't move."--"Ride quickly ...."--"Hold your tongue, Charles, you've been set aside like a lamb for the sacrifice, and have nothing to do with it," exclaimed Bräsig.--"No, never mind, the men are wiser than you, they're putting everything right down there."--"It isn't my fault, Sir," said Fred, "Mr. von Rainbow gave all the orders himself. The waggons are to go in a row, and are to move on quickly though they are overloaded."--"Then obey orders, and ride till your tongue hangs out of your mouth like a dog's," said Bräsig.--"He's on horseback over there on the heather-hill, and is overlooking and ordering everything himself."--"Then, I suppose, he has a telespope in one hand and a field-marshal's baton in the other like old Blücher in the hop-market at Rostock," said Bräsig scornfully.--"Ride on to the farm," interrupted Hawermann, "and see that each waggon sets off again for the field the moment it is emptied."--"I dar'n't do that," answered Fred, "the squire has given express orders that the waggons are all to go back to the field in a row as they came. He says that order must be maintained."--"Then you can tell him that I never saw a finer specimen of a donkey in all my life ....."--"Bräsig, take care what you say," cried Hawermann warningly.--"Than--than your little mule, Mr. Triddelfitz," added uncle Bräsig with great presence of mind.

Fred rode away to the farm.--"Charles," said Bräsig, "let us go too. We shall see everything capitally from your window."--"It's all the same to me," said Hawermann with a deep sigh, "where I am; whether here or there." So they went. The waggons all drove into the yard, the first right up to the barn, and the others in a row behind it. The forkers muttered that they were being worked to death; the labourers grumbled about the wet rye, and asked who was to thrash it out in winter; the men in charge of the horses laughed and played each other stupid tricks to while away the time they had to wait doing nothing, and Fred rode about the yard with a quiet conscience, for he was doing his duty, and carrying out his master's orders. As soon as the rye was all put in the barn, he placed himself at the head of the empty waggons and the procession moved off. The forkers and stackers closed the barn door softly to shade them from the sun, lay down and went to sleep, for they had plenty of time to enjoy a nap.--"What a delightfully quiet harvest time, Charles," said Bräsig, "the yard is as silent as death, and not a leaf is stirring! It's a great pleasure to me to see anything of the kind, for I assure you I had never thought such a thing possible."--"It isn't at all pleasant to me," replied Hawermann, "I see misfortune coming. Two or three mistakes of this kind will deprive the squire of the people's respect. As soon as they begin to see that it's really ignorance and not a new mode of farming that has brought about the changes, they'll begin to take their own way. I am very sorry for the unfortunate young squire, and still more so for his poor wife."--"There's Mrs. von Rambow coming out of the house, and there's the nursery-maid with the baby asleep in a perambulator. But, Charles--come to the window quick--what's all this?"--It was certainly worth the trouble of hastening to the window, there was now a stir and movement in the yard, which a moment before had been so still and quiet, Fred Triddelfitz thundered up to the farm on the old thoroughbred Bill, Alick followed about twenty yards behind, and shouted: "Triddelfitz."--"Coming," cried Fred, galloping out at the other gate with Alick still in pursuit.--"What the devil does all this mean?" asked Bräsig. He had hardly time to ask the question when Fred and Alick came back and recrossed the yard shouting: "Triddelfitz."--"Coming."--"Have you gone mad, Sir?" asked Bräsig as Fred galopped past the farmhouse, but he received no answer. Fred was sitting crumpled up like a sack in his saddle, and when he heard Bräsig's question could not help giggling from fright and misery. As he passed Mr. von Rambow he tried to touch his cap, but knocked it off instead, and Frida cried out anxiously: "Alick, Alick, what's the matter?" but got no answer, for Alick was too busy. Suddenly Bill jumped over the fence in front of the sheep's pen, and Fred was thrown head over heels into a heap of straw. Alick now drew in his horse and called again: "Triddelfitz."--"Coming, Mr. von Rambow," answered Fred from out of the straw.--"What devil drove you to ride so hard?" asked Alick.--"None," said Fred, getting up, and finding to his great joy that he had met with no injury, "I was riding one, that's all, and I think that Bill ran away with me."--"You're right enough there," said Christian, who had come out of the stable to see what was the matter. "You gee, Sir," turning to Mr. von Rambow, "the count used to ride Bill in steeple-chases, and when once the beast gets his head, he goes on till he finds a fence or hurdle to jump, and after he has had a good run he stands as quiet as a lamb. Just look at him now."--"Alick," asked Mrs. von Rambow, who now came up, "what is it?"--"Nothing, my dear; I had given Triddelfitz an order, and no sooner had he ridden off than a better plan occurred to me, so I followed him to make the desired change, but his horse ran away with him, and I went in pursuit."--"Thank God it was no worse," she said. "But, Alick, won't you come in and have some tea?"--"Yes," he said, "I've been working very hard to-day and am rather tired. Triddelfitz, just go on as we have been doing."--"All right, Sir," answered Fred, and then Alick went back to the house with his wife.

"Alick," she asked, when they were seated at tea, "I don't understand. The harvest waggons used always to come into the yard one by one as they were filled, at my father's place, but I see that you're making them come in a string of six."--"I know the old-fashioned way perfectly, Frida dear, but I think that it's a bad way, and one in which it's impossible to keep order; while if you have a train of six waggons you can easily maintain order."--"Did Hawermann arrange it in that way?"--"Hawermann? No. He has nothing whatever to do with it. I have at last found it necessary to emancipate myself from the bailiffs leading-strings, and have told him that I intend to bring in the harvest without his assistance."--"Alick, what have you done! He'll never stand that."--"He must though. He must learn that *I* am master here."--"He has always treated you as such. Dear Alick, what you have done to day cannot fail to do us a great deal of harm," and she leant back in her chair in deep and painful thought.--Alick felt uncomfortable and a little cross.--The door opened and Daniel Sadenwater brought in a letter: "With Mr. Hawermann's compliments."--"There it is," said Frida.--Alick read the letter: "The bailiff gives up his place at Christmas. He may go now for all I care. I don't require a bailiff. Besides that, I could get a hundred instead of him if I liked. I'm only sorry that it was he who gave up his place, not I who told him to go," and starting to his feet, he began to walk up and down the room. Frida sat still, and said nothing. Alick felt that her silence was meant as a reproach. He knew that he was in a difficult position, but that he must not confess it even to himself, and must lay the blame of what had happened on the shoulders of another, so he went on: "But it's your fault, it all comes of your taking that pretentious old scoundrel's part"--Frida made no answer; she rose and left the room.

That evening she sat by her little daughter's cradle and rocked her to sleep. Alas, who can rock his thoughts to sleep as she did her child! A baby comes straight from God, and still has the peace of heaven in its heart; but human thoughts come from earth, and are full of care and trouble and utter weariness; to such as are burdened with these, sleep is unattainable. Alick was right, he could easily get another bailiff, a hundred if he wanted them. But Frida was also right: they were losing a true friend.

CHAPTER XVI

There was great joy in Joseph Nüssler's house. Godfrey was elected, he was to have the living of Gürlitz. And to whom did he especially owe his election? Why to our good simple-minded old friend Pomuchelskopp, to be sure. His was the casting vote. Three divinity students preached one after the other, each anxiously struggling so to interpret the Word of God as to please the congregation, and prove himself most worthy of obtaining the living. "Henny," said Pomuchelskopp, when Godfrey had finished his sermon, and was passing his handkerchief over his white face, "Henny," he said, "we'll choose this one, for he's the stupidest."--"How can you be sure," asked his loving wife, "does one fool always know another when he sees him?"--"My chuck," said Pomuchelskopp, overlooking his affectionate wife's pleasantry, either because he was so accustomed to her little jokes, or because Godfrey's sermon had touched him, for Godfrey had preached on the text: "Forgive your enemies."--"Henny, listen. The first of these students, the one with the red face, is a son of old farmer Hamann, and custom is a great thing, you'll see that fellow will work his own glebe; the second, look, there he is, was seen examining the glebe by Gustavus, and was heard asking the parsonage-coachman, who had charge of the barns, for the roofs were in bad order. There'd be no hope with either of these; the rector's son is the man for us."--"He who reckons wrong, reckons without his host," said Henny drily.--"I hav'n't done so at any rate," answered Pomuchelskopp, "Mr. von Rambow and Nüssler have both given me a written agreement not to take the land, the young man can't farm himself, he's far too stupid for that, and the ground is too small to make it worth while for any one to take it by itself. He must let it to me, I am sure of getting it, and I can say to him: So much, and *not a penny more!*"--So Godfrey was elected, for almost all the votes were given to him, only one or two of the oldest labourers at Rexow gave their votes to their master, Joseph Nüssler. But that was merely an oversight and made no difference, for it was all in the family.

So, as I said before, there was great joy in Joseph Nüssler's house. The twins basked in the sunshine of happiness, and made plans for the future. Mina was quite as happy as Lina though she had not the same cause. Still she could not help remembering that her father had said one day when he came from the fields, that he found the sole management of the farm too hard work, and only wished that Rudolph were far enough on to be able to come and help him. Her mother had certainly answered that he ought to be ashamed of himself for saying such a thing, for he was still a young man, and he had replied that he would go on by himself a little longer. But still Mina saw that her father would really like to have Rudolph there, and so it would come to pass sooner or later. Lina's things were all ready, the trousseau was prepared, and Mrs. Nüssler's sitting-room looked more like a shop than anything else, Spinning, knitting, sewing, embroidering, crocheting were going on there, bales of goods were unwound and then wound up again. Every one was busy, even young Joseph and young Bolster. Young Joseph had to help to wind skeins of wool or cotton. He sat straight up with his pipe in his mouth, and a skein of knitting cotton over his hands, his wife stood in front of him, and wound it into a ball. Then he had a little rest, but when Lina or Mina came in he had to begin again. And young Bolster did not escape; if ever any one had cause to curse the marriage it was he; he was continually being tramped on and tumbled over, and at last came to the conclusion that it was better on the whole to take up his abode in the yard than in the parlour until the trousseau was finished.

"Well," said Mrs. Nüssler one evening as she laid her hands in her lap, "the marriage may take place to-morrow, Bräsig, for all I care. I'm ready."--"Then," answered Bräsig, "you needn't put off any longer, for no doubt the methodist and Lina are ready when you are."--"Ah, Bräsig, that shows how little you know about it. The chief thing is still wanting. The government hasn't given its consent--what's the right word for it--to the election as yet"--"Oh, yes, I know what you mean, 'confirmed his call,' as they say now-a-days; for my own part, I consider 'vocated' a better word, we always used it long ago when the late parson Behrens came to the parish, but it has gone out of fashion now."--At this moment Christian, the coachman, came in, and said: "Good-evening, Mistress, here are the newspapers."--"Wer'n't there any letters at the post-office?" asked Mrs. Nüssler.--"Yes," said Christian, "there was one letter."--"Why didn't you bring it?"--"Nay!" said Christian scornfully, as if to show that that was too great a piece of folly for him to have been guilty of, "they asked such a ransom for it, that I hadn't enough, money to pay for it."--"How much was it?"--"One pound four! What do you say to that? They said there was a post-mark, or a post-stamp, or something of that kind on it. It came in the mail-cart, and is addressed to the young gentleman, I mean our Miss Lina's bridegroom."--"Good gracious, Christian! What a dear letter! Who can it be from, I wonder?"--"I know," said Christian, "but I don't intend to tell," and he glanced at Bräsig.--"You may speak out before Mr. Bräsig," said his mistress.--"Very well," answered Christian. "It was from a woman, but I've forgotten her name."-

-"Mercy!" cried Mrs. Nüssler. "From a woman! To my future son-in-law! And costing one pound four!"--"A common occurrence!" said Bräsig. "A common occurrence, even amongst methodists!"--"So it is!" said Christian, preparing to leave the room.--"Christian," and Mrs. Nüssler rose, "you must take the rye to Rahnstädt tomorrow, ask particularly what name it is at the post-office, and I'll give you the money, for I must have the letter."-- "Very well, mistress," said Christian, going away, "if you want it, you shall have it."--"Bräsig," exclaimed Mrs. Nüssler, throwing herself back into her wicker-chair, and making it groan loudly, "what has my son-in-law to do with women's letters?"--"I don't know," said Bräsig. "I hav'n't the slightest idea, and I never trouble my head about secrets. Wait till the end, and you're sure to know."--"But," said Mrs. Nüssler, "Godfrey's such a quiet sort of fellow."--"Methodists ar'n't to be trusted," replied Bräsig, "never put faith in a Jesuit!"--"Bräsig," cried Mrs. Nüssler, springing to her feet so suddenly that her old chair gave a loud creak, "if there's any secret, I'll take my child back. If Rudolph had got into a scrape, I'd have forgiven him, for he's a thoughtless lad, but not hypocritical. But Godfrey! No. Not as long as I live. A man who pretends to be so much better than his neighbours, and then-- no, let him keep away from me and mine. I'll have nothing to do with a man of that kind."

When Godfrey appeared at the supper-table, his future mother-in-law looked at him from head to foot, and from side to side, as if he had been trying to cheat her into taking false coin for true. And when Godfrey begged Lina to bring a glass of fresh water to him in his room after supper, Mrs. Nüssler interposed and said, that Lina had something else to do, so he turned to Mary, the parlour-maid, and asked her to do it, but Mrs. Nüssler told him he had better go to the pump for it himself, it was no further for him to go than for Mary. Thus she drew a magic circle round him, over which no woman must venture.

The next day when they were all at dinner, the coachman came to the door, and signing to Mrs. Nüssler, said: "Oh, if you please, mistress, I want to speak to you for a moment."--Mrs. Nüssler at once signed to Bräsig, and the two old friends went out into the porch with Christian.--"Well?" asked Mrs. Nüssler.--"Here it is," said Christian, pulling a large letter out of his pocket, "and I know the woman's name too."--"Well?" asked Mrs. Nüssler again.--"Yes," whispered Christian in his mistress' ear, "her Christian name is 'Minnie,' and her family name is 'Stry.'"--"What? Mini--stry?" cried Mrs. Nüssler.--"Ha, ha, ha!" laughed Bräsig, pulling the letter out of Mrs. Nüssler's hand. "That comes of ignorant people meddling with outlandish words; this is the vocation from the ministry," and opening the parlour-door, he shouted: "Hurrah! You old methodist you! The marriage is to be next week."--And Mrs. Nüssler threw her arms round Godfrey's neck, kissed him, and said: "Godfrey, dear Godfrey, I've done you great wrong; but never mind, Godfrey, Lina shall bring you some water every evening, and the marriage shall be whenever you like."--"Bless me!" said Godfrey. "What is ....."--"Nay, Godfrey, I can't explain, it's too hard for me, but I'll tell you when you've been married three years."

So the wedding took place, and I might tell how Mina and Lina had a good cry together after the ceremony was over; how nice Godfrey looked when Lina had cut his hair properly; how Mrs. Nüssler assured every one who came near her that she was not bit tired, which meant that she was completely worn out. But I'll tell nothing about the marriage that I did not see myself, and there is one thing I can vouch for having seen it, and that is, that at half-past three the two old friends, young Joseph and young Bolster, lay down on the sofa together, and fell fast asleep.

Hawermann was at the marriage, but was very quiet and sad; Louisa was there also, her heart full of love for her little Lina, and she was very quiet too, but quietly happy. Mrs. Behrens had refused the invitation sent her, but just as all the company were giving three cheers for the bride and bridegroom, the door opened, and Mrs. Behrens came into the room in her widow's weeds. She threw her arms round Lina's neck, and said: "I am glad that you are to have it, very very glad; and I pray that you may be as happy as I was. You are now the nearest," Then she kissed her and patted her on the shoulder, and after that turned away and hastened out of the room without looking at any one else. As soon as she was in the passage she called: "Hawermann," but she need not have done that for he was already by her side, and after helping her into the carriage, he took his place beside her, and so they drove back to Gürlitz.

They got out of the carriage at the entrance to the church-yard, and walked together to the quiet green grave, there they stood hand in hand silently gazing at it and at the flowers that were growing on it. As they turned to go away little Mrs. Behrens said with a deep sigh: "I am ready now, Hawermann." They got into the carriage again and drove to Rahnstädt. "Louisa knows all about it," she said, "and will follow me tomorrow with the things." They went together into the new house, and little Mrs. Behrens kissed Hawermann, and thanked him for his kindness to her in having made everything look so like the dear old parsonage. She went to the window, and looking out, said: "Yes, it's very very like; all is here except the grave."--They looked out of the window for a long time in silence, at last Hawermann took her hand and said: "Mrs. Behrens, I have a great favour to ask of you. I have given Mr. von Rambow warning and am to leave him at Christmas. Will you let me have the garret, and will you allow me to board with you?"--If it had not been such a sad moment for them both' she would have asked a number of questions, and would have talked the whole thing over, but as it was she only said: "Your home is always wherever Louisa and I are. You are the nearest to us both."

It is ever thus in the world; what brings joy to one, brings sorrow to another, and marriage and death go side by side, although the difference between them is greater than between summer and winter. There are some people to be found with such beautiful dispositions, that in spite of their loss being the other's gain, or of their having gained by the other's loss, their love to each other forms a bridge over the abyss which might have separated them, but which their generous love has changed into a firm bond of union. And of this Mrs. Behrens and Lina were a bright example. Each clung to the other with a comprehending love and sympathy that never failed as long as they lived.

And our old friend Godfrey did his part to strengthen the ties binding Mrs. Behrens to her old home. In his first sermon also it must be confessed that he thought less of himself than of the example his predecessor had always showed, so that when Bräsig came out of church he stroked Lina's cheek and kissed Mina, saying: "He is growing much more sensible. Methodists are often quite reasonable mortals; but they're the devil's own. I once knew a Methodist, I mean parson Mehlsack, who was really a good sort of man, but he had given himself so completely to the devil that he no longer preached about God; and as for the parson over in the beautiful Cracow districts, he proved padagraphically that there are *three hundred and thirty three* separate devils rushing about the world, without counting the regular devil and his grandmother. Now look here, Lina, this is the chief discomfort for the like of us in such matters. Suppose that you, and some of your friends seat yourselves round a bowl of punch in Rahnstädt, and you finish that bowl, and then another, and another, and a gentleman in a brown surtout seats himself beside you--the devil always wears a brown surtout, it's part of the contract that he should do so--and talks to you pleasantly the whole evening, and when you wake next morning, you see the same gentleman standing before you, and he says to you, says he: 'Good morning, my friend, you signed a paper for me last night,' he then shows you his cloven foot, and if he's in a good humour, he lets you have a sight of his tail, and flips you playfully over the ears with it, and so you become his heritable property. That's the way with *honest* Methodists, and with the other's it's even worse I can tell you."

So Godfrey and his wife took up their abode at the parsonage, and Mina of course went to pay them a visit. It sometimes happened when Godfrey came into the parlour in the dusk that he gave Mina a kiss by mistake, but it did not matter, for it was all in the family. A short time after the young couple went to their new home, Pomuchelskopp, his wife, Mally and Sally went to return the clergyman's call, and to try to get the lease of the glebe. Pomuchelskopp offered Godfrey half as much as Mr. von Rambow had given for the land, and his wife declared that it wasn't worth a penny more, for Joseph Nüssler had refused to take it. Godfrey bowed, and was going to have said: "Yes," when Lina started up out of her sofa corner, and said: "Wait a moment! I've got something to say to that. We must ask the advice of some one who understands the matter," and she called out at the door: "Uncle Bräsig, please come here."--So he came in dressed in a loose linen coat, and taking his stand right in front of his old school-fellow who was wearing his blue coat and brass buttons, asked: "What's the matter?"--Lina went up to him: "Uncle Bräsig," she said, "*need* the glebe be let. I should so like to farm it myself."--"Then it shan't be let, my dear little Lina," he said, stooping and kissing her, "I will farm it myself."--"I won't have any small tenant," cried Pomuchelskopp.--"Don't be afraid, Samuel--a--don't be afraid, Mr. Samuel, I am only going to be his reverence's bailiff."--"Mr. Nüssler signed a paper giving me the land...."--"No, showing what a fool you are," said Henny, thrusting her husband out of the room.

"My dear parson," said uncle Bräsig as he and Godfrey were walking in the garden, "you have not to thank me for having made this arrangement, it was all Lina's doing. It is a marvel to me how positive these innocent little creatures grow when once they're married. Well, perhaps it's better to trust everything to them, they always know best. Most probably you will wish to talk me out of my hatred of certain people, for you no doubt preach from the Christian standpoint of holding out your left cheek to the man who struck you on the right cheek, but I tell you that there must be hatred; where there is no hatred there can be no love, and I don't at all approve of the story of the right and left cheeks. I confess that I can hate; I hate Samuel Pomuchelskopp!--How?--What?--Why?--Wouldn't you hate him if he treated you as he treats me?"--"My dear Sir, the wickedness of the principles you have just ....." he was about to have vindicated his right to be a clergyman by giving the old bailiff as severe a lecture, as he had done on a former occasion about fishing, when fortunately Lina came up and throwing her arms round her old friend's neck, exclaimed: "Uncle Bräsig, dear uncle Bräsig, how are we ever to thank you for giving up your quiet life for our sake."--"Don't distress yourself, Lina. Love is as strong as hatred. Did you notice that I called Pomuchelskopp, Mr. Samuel, although he was really christened Samivel, which is a much grander name."--"No, no," interrupted Godfrey, "he must have been christened Samuel."--"No, reverend Sir, 'Samuel' is a Jewish name, and although he is really a Jew, that is, a white one, he was christened *Samivel*, and his wife's name is Canary."--"Uncle Bräsig," laughed Lina, "what a funny way of pronouncing it. Her name is Cornelia."--"It's quite possible, Lina, that she may call herself that now, for she may well be ashamed of the ugliness of her real name, but I know that I'm right. When the old parson at Bobzin died, and the clerk was taking the register-books for the new clergyman to look at, I saw amongst the entries: 'Mr. Samivel Pomuchelskopp to Miss Canary Kläterpott,' so you see that you see she was a Kläterpott, and a Canary too.--But that's enough of her, Lina, she has got nothing to do with us, and you and I will do everything capitally together and will have a happy union in farming matters. You must give me the small corner room overlooking the yard, and the devil himself must take part against me, if Godfrey isn't able to farm his own land after a year and a day. Good-bye, for the present. I know of two good milch-cows which I shall at once secure, then I'll get those two horses from old Prebberow, and we'd better keep George, Mr. Behrens' former servant, for he's a splendid dickshun'ry of the management of horses and cattle. Good-bye," and he went away, old heathen that he was, in his clinging to his hatred.

Whoever maintains that he has a right to hate another man, must be content to be hated in his turn, and no one was so hated on that day as uncle Bräsig himself.

When the Pomuchelskopps were at home again, Henny began to stroke the quiet father of the family and Mecklenburg law-giver the wrong way, and stung him with her sharp words as though with thorns and nettles. She continually taunted him in the words of her favourite proverb: "Ah, yes, Kopp," she would say, "you're as wise as the Danish horse which always came home three days before it began to rain!"--At last the much enduring man could bear it no longer, he sprang to his feet, exclaiming: "Mally, have I not always been a kind father to you?"--But Mally was too deeply ingrossed in the Rostock paper to be able to answer.--"Sally," he cried, "can I help the world being so wicked?"--But Sally stitched and sewed the body of a little cupid in her worsted work so diligently that she could only sigh and look as if she were sorry her father was not like the cupid in her work that she might run her needle into him after her mother's example. Gustavus then came in clattering a slate against a board, as if he had been sent for to play an accompaniment to the family drama.

But when things get to a certain pass they become unbearable! Human nature cannot deny the argument of a stick, and our old friend was now determined to show his rebellious family that he was master in his own house; having thus asserted himself he rushed out of doors and left them alone. He hastened into the garden, and up to the sundial, but he found no comfort there. He had certainly showed his own flesh and blood that he would not be bullied, but that did not make him happier, for there before his very eyes lay the glebe, the beautiful glebe. And beyond that was Pümpelhagen. Both of these were his by rights, for had he not paid three hundred pounds for the glebe, and how much more to Slus'uhr, to David and to that wretch Mr. von Rambow! He could not bear the sight, and turning round, gazed up into the blue sky, and asked himself if there was any justice on the face of the earth. At that moment Phil came to him, and pulled him by the tail of his blue coat--for in putting Henny down, he had for the time being put an end to all order in the house--and told him that Mr. von Rambow was there, and wanted to speak to him.

Mr. von Rambow? Ah, ha! He had some one now whom he could bully, he would make him pay for all the discomfort he had suffered that morning at the hands of his own family. Mr. von Rambow? Well! He was about to have gone to him, when his visitor stood before him: "Good morning, Mr. Pomuchelskopp. I hope I see you well--I came to hear what arrangements you had made about the glebe."--Ah! The glebe! Wait, I mustn't let him guess, and Pomuchelskopp looked slyly down to the point of his nose without making any reply.--"Well," said Alick, "how is it settled?"--But Pomuchelskopp made no answer, and continued to gaze down his nose as if it were a mile long, and he had not nearly reached the end of it yet.--"What's the matter with you, neighbour? I hope it's all right."--"I hope so too," answered Muchel, stooping to pull up a weed, "at least the three hundred pounds I lent you are all right?"--"Why?" stammered Alick in amazement, "but what has that to do with it?"--Wait, Alick. Do not be in such a hurry. Wait. He wants to plague you a little. What must be, must be.--"Mr. von Rambow," said Muchel pulling up another fine weed, and then turning to his visitor with a flushed face, "Mr. von Rambow, you got the three hundred pounds, and *I* was to have had the glebe, but I hav'n't got it."--"Why, you were so sure of it ..." began Alick.--"Not nearly so sure as you. You got the three hundred pounds--didn't you now? You got the money I say--and I," here he tapped his left foot impatiently on the ground and muttered the next words in a low gruff tone that seemed to come from the lowest region of his stomach, "and I, have been taken in!"--"But ...."--"You needn't say 'but' to me, I've heard enough 'buts' this morning. Let us talk of bills instead," here he groped in his pocket, "Oh, Ah, I see I have another coat on, my pocket-book isn't here. I've had one of your bills for the last three weeks."--"But, Mr. Pomuchelskopp, pray--why do you speak to me about it to-day? It isn't my fault that you didn't get the lease of the glebe."--It was all of no use. He had better have been quiet. Pomuchelskopp had heard too much that day of the glebe, so he pretended not to hear Alick's last words, and said: "I am a kind-hearted man, and am always willing to do what I can for my friends. People say that I'm rich, but I am not rich enough to be able to throw away money. There's time enough for that, But, Mr. von Rambow, I must *see*, I must *see* something. I must see to my business, and when a man signs a bill, he must see ...."--"Oh, Mr. Pomuchelskopp," cried Alick in great anxiety, "I forgot all about it. Indeed ..... I didn't remember."--"Oh," said Muchel. "You didn't remember? But a man ought to remember such things, and ...." he suddenly stopped himself before he had said too much, for his eye fell on Pümpelhagen--no--He must take care--He must not shake the tree before the plums were ripe. "And," he went on, "I have to thank that fellow Bräsig for my disappointment. That's all the reward I get for the kindness I showed the man when he was a lad. I lent him money to buy a watch. I gave him trousers when his own were torn, and now? Ah! I know what it is, it's all that sly rascal Hawermann's fault."

If you give the devil *one finger*, he seizes your *whole hand*, and then he leads you where he wills, and if he desires it, you must fall on your knees before him, and entreat him for mercy in your abject misery and gnawing pain. So it was with Alick. He was obliged to agree with Pomuchelskopp, for he had now to row in the same boat with him, and so he joined him in his accusations of Bräsig and Hawermann. Why? Because Pomuchelskopp held his bills and had therefore the whip hand of him. The light-hearted, gallant young officer of a few years back, was gone, and in his stead was a broken spirited man who tried by telling all the scandalous stories he had heard of the two old bailiffs to propitiate the Moloch who stood beside him in a blue coat and brass buttons. He had betrayed his best friend. He had spoken falsely. As he thought of what he had done while he was riding home, he felt a bitter contempt of himself rising up in his heart, and he rode quickly in order to leave the house where he had behaved so basely as far behind him as possible.

He rode home, and when he came to his fields where Hawermann was at work, he saw the old bailiff standing in the full heat of the sun beside the sowing machine, getting everything in order. When he saw that, he felt as if coals of fire were burning his head. When he had gone a little further he met a man in a linen coat, and saw that it was uncle Bräsig. Bräsig was standing by the wall and shouting across the field: "Good day, Charles. Here I am at the old work, I'm going to buy some cows, and everything is getting into good order. We're going to farm ourselves, and Samuel Pomuchelskopp is out in his reckoning." At that moment he heard Alick's horse, and turned round to see who was there. The remorse Alick felt for what he had done made him speak more kindly than usual: "How d'ye do, Mr. Bräsig. You're always on your legs?"--"Why not, Mr. von Rambow? They do me good service in spite of gout now and then, and as I've undertaken to manage farming matters for the young people at the parsonage, I am on my way to Gülzow, to get a couple of milch-cows from farmer Pagel for the parson."--"You know all about such things of course, Mr. Bräsig," said Alick wishing to be civil.--"Yes, thank God, I know pretty well. We farmers have only to give a glance at a field and we can see whether it has been properly treated. Look, I was over there yesterday," pointing to the paddocks, "I went past the fence, and I saw that the mare and foal were quite starved, and no wonder. Some one steals the oats out of their manger and if you want to put a stop to that, you'll have to have a lock put on it."--Alick looked at him; was it not pure love of aggravation that made him say that? Naturally! He gave his horse a touch of the spur: "Good-bye," he said and rode away.--Bräsig looked after him: "If he's too great a fool to take the hint, he needn't do it. I meant him well. It seems to me as if the young nobleman does not want God's .... nay, I oughtn't to say that. He'll come to his senses at last, but he'll have much to suffer first. Charles," he shouted across the field, "he has given me another hint to mind my own business!" Then he went away to buy the cows.

CHAPTER XVII

Winter had come again, and the earth had to consent, with or against her will, to receive her rude visitant. It is all very well when winter comes in pleasantly with bright frosty weather, but when it brings a nasty cold rain at Christmas time, it is very disagreeable. This year, however, it came in merrily as I have often known it do, with the cracking of whips and tinkling of sledge-bells. I remember well how William of Siden-Bollentin drove up to my door in a sledge, his horses smoking in the frosty air. He sprang to the ground, rubbed his cold blue cheeks, slapped his arms once--twice--thrice, across his chest to warm himself, and said: "Good-morning, Mr. Reuter, I've come to fetch you. My master and mistress send their compliments, and you've nothing to do but to get into the sledge, for the foot-bags and cloaks are lying in a heap on the seat ready for you. To-morrow's Christmas, and little Jack told me to drive as hard as I could."--When winter comes like that my wife and I rejoice and welcome it with delight, so we gave the old groom a glass of wine, seated ourselves in the sledge, and off we went at the rate of ten miles an hour--and yet when we got to the front-door at Bollentin, Fred Peters greeted us with: "What the devil has made you so long in coming?"--His wife embraced my wife, took off her hood, and said to me; "Uncle Reuting, I have a nice little dish of cabbage and sausage ready for you."--And the two girls, Lizzie and Annie, whom I have so often carried in my arms when they were little babies, ran up to me, gave their old uncle a hearty kiss, and then threw themselves into my wife's arms. Fred and Max, who were now great school-boys, came and shook my hand in the old high-school fashion, and while they were doing so, Jack was watching his opportunity to spring out upon me. As soon as he caught me, I gave him a ride on my foot, and would have liked to have been his playfellow for the rest of the evening. Then little Ernest, the baby, was introduced to me, and we all stood round that wonder of the world, and exclaimed at his look of wisdom, and at his being able to take so much notice. Last of all came the old grand-mother. After that the amusements of the evening began. The Christmas tree was lighted up. The Julklapp knocked, and the first thing it threw in was a poem written by my wife, the only one she ever made, and which was as follows: "Here I sit, and am so hot; and ask naught by day ....." There it ended, and it was no matter, for it was perfect as a fragment. Then Christmas day came with a solemn hush into the world, and God scattered His soft snow-flakes like down upon the face of the earth, so that no sound was to be heard without. On the next day parson Pieper and his wife, and the superintendent and his wife came, and Anna too, who is a great pet of mine, for she was once my pupil. Then came Mrs. Adam, the doctor's wife, and Mrs. Schönermark, the sheriff's wife; they brought Lucy Dolle with them, and she had rather an uncomfortable seat between the two ladies. After that another sledge drove up, out of which Dr. Dolly lifted a great round bundle, beside which he had been sitting, and handed it over to the two parlour-maids, who were standing ready to receive it. When the bundle was unrolled, and all the furs, cloaks, shawls and foot-bags which composed its outer covering had been removed, Mr. Schröder, the barrister, was disclosed to view. He was not ready even then, for he seated himself on one of the hall-chairs, and Sophie took possession of one leg, and Polly of the other, and then they pulled off his fur-boots, while I held him firmly, lest his legs should be tugged off. Then came another sledge, and out of it sprang Rudolph Kurz--he jumped right over the reins the coachman was holding in his hand, and after him came Hilgendorf. Do you know, Hilgendorf? Hilgendorf, our Rudolph's teacher? No? Well, it is not necessary that you should. To describe him in a few words: Hilgendorf is a natural curiosity, his bones are made of ivory--"pure ivory." He is so hard that any one thumping him on the shoulder or knee has his hand badly bruised--because of his ivory bones.

Then coffee was drunk, and the barrister told stories, very good stories they were too, and he told them with fire, that is to say, his pipe was continually going out while he was talking, and he had to light it again every now and then, so that before long he had smoked a whole boxful of matches. Max was deputed to sit beside him, and see that he did not catch fire during his consumption of matches. After that there was whist with van der Heydt and Manteufel, and various other things of the sort, for that was the barrister's usual play. During supper, whilst he was disposing of roast goose and other good things, the barrister made all kinds of beautiful poems out of the most extraordinary rhymes; for instance, "Hilgendorf," "Schorf," and "Torf," and when given "Peters," he made the next lines end with "Köters," and "versteht er's." When we at last separated, we all shook hands, and parted in peace and good-will, every face saying: "Till next year!"

The day after Christmas passed very differently at Pümpelhagen. The weather was bright and beautiful there also, but the peace and good-fellowship that should have made the day a happy one, were wanting. Each member of the household was busy with his or her own private thoughts, with the exception of Fred Triddelfitz and Mary Möller, who spent the afternoon together eating ginger-bread-nuts. Fred said after a time: "I can eat no more, Polly, for I have to go on a journey to-morrow. I am to take three loads of wheat to Demmin, and if I eat more ginger-bread I may be ill. I shouldn't like that you know, especially as I want to make up the parcel of our reading-books for the library, that I may change them in Demmin, and so let us have something to read in the evening." He then rose and went out to visit his sorrel-mare, and Mary Möller felt that his heart was not entirely hers, for he divided it between her and his mare.

Hawermann was sitting alone, buried in thought. He was very grave, for he felt that his active work in the world had now come to an end, that he might fold his hands on his knees, and take his rest. He was sad when he thought of how his life at Pümpelhagen had ended, and how all his joy in the place had turned to sorrow.

Alick and Frida were sitting in another room. They were together, and yet they were alone, for they thought their own thoughts, and did not confide them to each other. They were silent; Frida calm and quiet, and Alick rather cross. Suddenly sledge-bells were heard outside, and Pomuchelskopp drove up to the door. Frida picked up her work and left the room, so Alick was obliged to receive his visitor alone.

The two gentlemen were soon busily engaged talking of farming matters, such as horse-breeding, and the price of corn. The afternoon would have passed innocently and peacefully, if Daniel Sadenwater had not brought in the post-bag. Alick opened it, and found a letter for Hawermann. He would at once have given it to Daniel, but he saw his own crest on the envelope, and on looking more closely, he discovered that it was addressed in his cousin's hand-writing. "Is that confounded plot still going on behind my back?" he exclaimed, as he threw the letter to Daniel, almost hitting him in the face with it: "Take that to the bailiff."--Daniel went away looking rather dazed, and Pomuchelskopp asked Alick sympathisingly what had put him out.--"Isn't it enough to make any one angry to see how that idiotic cousin of mine has allowed himself to be caught in the toils laid for him by that old rascal and his daughter, and how obstinate he is in carrying on that foolish love-affair?"--"Oh," said Muchel, "I thought that was over long ago. I was told that your cousin had broken off all connection with these people as soon as he heard what every one was saying about them."--"What is it?" asked Alick.--"Oh, what is said about your bailiff and the labourer, Kegel--isn't that the man's name--and the three hundred pounds."--"Tell me, what do people say?"--"You know. I think that was why you gave the old fellow the sack."--"I don't understand. Tell me what you mean."--"Everyone knows it. It is said that Hawermann and the labourer had made a compact together.

That Hawermann let the labourer escape, and that he got half of the money for doing so. That he gave him an estate-pass, which enabled him to get an engagement as ordinary seaman at Wismar."--Alick paced the room with long strides: "It isn't possible! He can't have deceived me so shamefully!"--"Ah, people even go so far as to say that he and the labourer had arranged about the theft from the very first, but I don't believe that."--"Why not? What was the old sinner talking secretly to the woman for? What made him take such a prominent part then, when he is generally so very retiring."--"If there had been anything in that," said Pomuchelskopp, "the mayor of Rahnstädt would surely have noticed it"--"The mayor! I have very little confidence in his judgment. They make out now that the wife of a poor weaver was the thief who stole the money from the labourer on the public road. And why? Because she tried to get change for a Danish double Louis d'or which she had found. She declared that she had found it, nothing would make her change her story, and so the wise mayor of Rahnstädt had to set her free."--"Yes," answered Muchel, "and the man who saw the Louis d'or was Kurz, the shopkeeper, and he is a relation of Hawermann's I think."--"I'd give another hundred pounds with pleasure," cried Alick, "if I could only get to the bottom of this villany."--"It would be difficult to manage," said Pomuchelskopp, "but, first of all I'd--when does he go?"--"Hawermann? To-morrow."--"Well, you should go over his books very carefully, you can't tell whether they're in good order or not. Be particular to add up the columns of figures yourself, and you may perhaps find something wrong, at any rate it's the best check. He must have feathered his nest pretty well, for I hear he is going to live in Rahnstädt on his savings. Certainly he has been receiving a high salary here for a number of years, but I know that he had to pay off a good many, and rather considerable debts, when he first became your father's bailiff. After that he--as I hear from attorney Slus'uhr--lent out his small savings, and perhaps some of the estate-money at usury, and has made a good thing of it."--"Oh," cried Alick, "and when I asked him once ....." but he stopped short in order not to betray himself, but he felt as if he hated Hawermann for not having helped him when he could so easily have done so, for having refused him assistance because he had not offered him a high enough percentage on the money he had wanted to borrow.

 After this there was very little more conversation, for each of the gentlemen had too much to think of to care to talk, and when Pomuchelskopp at length drove home, he left young Mr. von Rambow a prey to all kinds of suspicious fancies, which made him so restless and uneasy that he could not go to sleep the whole night.

In an upper room in the Pümpelhagen farm-house Hawermann was sitting over his desk, with his account-book open before him. He was going over the last months' accounts to make sure that they were all right, and corresponded with the quantity of money he had in his safe. Since Alick had come into the estate, he had taken him the books every quarter to be examined, but the young squire sometimes said he had no time to look at them, and sometimes without looking at them, had returned them, saying, he was sure they were all right, and that it was not necessary to show them to him. Hawermann had not made use of this carelessness of his master, but had been even more particular than before, and had kept his books as he had been accustomed to do from his youth up. He had taught Triddelfitz to keep an account of the corn used, and to bring it to him every week; if ever the lad made a mistake in his report he scolded him for it far more severely than for any carelessness in other things.

While the old man was sitting at his desk Fred came in, and asked his advice about this or that concerning his journey to Demmin. When all was settled, and Fred was about to leave the room, the bailiff called him back: "Triddelfitz," he said, "I hope you have your corn-account ready."--"Yes," said Fred, "that's to say, very nearly."--"Didn't I ask you to be particular about having it ready for me to-night, and to be sure that you added it up properly?"--"All right," said Fred, leaving the room. Daniel Sadenwater came in, and brought the bailiff a letter; and as it was growing dark Hawermann took it to the window. When he saw that it was from Frank his heart beat quicker, and as he read it, his eyes shone with pride and joy, and his heart softened and thawed under the influence of the young man's affection, in the same way as the snow on the roof melts in the sunshine, and before he had finished the letter a few tears had fallen from his eyes upon the paper.

Frank wrote that he had heard that Hawermann was going to leave Pümpelhagen, that he was now free, and must consent to his sincere desire to write to Louisa at once. The enclosed letter was to be given to her, and Frank hoped that it would lead to three people being happier than before.

The bailiff's hands trembled as he put his daughter's letter into his pocket-book, and his knees knocked together as he thought of the future happiness or unhappiness of his only child being thus in his hands. He seated himself on the sofa, and considered what he ought to do. In the morning the sea sometimes rises in wild billows, at noon it is calmer, but still gloomy and uncertain looking, but in the evening the blue sky is reflected in the smooth mirror of the water, and the setting sun encloses the picture in a golden frame.

Something of this sort was going on in the old man's spirit. At first his thoughts were tumultuous and confused, then he grew calmer, and was able to think whether he should be failing in his duty to Mr. von Rambow if he consented to do as Frank wished him. But what duty did he owe to the man who had returned him evil for good, and who was even now driving him away by his conduct? None. And he raised his head proudly, feeling that his conscience could not reproach him for his actions or thoughts, and then he determined that he would not sacrifice his best and dearest for the sake of a foolish boy, that he could not make his child suffer because of unjust social prejudices. Then he pleased himself by thinking of the happy future before Frank and Louisa, and lost himself in a delicious day-dream.

While he was thus engaged the door opened, and Christian Degel rushed into the room, exclaiming: "Oh, sir, you must come at once, the Rubens-mare has been taken very ill, and we don't know what to do." The bailiff rose and hastened to the stable.

Scarcely was he gone than Fred Triddelfitz came in carrying a portmanteau, club-books, shirts, and clothes of all kinds. He laid the portmanteau on a chair by the window, and began to pack up his things that he might be able to cut a figure in Demmin, when he caught sight of Hawermann's farm-book; for the old man had forgotten in his excitement to shut his desk.--"That'll, do for me," said Fred, and seating himself in the window as it was beginning to grow dark, he set to work to enter the corn-account.

Before he had quite finished Christian rushed into the room again: "Mr. Triddelfitz, you must go at once--this very moment--and fetch a rape-cloth from the granary, we are going to pack the mare in wet sheets." When Fred heard footsteps coming he hid the book behind him on the chair, and when Christian thrust the key of the granary into his hand, he left the book lying on the chair and went away with the groom. He met Mary Möller coming from the cow-house just as he got to the granary door; "Mary," he cried, "will you be so kind as to put up my things for me. You'll find them with the portmanteau on the chair at the parlour window; be sure you don't forget the books."--Mary did as she was asked. It was very dark and she was in love, so she packed Hawermann's farm-book as well as the novels from the lending library.

When Hawermann came back from the stable he locked his desk without noticing that anything was missing, and next morning Fred Triddelfitz set off at cock-crow for Demmin with his wheat and portmanteau, never thinking he had anything with him that he ought not to have had.

After the old bailiff had given the labourers their orders for the last time, he returned to his house to collect and pack his things so that he might leave that afternoon, but before he was quite ready, Daniel Sadenwater came in, and desired him to come to Mr. von Rambow.

Alick had spent a very restless night; his best thoroughbred mare in which he had placed his hopes had been taken ill; the suspicion Pomuchelskopp had aroused, troubled him; the difficulty of farming by himself overwhelmed him, and then he must pay Hawermann's wages at once, to say nothing of various small sums he had got the bailiff to pay for him to the labourers, and the total amount of which he did not know. The bailiff had given him warning, not he the bailiff, and he must try to think of some pretext to put off paying him at once what he owed him. A good reason for such conduct is difficult to find, but a subject of quarrel is always to be had, and may be made to serve as a pretext for putting off the payment of one's debts. It is a wretched means to gain such an end, but a very common one! And Alick determined to make use of it, thereby showing how much his pride as a man and a gentleman had been lowered. Nothing has so much influence on a weak man's character as being short of money, especially when he wants to keep up appearances. "Needy and bumptious" is a true proverb.

When Hawermann came in, he turned to the window, and asked while he looked out into the yard: "Is the mare quite well again?"--"No," said Hawermann, "she is still ill, and I think you should send for the vet."--"I will see that he comes. But," he added, still staring out of the window, "she would have been quite well if the stables had been properly looked after, and if she had not been fed on that bad, mouldy hay."--"Mr. von Rambow, you know that the hay got a good deal of rain this summer, but still it's by no means mouldy. And you took the entire charge of the thoroughbreds into your own hands, for when I made a slight change in the stable a few weeks ago, you forbade my order being obeyed, and undertook to manage the horses yourself."--"Of course! Of course!" cried Alick beginning to walk up and down the room, "we know all that. It's the old story over again." Suddenly he came to a stand-still before Hawermann, and looking at him a little uncertainly, went on: "You're going away to-day, ar'n't you?"--"Yes," said Hawermann, "after our last agreement ...."--"I needn't," interrupted the young squire, "let you go before Easter unless I choose, and I insist upon your staying here until the second of January."--"You're right, but ....."-- "That isn't so much longer for you to stay," interrupted Alick, "and we must go over our accounts. Go and get your book now."--Hawermann went.

Alick was determined to save his money a little longer if he could. When Hawermann came back with his book, he might say that he had not time to look at it at that moment, and if the bailiff begged him to do it, he might get on his high horse, and say that the second of January would be time enough. But matters were to go more easily for him than he had thought. Hawermann did not return. He waited, and waited, but still Hawermann did not return. At last he sent Daniel Sadenwater to seek him, and then he came back with the butler. The old bailiff was pale and excited, and as he entered the room, he exclaimed: "I don't understand it. How can it have happened?"--"What's the matter?" asked Alick.--"Mr. von Rambow, I was busy finishing my book yesterday afternoon, and when I had done I put it in my desk, and now it is gone."--"A nice story forsooth," cried Alick scornfully, and the seed Pomuchelskopp had sowed in his soul began to grow, "yes, it's a nice story. When no one wanted the book it was always ready, and now that it is asked for, it has disappeared."--"I entreat of you," urged Hawermann, "don't judge so quickly. It will be found; it must be found," and he hurried away.

After a time he came back, "It isn't there," he said mournfully, "it has been stolen from me."--"That's a good joke!" working himself into a rage. "My three hundred pounds were not stolen, at least you said they were not, and now you say your book is stolen, because it suits you to say so."--"Oh God!" cried the old man, "give me time!" He clasped his hands together: "Oh God, my book is gone."--"Yes," cried Alick, "and the labourer Regel is also gone, and everyone knows how he escaped. My three hundred pounds are also gone, and everyone knows where they are to be found. Have you noted them in the book?" he asked advancing close to Hawermann, and looking him full in the face.--The old man stared at him, and then looking all round as if to make sure where he was, let his clasped hands fall to his side. He shivered from head to foot as does a giant river when about to break its icy fetters, and the blood rushed through his limbs and tingled in his face, like the waters of the great river, when they have freed themselves from their bonds, and rush swiftly on their course carrying all before them. Beware of such times, children of men! "Scoundrel!" he shouted, springing upon Alick, who had: retreated a few steps when he saw the expression of the other's face. "Scoundrel!" he cried, "my honest name..." Alick got into a corner and seized the weapon that was always kept there. "Scoundrel!" cried the old man, "your gun and my honest name!" And now began a violent struggle for possession of the gun, which the bailiff caught by the stock and tried to wrench out of his opponent's hand. Bang! The gun went off.--"Oh

Lord!" cried Alick, falling back upon the sofa. The old man stood beside him with the gun in his hand.--The door opened, and Mrs. von Rambow rushed up to her husband: "What is it? What's the matter?" she exclaimed, and all the love she had ever felt for him came back with a rush. "Oh, what is this? Blood!"--"Never mind," said Alick, trying to raise himself, "it's only my arm."--The old man stood motionless with the gun in his hand. His fury was calmed, but he felt that he had done an evil deed that he could never wash out however long he might live.--Daniel and the housemaid both ran into the room, and with their help Alick's coat was taken off and he was laid upon the sofa. His arm was much lacerated by the shot, and the blood dripped upon the floor.--"Go for a doctor," said Mrs. von Rambow, while she tried to stop the flow of blood by binding handkerchiefs round her husband's arm. She had not enough to be of any use, so she rose to fetch more. She had to pass Hawermann on her way to the door. He was standing pale and motionless by his master's side. "Murderer!" she said as she went out, and again when she came in she repeated: "Murderer!" The old man made no reply, but Alick raised himself, and said: "No, Frida, no. He is not that," for even an unrighteous man speaks the truth when he feels that he has escaped death by a hair's breadth, "but," he added, still harping on the old theme, "he is a cheat and a thief. Get out of my sight as quick as you can," he said addressing the bailiff.--The old man's face flushed, he opened his mouth as if to speak, and then seeing how Mrs. von Rambow shrank from him, he staggered out of the study.

He went to his own room: "A cheat and a thief," the words rang in his ears. He went to the window and looked out into the yard. He saw everything that went on there, but he saw it as in a dream. "A cheat and a thief," that was the only thing he could understand, that alone was real. He saw Christian Degel driving out of the yard; he knew that the man had gone to fetch the doctor; he threw the window wide open and was about to desire him to drive as hard as he could; but--"a cheat and a thief" was what he involuntarily called out instead of the order he had intended to give; he shut the window again. But the book! The book must be found--the book! He pulled everything out of the boxes he had already packed; he strewed all his possessions about the floor; he fell upon his knees--not to pray, for he was "a cheat and a thief"; he poked about under his desk with his stick, under his chest of drawers, and under his bed; the book must be somewhere, the book! All in vain! "A cheat and a thief." He once more took his stand in the window, and looked out; he still had his walking stick in his hand, was he going out, or what did he want with the stick? Yes, he would go out, he would go away from here, far away! He snatched up his hat, and went out. Where should he go? It was all the same to him, all the same, but habit led him to Gürlitz. As he went along the familiar road, old thoughts came back to him: "My child! My child!" he cried, "my honest name!" He felt his breast pocket--yes, he had put his pocket-book there, he had his daughter's happiness safe. What was the use of it now? He had destroyed the power that letter contained of making her happy, his honesty was doubted, and that shot had made matters even worse than they were before. A few bitter tears were wrung from him in his agony of spirit, and the tears brought him comfort; he knew that he had only meant to wrest the gun from Alick, not to hurt him; his conscience acquitted him of that crime, and he breathed more freely--but his honest name was gone and with it the happiness of his only child. Oh, how distinctly he remembered his joy yesterday when he had read and thought over that letter in his own room, when he had indulged in day-dreams of his daughter's future happiness, and now, all was changed and lost. The brand attached to his name would sink into his daughter's heart and bring her sorrow and shame. But what had his child to do with it? Alas! The curses and brands that rest on the father descend to the children even to the fourth generation, and the same hedge of thorns which separated him from all honest men came between his daughter and happiness. But he was innocent. Who would believe him if he were to say so? He, whose white robe of innocence has been, however unjustly, smirched, may go on his way through the world, no one will wash him clean; even if God were to proclaim his innocence by signs and wonders--the world would not believe. "Oh," he cried, "I know the world!" Then his eyes fell on Gürlitz manor, Pomuchelskopp's home, and out of a corner of his heart, a corner he thought he had closed and barred for evermore, rose the dread figure of Hate, the tears he had shed for his child dried on his cheek, and his voice which had before uttered the words involuntarily, now repeated them, "a cheat and a thief," and angry thoughts rose thick and fast in his mind: "he is the cause of it all, and we must be quits some day!"

He went through Gürlitz, but saw nothing on the right hand or the left. All he had loved there were gone from the place, he had only to do with his hate, and had only one object to set before him in life.--Bräsig was standing by the parsonage barn, and seeing his friend went forward to meet him: "Good morning, Charles. Where are you going? But what's the matter?"--"Nothing, Bräsig! But leave me, leave me alone. Come to Rahnstädt to-morrow, come to-morrow," so saying he walked on and left him. When he came to the hill on the other side of Gürlitz, from the top of which Alick had first shown his young wife his beautiful estate of Pümpelhagen, and where she had shown such unaffected pleasure in what she saw, he stood still. It was the last point from which he could see the place where he had been so happy, and where he had as it were wept tears of blood when his honour and his name had been so cruelly tarnished. His whole soul rebelled against his fate: "The miserable liar!" he said. "And she--she called me a 'murderer' once, then she said it again: 'murderer,' and turned from me in horror.--Your day of sorrow is coming upon you all. I could have saved you, and I would have saved you. I watched over your interests and served you as faithfully as a dog, and you have thrust me from you like a dog; but ...." and he turned to resume his walk to Rahnstädt, hatred still possessing his soul.

FOOTNOTES

Footnote 1: *Note.* The housekeeper in a large farm in N. Germany is a person of great consequence, and is always called Mamselle.

Footnote 2: *Note.* In Germany the wife has to provide, as well as her own trouseau, all the house and table-linen, and all the furniture even tables and chairs.

Footnote 3: *Note.* "Fasan"--"Vasall."

Footnote 4:

> "Vinum, the father,
> And cœna, the mother,
> And Venus, the nurse,
> Make gout much worse."